To Ka[...]

Hope you enjoy this

tasty bite of...

FAT-FREE
AND FATAL

▲

... death!

JAQUELINE GIRDNER

Jaq [signature]

DIAMOND BOOKS, NEW YORK

This book is a Diamond original edition,
and has never been previously published.

FAT-FREE AND FATAL

A Diamond Book / published by arrangement with
the author

PRINTING HISTORY
Diamond edition / July 1993

ISBN: 1-55773-917-X

Diamond Books are published by The Berkley Publishing Group,
200 Madison Avenue, New York, NY 10016.
The name "DIAMOND" and its logo
are trademarks belonging to Charter Communications, Inc.

PRINTED IN THE UNITED STATES OF AMERICA

10 9 8 7 6 5 4 3 2 1

KATE JASPER MYSTERIES from Diamond Books

ADJUSTED TO DEATH
THE LAST RESORT
MURDER MOST MELLOW
FAT-FREE AND FATAL

For my parents,
Bill and Audrie Girdner

- One -

MURDER WAS NOT far from my mind when I said goodbye to Wayne's mother, Vesta, at my front door. Vesta Caruso didn't bother to return my attempt at an amiable farewell. Her only reply was to cross her bony arms over her equally bony chest and squeeze her eyes into two malevolent slits. My stomach clenched. I stomped down my front stairs angrily, then took a deep breath, forced my face into a smile and turned back, willing to give sociability one more try. This was my sweetie's mother, after all. But Vesta wasn't glaring anymore when I turned. Her homely face was lit with a rare expression of happiness.

"And good riddance," she cooed. Was this her belated version of goodbye, or was she trying to tell me something?

And that smile. My mind wheeled into a panic. What was she planning to do while I was gone? Burn my house down? Poison the cat?

My cat, C.C., came racing down the stairs after me as if she had heard my thoughts. She took one look back at Vesta, then streaked across the yard and over the fence. She wasn't going to stay alone in the house with that woman. Well, neither was I.

I stomped the rest of the way to my car, telling myself that even Vesta wouldn't stoop to arson or cat poisoning in my absence. She liked an audience too much. And I really was looking forward to the vegetarian cooking class that my friend Barbara had talked me into. If nothing else, it would get me out of the house on Monday evenings. Out and away from Wayne's mother.

I climbed into my old brown Toyota Corolla and took a peek back at Vesta as I set my rearview mirrors. I watched her skinny backside disappear into my house, then started my car, letting out a long, noisy sigh as the engine turned over. I wasn't even married and I had mother-in-law problems. Last year, Wayne Caruso and I had celebrated his move into my home with sparkling apple juice and ecstatic embraces. But in June of this year, Vesta Caruso had been released from The Shady Willows Mental Health Facility and had come directly home to live with us. Wayne had assured me that the arrangement was only temporary. Now it was late August.

I pulled out onto the street, remembering the days when we had visited Wayne's mother at Shady Willows and watched her drooling mindlessly in front of the TV set in the recreation room. With a pang of guilt, I realized how much I missed those days. But an observant social worker had put an end to all that when she discovered that Vesta had been overmedicated by the Shady Willows staff for the past twenty years. I had been filled with indignation for Vesta's sake when I heard about the malpractice. But after two months in her malicious presence I was beginning to understand exactly why the staff had overmedicated her.

Vesta hated me. I'm not exaggerating. Her hatred for me was as pure and visceral as a banker's love of money. And she wasted no time in letting me know about her feelings. And in letting me know that if and when she left my house, she would take Wayne with her. She had driven a wedge between Wayne and myself that bit deeper each day. And she was enjoying the exercise. Immensely.

I put Vesta out of my mind as I pulled up to Barbara's apartment building. I was going to enjoy the evening . . . if it killed me.

Barbara Chu was already at the door when I knocked, looking gorgeous in a hot-pink jumpsuit.

But then again, Barbara looked gorgeous in dirty overalls. She was small and slender, with perfectly proportioned Asian features under asymmetrically cut black hair. She could have been a model if she were taller, except that her eyes were too alive for that model's look of ennui. But she wasn't a model. She was an electrician. She was also a practicing psychic.

"So how's Vesta Caruso, the wicked witch of the West?" she asked, her sparkling eyes peering into mine knowingly.

I groaned. She opened up her arms sympathetically and pulled

me into a deep hug. A moment later, she released me to peer into
my eyes again. This time, her brows were pinched together in a
look that combined both concern and curiosity. Damn. Having a
psychic for a friend has its drawbacks.

I did the only thing I could do. I changed the subject. "So,
what about this class we're going to?" I asked.

Barbara stared at me for a second longer, then cheerfully ushered me out the door and down the stairs as she answered my
inquiry.

The class we were going to was a vegetarian, low-fat, low-
cholesterol cooking class, she told me. She had seen the ad for
it in the *Marin Mind*. It was going to be held from six to nine on
Monday nights at the Good Thyme Cafe in San Ricardo, which
sounded like bad news to me. I'd eaten at the Good Thyme. The
food was vegetarian, greasy and uninspired. However, the news
got better when Barbara assured me that the Good Thyme people
weren't giving the class; they were only renting the space to the
cooking teacher. And the teacher was going to provide free sam-
ples of the food she was teaching us to cook. That part sounded
even better to me. But I took a moment to wonder why it
sounded good to Barbara. She was no vegetarian.

"So, why are *you* going?" I asked as we walked to the Toyota.

Barbara's taste ran more to barbecued ribs and bacon burgers
than tofu. She never gained a pound. I, on the other hand, on my
healthful, low-fat, vegetarian diet, could gain a pound just sniff-
ing the aroma of fresh-baked whole grain bread.

"Because of Felix," Barbara answered as we got to the car.

"But Felix isn't a vegetarian either," I objected. He certainly
wasn't. Barbara's reporter boyfriend ate meat and plenty of it. He
had the nerve to be thin, too.

"Well, he's going to be a vegetarian now," Barbara said, her
face tightening with determination. "Kate, you wouldn't believe
it. Not only is Felix's cholesterol as high as the audience at a
Grateful Dead concert, but Felix has gout. Too much rich food.
I mean *gout*, for God's sake! This is the twentieth century. I
asked him to come to this class, but no way. He's so
stubborn . . ."

By the time we had reached the Good Thyme Cafe I was convinced that Felix's meat-eating days were numbered. Poor guy.
As much as he had driven me crazy in the past with his fevered,

journalistic inquisitions, Felix Byrne was still a human being. At least I thought so. I stole a look at Barbara's face as we got out of the car, and made a mental note to send Felix a sympathy card.

Barbara pushed open a glass door that held one sign stating CLOSED MONDAYS and another reading "Welcome, Vegetarian Cooking Class Tonight." I followed her through the door, noting that the restaurant looked pretty much like it had the last time I'd visited, a sea of wooden chairs at tables covered with white vinyl tablecloths. The only difference was that now the chairs and tables were empty.

The only people in the restaurant were three women and a tall black man standing in an aisle at the edge of the tables. As we started toward the group, one of the women looked up at us eagerly. She was plump, with a friendly, heart-shaped face that was defined by a kewpie-doll mouth and dark impish eyes. And she was well-dressed, in a silky magenta pantsuit scattered with black stars that matched the color and sheen of her neatly trimmed black hair.

I began to feel a little outclassed in the corduroys and San Diego Zoo T-shirt that clothed my own short, A-line body. In a last-minute attempt to spruce up, I ran my fingers through the inch or so that was left of my recently hacked curls.

"Hi there, I'm Alice Frazier," the plump woman bubbled enthusiastically. "Are you here for the class?"

"You bet," answered Barbara, matching her enthusiasm.

"Oh, goodie!" Alice danced over to one of the tables and picked up a lined notepad, which she handed over. We wrote our names and phone numbers on it dutifully. Then she asked for our money.

As I handed over my fifteen dollars, I hoped for her sake that more people were coming.

"So, is this the first class you've taught?" I asked conversationally.

"Oh, I'm not the teacher," Alice said, giggling. "My friend Meg Quilter is the teacher. I'm just helping her out." She turned and shouted, "Yo, Meg!"

The young woman who turned our way was too thin, and not nearly as well dressed as her friend Alice. I began to feel a little better about my T-shirt.

Meg Quilter wore dark baggy pants and a high-necked white blouse that did nothing to add color to her pale, freckled skin. Her large sea-green eyes looked faintly bewildered under invisible eyebrows. Her silky blond hair was pulled back in a haphazard ponytail.

As Meg walked toward us, I saw that she wasn't as young as she'd seemed at first glance. She was probably about thirty, I estimated, younger than my forty-one years in any case. Younger than Alice, too. And not happy about meeting new people, if her slumped shoulders were any indication.

"Meg," said Alice as the woman reached us, "Say hello to—" She paused for a moment to look at the notebook. "To Kate Jasper and Barbara Chu," she finished with a big smile.

"Hello," Meg said softly. She smiled vaguely at a point somewhere between Barbara and myself. Then she sniffled and looked away.

Wonderful, I thought. I just paid fifteen dollars and the teacher is too shy to look at us. I wondered what her lecture would be like.

"I'm Paula Pierce, friend of Meg's," came a rapid-fire voice from behind me, breaking into my thoughts.

I turned and got a good look at the last of the three women. She was a short, stocky woman with cropped salt-and-pepper hair, high cheekbones and a determined, tight mouth. She wore a navy blue business suit that strained over her shelf of a bosom.

Before I had a chance to introduce myself, she nodded at the tall, thin black man who stood behind her. "My husband, Gary Powell," she said brusquely.

At least her husband was dressed casually—in a polo shirt and jeans. I smiled up at him. Gary smiled back down at me, a kind smile that stretched all the way across his face and crinkled the edges of his warm brown eyes.

"Kate Jasper," I said.

Paula took it from there. I watched Barbara out of the corner of my eye talking to Meg and Alice, as Paula rattled off information. She and Gary had known Meg for years, she assured me. That made Barbara and me the only ones that weren't personal friends of Meg's, I realized. Meg was very creative, Paula went on. A wonderful artist as well as a good cook. Paula herself was an attorney. And Gary taught mathematics at U.C., Berkeley. I nodded.

My shoulders began to loosen as Paula went on. Then my mind began to drift. It's so much easier to socialize when someone else has both sides of the conversation covered. A look at Gary, still standing behind Paula, told me that he had drifted off too. His eyes were unfocussed and he was playing with something in his hand. What was it? I bent down to look.

But Gary's hand closed just as I got it into focus. Then I realized that Paula had stopped speaking. I brought my eyes back to her face quickly. By her expectant look, I guessed that I had missed a question.

I could hear Alice talking to Barbara behind me. "It was so neat, with me knowing Dan and Sheila and all. They're the owners of the Good Thyme . . ."

"I'm sorry," I said to Paula. "What did you say?"

"What kind of work do you do?" she repeated crisply.

"Uh, Jest Gifts," I mumbled in embarrassment. My profession stacked up against an attorney's and a math professor's about as well as my T-shirt did against Paula Pierce's navy suit.

"Jest Gifts?" repeated Paula inquisitorially. I'd have bet she did trial work when she wasn't taking cooking classes.

"I own a gag-gift company," I explained. "We sell mail-order to various professionals." Like you, I thought. I looked into her serious eyes and wondered if she had ever bought one of my shark mugs.

Someone else walked in the door before I had a chance to ask. I turned to look.

The newcomer was a good-looking older woman whose silver hair was arranged in an elaborate French twist. She wore an Indian squash-blossom necklace over a beige linen pantsuit that looked expensive. What was with these people? Didn't they expect to get messy food all over them? This was supposed to be a cooking class.

"Oh my," she trilled as she walked in. "This must be the place. What a wonderful atmosphere!" I looked around at the uninspired tables and chairs and wondered what she was used to.

Alice looked excited as she picked up her sign-in notebook. Maybe this newcomer wasn't a friend of Meg's.

I turned back to Paula, who was still eying me inquisitively.

"I make stuff for attorneys, too," I continued. "Like coffee mugs in the shape of a shark."

Her mouth tightened. Skip the shark mug, I thought. "And for Christmas, I have the Faw-law-law line . . ."

I was desperately wondering how to get myself out of this conversational hole when the woman with the silver French twist strode up to our little group. She was a handsome woman with strong facial features, widely spaced blue eyes and the posture of a retired dancer.

"I'm Iris Neville," she announced, her voice high and musical with a touch of something aristocratic. "And you are . . . ?"

Paula did the introductions, but surprisingly she couldn't hold the floor. Iris met her introductions with a flood of reminiscences about the city of San Ricardo.

"Do you remember Mayor Neumann?" Iris was asking a couple of long minutes later. "Such a delightful man. I was a friend of his dear wife, Nancy. Such a wonderful soul—"

Iris stopped as if someone had kicked her. I followed the direction of her narrowed eyes, looking for the cause.

Two men had just entered the restaurant. The younger of the two wore glasses and a gray pinstripe suit that didn't seem to fit his pear-shaped body. The older man was heavier, with dark shoulder-length hair and a Vandyke beard. He was wearing a beige linen suit. He met Iris's gaze with his own glare. What was going on here?

I looked back at Iris for an answer. Then I saw it. His suit and hers were identical. I caught a glimpse of amusement in Gary's brown eyes; then Iris took a breath and began to speak again. "Such a shame when men dress in women's clothing, don't you think?" she asked in a high, ringing voice. Damn. If I had wanted this kind of evening, I could have stayed home with Vesta.

"Personally," Paula fired back, her head thrust forward eagerly, "I am thankful for the right of free expression that we presently enjoy in this country. If the Moral Majority, which is neither moral nor a majority, was to have its way . . ."

As I listened to Paula expound, I realized she probably hadn't even noticed the man's suit. Iris didn't wait long to regain the upper ground, though. When Paula stopped to inhale halfway through her brief, Iris was ready.

"I remember meeting Justice William O. Douglas just before he retired. Such a delightful man," Iris interrupted. "Of the Supreme Court, you know—"

"I know who Douglas was," Paula said between clenched teeth.

"Of course you do, dear," agreed Iris, her wide blue eyes round with innocence. "Such a similar philosophy to yours. And such a unique way of expressing himself."

Paula closed her mouth, seeming to accept defeat. Gary wrapped a long arm around her stocky shoulders and gave them a squeeze.

Iris turned her eyes to Gary. "And you, Mr. Powell, you're a professor of mathematics. Such a difficult field, I would think . . ."

I wasn't going to wait around until she got to gag gifts. I smiled politely, then turned to rejoin Barbara. And ran smack into the man in the beige linen suit.

"Well, hello, sweet thing," he murmured with a lecherous smile. I should have smelled him coming. He reeked of partially metabolized wine. "You can bump into me anytime, honey."

I glared into his leering face. I don't mind when waitresses call me honey, but this guy was a different story. His close-set eyes were gleaming with lewd pleasure. He stroked his beard slowly. I had a feeling he was trying for a devilish image with that Vandyke beard and long hair, but he looked like an aging Maxwell Smart in disguise to me.

"Call me Leo," he murmured suggestively and tossed his hair back with a flick of his head.

"Fine, Leo," I said and stepped around him.

"Wait a minute," he called. "You gotta meet my main man, Ken." He nodded to the younger man in the pinstripe suit, who goggled at me through thick glasses as he cracked his knuckles.

"Nice to meet you, Ken," I said and almost ran the last step to Barbara's side. She was still standing with the pale cooking teacher and her plump friend Alice.

"And Meg's artwork is so neat . . ." Alice was saying.

"Bad vibes, huh?" Barbara whispered out of the side of her mouth. I nodded fervently.

"You wouldn't believe what Meg can do with tofu . . ." Alice continued.

Well at least I wasn't at home, hanging out with Vesta, I told myself. Nothing could be worse than that.

Then Leo and his friend Ken joined us.

"Haven't I met you somewhere before?" Leo asked Meg.

Meg gazed at him, her sea-green eyes wide with bewilderment.

"I don't think so," she answered softly. Then she dropped her gaze and went back to sniffling.

I was better off with my original group. I turned back to Paula, Gary, and Iris with new appreciation. Paula was listening to Iris with apparent interest now, though Gary's eyes were half closed as he stood behind her.

"Some of the most interesting people are vegetarians," Iris told us. "Carlos Santana, dear Carlos, such a really nice man. Do you know him? And Dennis Weaver, Dick Gregory. And historically, of course, George Bernard Shaw, Ralph Waldo Emerson—"

"Hitler was a vegetarian, too," came a loud voice from down the dark hallway that led to the kitchen and rest rooms.

It took a few more seconds for the woman who was attached to that voice to emerge into the light. But when she did, it was worth the wait. She was tall and slender with long, blow-dried hair, heavy eye makeup and large, round breasts prominently displayed in a tight red-and-white striped top. The rest of her outfit consisted of a pair of red short-shorts and spike heels. Suddenly, I was feeling okay about my T-shirt.

The two separate social groups that had formed earlier congealed into one as everyone turned toward the newcomer.

"Sheila . . ." said Alice. She stared at the woman, presumably Sheila, without finishing her introduction, her mischievous eyes subdued now.

Leo recovered first. He stroked his beard, eyed Sheila appraisingly and said, "Say, honey, don't I know you from somewhere?"

"Well, I certainly don't know you," Sheila snapped. She crossed her arms under her large breasts and squinted her black-rimmed eyes. "But I'll bet I know your sign. You've just gotta be a Sagittarius."

Her tone gave me the feeling this wasn't a compliment. Leo

must have felt it too. His face was red above his beard as he turned away.

Iris recovered next.

"I don't believe Hitler was really a vegetarian," she objected, her musical voice cracking on a high note.

"Fine, believe what you want to," answered Sheila, shrugging her shoulders. "So, Alice, introduce me," she ordered.

Alice didn't look enthusiastic anymore as she dutifully introduced the woman to each of us. Her name was Sheila Snyder. She and her husband owned the Good Thyme Cafe. Sheila's eyes stopped and fastened themselves on Gary Powell before the introductions were even finished. In her high spike heels, she was eye level with the tall black man.

"I'll bet you're a Gemini," she said to him. Her voice was low and intimate, but still quite audible. "You remind me of an old friend who was Gemini. Very mental." She ran her gaze down his body. "What's that you have in your hand?" she asked him.

"A crystal," he muttered, then added more clearly, "This is my wife, Paula."

Alice straightened her plump shoulders and jumped into the fray.

"Meg and I certainly enjoyed visiting you and the kids yesterday," she said to Sheila with forced friendliness. "Though I was sorry to miss Dan. How's he doing?"

"Oh, Dan's fine," Sheila said. "Getting fat, though."

The blush that rose slowly up Alice's neck and into her heart-shaped face matched her magenta pantsuit perfectly.

"Of course, I never gain any weight," Sheila went on. "I eat ice cream, butter, cheese, the whole bit. But I've just got one of those bodies."

I sighed. She certainly did.

"But those are dairy products," announced a shrill voice from behind me. It was the young man in the pinstripe suit, the friend of Leo's. What was his name?

"Ken," Barbara whispered in my ear. Psychic friends are useful that way.

"There are all kinds of poisons in dairy products," he told her, his eyes earnest behind thick glasses. "The antibiotics they put in milk, for instance, can give an allergic person hives, headaches—"

12   *Jaqueline Girdner*

"Well, I don't have any hives or headaches—" Sheila interrupted impatiently.

"But growth hormones—" Ken insisted.

"Oh, please," Sheila groaned. "I don't want to hear about
growth hormones." She shook her head. "I don't even know why
I came tonight. I certainly don't need a cooking class. I've done
the cooking here at the Good Thyme since we opened."

I felt a nudge from Barbara and stifled a snort of laughter. So
this was the woman responsible for the two wretched meals I had
eaten here. I saw two little girls emerge from the dark hallway
behind Sheila. Were these her kids?

"But when Alice asked to use the place, I thought, why not?"
Sheila continued. "Dan is out with his friend Zach tonight, anyway, so—"

"Mom, we're hungry, can we have the leftovers in the
fridge?" interrupted the taller of the two little girls.

Sheila jumped, startled. Then her face darkened. She whirled
around and slapped the girl across the face.

The girl stumbled to one side, then regained her footing.

"What are you, stupid?" Sheila shouted at her.

- Two -

THE SOUND OF the slap still reverberated in my mind as Sheila berated the little girl. I could almost feel its sting.

"Goddammit, Topaz! Why do you sneak up on me like that?" Sheila demanded.

The girl was still now, frozen. Her face was splotched with red where she had been struck. She couldn't have been more than ten years old, but her eyes were already dead. There was no feeling visible in them, except for the long-suffering vacancy of an old woman. Her arms were alive, though. They lifted hands bunched into fists, then dropped them, then lifted and dropped them again, and again, in a slow, rhythmic cycle. A shiver prickled the skin on my own arms into goose flesh.

"Look, I'll be up in a minute," promised Sheila, her tone more placatory than angry now. As she let out a long sigh, she seemed to diminish in size. Even her prominent breasts sagged into insignificance. "Okay?" she asked softly.

The girl muttered, "Yes, Mom," and turned to make her way back down the darkened hallway. The smaller girl stared at Sheila with round eyes for a moment, then turned and raced after her sister.

It was only after the children were gone that I remembered the rest of the audience to this family drama. I sneaked a peek at the faces around me as I struggled with my own churning feelings. Each face bore the imprint of what we had witnessed, some more starkly than others. Barbara's and Paula's faces were tight with rage. Even Meg's wide eyes were narrowed fiercely in her pale face. And Iris—

"Hey!" Barbara barked. "You don't need to hit a kid to get her attention."

"So, what's it to you?" Sheila shot back defiantly. She glared at Barbara for a moment, then drew herself up to her full height, turned on her red spike heels and clattered back down the hallway.

As I let out the breath I hadn't known I was holding, I heard one or two others echoing my relief. Then I heard a nervous giggle. I turned and caught Ken in the act, giggling behind his hand. Paula and Barbara were still glaring, but everyone else had pasted their social faces back on.

"Is it time to start yet?" Meg asked Alice softly.

Alice looked at her watch. "It's time," she confirmed, her plump, heart-shaped face smiling again.

Meg gave out a miserable sniffle and murmured something about getting it over with.

Alice patted Meg's arm and took charge. Switching on the hallway light, a single bare bulb that couldn't have been more than forty watts, she led the group forward, pointing like a tour guide to the rest rooms and pantry on the left, the kitchen on the right and the stairway at the end of the hall that led to the Snyders' flat.

The kitchen, behind swinging doors, was better lighted than the hallway. And very well outfitted. Someone had put some money into this kitchen. Too bad they hadn't put the money into a better cook.

I saw at least a dozen burners on the waist-high stoves, with ovens underneath and cabinets above that stored bottles, canisters and shakers. Stainless steel sinks gleamed under shelves of dishes, pots and pans. A bank of refrigerators and another row of shelves filled the far wall. In the center of the room a twelve-by-four butcher-block table sat with some dining room chairs scattered haphazardly around it. And just past the end of the table stood a ratty-looking podium and a large pad of paper on an easel.

"So, take a seat, everyone," Alice ordered cheerfully, waving her arms.

I took a chair and found that the table was chest-high once I was seated. I looked around as the others sat down. The butcher block was obviously meant for standing and cutting, not for sitting. Even Gary, the tallest of our bunch, looked like a kid at the grownups' table as he sat next to his even shorter wife, Paula.

Alice's smile faded as she joined us at the table. Had she only now realized the inadequacy of the seating arrangements? People began pulling out notebooks, and *I* realized the inadequacy of my note-taking arrangements. Leo and I were the only ones who hadn't brought anything to write on.

Meg closed her eyes for a moment, then straightened her back and strode up to the podium. As she turned to face us, I saw new color in her pale cheeks. Between the color and the improved posture, Meg managed to look elegant in her baggy pants and white blouse instead of too thin.

"Thank you all for coming this evening," she began, her voice crisp and clear now. "Tonight we'll talk about the basics of vegan cooking. As you may know, a vegan diet is one without any animal products, be it meat, dairy, fowl or fish . . ."

I was impressed with Meg's delivery. When she was on, she was on. Maybe the class wouldn't be a total fiasco, after all.

"There are numerous advantages to the vegan diet," she went on. "It is healthier, lower in cholesterol—"

"And saves the lives of innocent animals," Paula Pierce pointed out. I groaned inwardly, hoping that Paula wasn't planning to go into details.

"You don't have to worry about growth hormones or antibiotics either," added Ken. "But then with vegetables and grains, there's always the risk of pesticides—"

"We will talk about those risks later," Meg interrupted briskly.

All right, Meg! I cheered silently.

"Tonight, I'd like to start with some of the staples of a vegan pantry," she told us, turning to the pad of paper on her easel. As she spoke, she wrote in a graceful cursive hand. "Grains, legumes, soyfoods and vegetables—"

"Say, how about a drink while we listen?" Leo suggested. He stroked his pointed beard thoughtfully. "There's gotta be some wine, or something, somewhere in this joint."

Iris shook her head and clicked her tongue. I thought I heard her murmur "such a shame." She probably still hadn't forgiven him for wearing the beige linen suit.

"I'm sure you can get a glass of water from the tap," Meg said in a voice that could have frozen the water into ice cubes.

I tallied up another point for Meg.

She continued uninterrupted, telling about the different kinds of vegan foods, beginning with grains and ending with sea vegetables. She showed us some of the special tools of the vegetarian cook: juicers, grinders, steamers and a cute little handheld electric appliance called a SaladShooter whose cord plugged into the wall and shredded fresh vegetables in a matter of seconds. Was this an end to scraped knuckles?

Then came the best part. Meg passed around trays of some of the appetizers we would learn to cook, along with three pitchers of herbal iced tea.

"Oh my, this is simply delicious," Iris declared after tasting the lentil-walnut pâté on rye toast. "Such a deft hand with the seasoning. Is that marjoram I taste?"

Meg nodded.

"Mrmph," I added in approval as I stuffed barbecue-flavored soybean riblets into my mouth. I wasn't going to say any more than that until I got my share of all the food that was being passed around.

Which wasn't going to be easy. There was a stiff competition for the appetizers. Leo was loading up squares of cracked wheat bread with large portions of both hummus and herbed tofu dip.

"Doesn't seem right without wine," he complained as he stuffed a chunk of dip-laden bread in his mouth. He swallowed, stroked his beard for a moment, then scraped the bowl of hummus clean with the rest of his bread.

Paula Pierce grabbed what was left of the tofu dip before Leo could finish it, and scooped it up with the homemade sesame herb crackers she had already snagged. Barbara was gobbling curried mushrooms and eyeing the tray of Mandarin vegetable kebabs that Gary and Alice were decimating. Only Meg and Ken seemed aloof from the frenzy.

"Are these organic?" Ken asked suspiciously as he pointed at the untouched platter of raw vegetables.

"I always use organic foods," Meg assured him.

Ken took two carrot sticks and nibbled cautiously. At least *he* wasn't going to eat more than his share.

Meg continued with her lecture as the rest of us ate. It was no wonder she was so thin if she could ignore food this good. Once the food was gone, she finished up with a promise to teach us how to cook all the things we had tasted and told us it was time for a break.

"Good, I need a drink," boomed Leo, rising. He made a quick exit out the kitchen doorway. Ken looked back at the rest of us briefly through his thick glasses, then followed Leo out.

As Meg walked away from the podium she closed her eyes. When she opened them again a moment later, they held her old expression of faint bewilderment. Even her body was drooping once more. Poor thing, I thought. Public speaking was bad enough, and she had spoken for close to an hour and a half.

"I did so enjoy your lecture," Iris told her. "You have such an imaginative touch with vegetarian foods."

Meg looked down at her feet and mumbled a thank-you.

"Now, how long a break should we take?" Iris asked briskly as she stood, smoothing the wrinkles out of her pantsuit.

Meg turned to Alice for an answer.

"How about fifteen minutes?" Alice suggested. A smile curled the sides of her Kewpie-doll mouth. "Then I can do a quick jog around the block and burn off some of these delicious calories."

"Fifteen minutes sounds perfect," Iris agreed. "The park across the street is one of the nicer ones in the area. I've spent many a quiet afternoon there reading. Such a peaceful atmosphere."

As Iris turned to go, Paula Pierce strode up and put an arm around Meg's slumped shoulders. "You did great, honey," she said.

"A very well organized lecture," Gary added from behind Paula.

I didn't wait for any more rave reviews. I needed some fresh air. Actually, I wanted to talk to Barbara about the evening's events. The two of us walked out of the kitchen, back down the dimly lit hallway and through the dining room, whispering back and forth.

"That woman ought to have her children taken away," Barbara hissed as we emerged into the cool evening air.

I didn't ask who Barbara meant by "that woman." I knew she meant Sheila Snyder. Maybe I was getting psychic too. I looked out across the street and saw Iris seated on a bench in the little park she had recommended, her silver hair shimmering in the luminous twilight as she turned a page of the book in her lap.

"I'm going to call Social Services tomorrow," Barbara muttered as we crossed the street.

We sat down on the grass under an old, gnarled oak tree on the other side of the park from Iris. When I took a good look at Barbara, I saw lines of anger creasing her usually peaceful face. There was no humor left in her eyes. They looked old without it.

"My father used to hit me like that," she said, and then I understood the intensity of her anger.

"You don't know how that can mess a kid up," she went on. She pulled up a handful of grass and dropped it again. Her face softened into sadness. "Those poor kids. Who knows what she does to them in private."

She lay down full-length on the ground, her pink jumpsuit a crisp contrast to the bright green grass. "It will take them years to find their self-worth. It did me."

I lay down beside her and stared up at the twilit sky, waiting for more. But Barbara was quiet. Barbara was never quiet. I began to worry.

"You came out pretty well, if you ask me," I said softly.

She laughed. "I put on a good show, don't I?"

I didn't know what to say. I reached out and patted her hand.

"Thanks, kiddo," she murmured and sat up.

I sat up too and scanned her face once more. I relaxed when I saw her eyes crinkling with their customary humor. She snaked an arm around me and squeezed my shoulders briskly.

"Hey," she said, her voice filled with mischief. "I could use an ice cream cone. How about you?"

"Barbara!" I objected. "What's the use of a low-fat, vegan cooking class if you top it off with an ice cream cone?"

But before I could stop her, Barbara was up and off to the ice cream parlor she had spotted on the corner. I watched her hurry up the street, almost colliding with Alice, who came jogging down the other way. Then I smiled and lay back down. My disapproval would make the ice cream cone taste all the better to her.

Ten minutes later, I had closed my eyes and drifted into a half dream about new gag gifts. A whistle jerked me awake. I sat up and looked around me. Paula and Gary were sitting on the bench where Iris had been. A young woman in shorts and a halter top was walking by. And Leo and Ken were standing across the street in front of the restaurant. Leo, I should have known.

He took a sip out of something in a brown bag and shouted, "Great legs, honey!"

I once knew a dog whose vocal cords had been cut to prevent him from barking. His mouth would move, but all that would come out was a little mewling sound. It had seemed heartbreaking to me at the time. Now, I was wondering if the same operation could be performed on Leo, preferably without anesthetic.

The young woman gave Leo the finger without breaking stride. I chuckled at the forlorn expression on his face, and issued a silent *Right on, sister*. Spoken aloud, the words of support would probably be meaningless to this young woman of the nineties.

Paula Pierce wasn't chuckling. She rose and crossed the street, bearing down on Leo, oblivious to a BMW which slowed down to let her by. Leo saw her coming and quickly headed back into the Good Thyme Cafe. Whatever he had found to drink, it hadn't slowed his reflexes.

I lay down again and stared at the darkening sky.

"Hey, the pecan praline was great," I heard a few minutes later. Barbara was smiling down at me. "It's time to get back, kiddo," she added.

It was past time. We rushed back into the Good Thyme and down the dark hallway, now lit only by the glow from the kitchen. Someone had turned off the hallway's one dim light bulb.

"I've gotta go to the bathroom," Barbara whispered as we were almost to the kitchen.

"Me too," I whispered back. All that iced herbal tea was weighing heavily on my bladder. I could hear more than one voice coming from the kitchen. Apparently, Meg hadn't resumed the lesson yet. Were they waiting for us to reconvene?

Barbara crossed the hallway, giggling.

"Is this the ladies room?" she asked, pulling open the first door she got to.

"You're the psychic," I teased softly, walking up behind her. "You tell me."

"Whoops," Barbara said as she took a step in. "I think this must be the pantry. I tripped over something."

I followed her in, felt for the light switch and flipped it on.

As my eyes adjusted to the light, I saw that we were in fact in the pantry. The walls of the small room were lined with shelves holding an assortment of oversized jars, bags and boxes.

Then I looked down and saw what Barbara had tripped over. It was a red high-heeled shoe.

I didn't want to look any further, but my eyes traveled without permission to the foot the shoe had fallen from, and then moved swiftly up one long, crumpled leg to the seat of a pair of red shorts, passed the buttoned back of a red-and-white striped top, and came to rest on a mass of blow-dried hair lashed with loops of white electrical cord to what I now realized had to be Sheila Snyder's neck. A SaladShooter hung from the end of the electrical cord like a haphazardly placed bow on a hard-to-wrap package.

No! my mind screamed. The room shimmered, then swayed as my stomach turned over. *No*, I told myself, closing my eyes, *I will not pass out*. Or vomit. My ears began to buzz.

A gurgling sound broke into the buzzing. I opened my eyes. Was Sheila still alive?

- Three -

I TOOK A deep breath, and the room stopped swaying. I let the breath out and pushed past Barbara, dropping to my knees beside the body.

I grabbed Sheila's wrist to feel for her pulse. The instant I touched her flesh, I knew I wouldn't find one. Her body was too inert to be alive, her arm too heavy. But I desperately pressed my fingertips to her radial artery. I was right; no pulse. I laid my ear against her back and listened for breathing, in vain. I wondered frantically if I should turn her over. Bile rose in my throat. I didn't want to see her full face. I had already glimpsed its blue-gray edge under her mass of blow-dried hair.

Should I try to unwind the electrical cord from around her neck? A look told me it was wrapped too tightly. It was too late. She was dead. She had to be.

I stood back up. I needed help.

Then I heard the gurgling sound again. But it wasn't coming from Sheila. It was coming from Barbara. She bent over Sheila, then knelt down where I had knelt a moment before.

"Barbara . . ." I tried to say, but my voice didn't make it past my throat.

Barbara wasn't listening, anyway. She clawed at the loops of cord wrapped around Sheila's neck, failed to loosen them, then grabbed Sheila's shoulder and shook it hard.

"Barbara, we'll get help," I said, my voice shaking but audible now.

She whipped her head around in my direction. Her eyes were wide and empty of reason.

Then she screamed, a long, shrill scream of pure terror.

At least I didn't have to go for help. The scream brought all the help I needed running to the pantry.

Alice was the first one through the doorway. I watched her heart-shaped face change expression as she took in the scene. Her eyes widened and her plump hand leapt to her face as her skin lost color. Then she looked at Barbara, who was still on her knees next to Sheila. Alice's eyes narrowed. Did she think Barbara was the murderer?

"Barbara!" I ordered loudly. "Get up."

Barbara stood and looked into my eyes blankly. I put my arms around her and held her close to me. Looking over her shoulder, I saw more faces crowding the doorway.

"Does anyone have medical training?" I called out.

"I do," came Iris's voice, clear and calm.

The faces in the doorway shuffled and disappeared as Iris made her way into the room, her silvery head held high. I didn't have to point out the body. Her gaze landed on it immediately. There wasn't enough room for all of us in the small space, so I squeezed past Iris and Alice, pushing Barbara ahead of me through the doorway into the hall.

Grisly as the scene had been inside the pantry, it wasn't much better outside in the hallway. First Leo shoved his way into the pantry. Then Paula demanded to know what had happened. Before I could answer, Leo rushed back out the doorway, his hand over his mouth. He made it two feet beyond us and threw up. Ken went goggle-eyed behind his glasses and asked Meg with apparent seriousness if this was part of the class

"That woman was killed," said Barbara softly to Paula. I took a quick look at Barbara's eyes and saw with relief that there was intelligence in them again.

"What woman? What do you mean, killed?" questioned Paula, her voice shrill with urgency. Gary walked up behind her and laid his hand on her shoulder.

"Sheila Snyder, the woman who owns the Good Thyme," I explained. "Strangled." Sheila's body rose up in my mind's eye. My own body began to shake.

This time it was *Barbara* who put her arms around *me*. She was still holding me when I remembered that I had been on my way to the bathroom an eternity ago. I returned her embrace for a few more heartbeats, then broke free to complete my original mission as Paula rushed to the phone to call the police.

Sitting atop cold porcelain, I tried to breathe away my nausea, tried not to think about what was going on outside. But through the thin bathroom door I could hear Iris as she announced that Sheila was past help. And Alice as she asked Barbara whether she had killed Sheila. Barbara's high-pitched denial brought me out of my imperfect refuge. I came back into the hall in time to see tears running down Barbara's stricken face. I helped her to a seat at one of the tables in the dining room and sat down beside her.

By the time we heard the police sirens, Paula had shepherded the stragglers into the dining room with us and told everyone to sit down and keep quiet. I took a deep breath and glanced furtively at the silent members of the Monday evening vegetarian cooking class, now scattered at tables around the room. One of this group's members might be a murderer, I thought. Which one?

Leo didn't look much like a murderer. His face was a sickly greenish color from the beard up, and totally devoid of its usual arrogant lechery. Nor did Meg, her face pale, her eyes more bewildered than ever. Her friend Alice refused to sit, pacing frantically around the dining room instead. She was no longer eyeing only Barbara, but peering into each and every one of our faces as if looking for evidence of guilt. Paula's face was grave, her mouth pursed and trembling. She placed her hand gently on the back of her husband Gary's bent neck. He reached over without looking and patted her navy-blue-suited thigh with one hand, while continuing to caress his ever-present crystal with the other.

Ken's expression was the most disturbing. He wore a half smile as he watched the rest of us watch each other. Why was he smiling? Was he nervous? Was he psychotic? I shivered violently, seeing Sheila in my mind again, strangled with electric cord, the Salad Shooter hanging from her neck. Someone was psychotic. Someone had to be.

Only Iris held her head high. Her handsome features were calm now, even serene, her hands folded gently in front of her.

Why serene? I wondered, and then the police burst into the dining room.

"Who placed the call?" demanded the first officer, a tall, uniformed Hispanic man, holding a gun with both hands straight out in front of him. Behind him was a muscular young policewoman, also pointing a gun in our direction.

"Please lower your weapons, officers," Paula said, her voice filled with authority. She rose to her feet and frowned in their direction. "The guns are unnecessary."

The Hispanic officer lowered his gun reluctantly until it pointed at the floor. The female officer followed suit.

"I called," Paula told them. "I think—"

"Where's the injured party?" the woman in uniform interrupted her.

"I think she's dead," Paula said.

"Where?" repeated the policewoman.

Paula shrugged and pointed down the hallway. "Down the hall to your left, in the pantry," she answered.

The Hispanic officer nodded to his partner, who raced down the hallway. I hoped she had a good stomach. Only when she was gone did the policeman holster his gun. He kept his hand on it though, and remained standing, glaring silently at the lot of us. Paula sighed and sat back down.

"Officer," began Iris, "perhaps—"

Her speech was abruptly canceled by the arrival of the paramedics. They flashed through the door and past us into the hallway in the time it took for the policeman to direct them with a pointed thumb.

"Possible crime scene, careful!" the officer warned as they disappeared down the hall.

No one spoke as we waited. The muscular policewoman came back, gun holstered. She gestured to her fellow officer and they stepped a few yards away from the rest of us to hold a hasty, whispered conference. Then she went back down the hallway again.

When the paramedics came back, they were no longer rushing. One of them shook his head and they left by the front door.

"Oh," said the policeman watching us. It was not a happy sound. He shook his head, then turned back to us, his face angry.

"So, what happened here?" he demanded.

No one answered. The silence was absolute among the members of the cooking class. The only sound was a tapping from behind me. I turned. Alice was finally seated, and tapping her fingers on a vinyl-covered table.

"Did anyone see who did it?" he pressed.

Again, no one answered.

The officer sighed. "It's gonna be a long night," he predicted, his voice human for a moment. Then he got professional. "You'll have to be patient, you will each—" he began.

The policewoman interrupted him as she emerged from the hallway. "All the outside doors are locked," she said. She turned toward us. "What's up those stairs?"

"Oh dear," said Iris. "I forgot about the two little girls." Her face lost its serenity, crumpling into concern.

"I think the family of the dead woman lives upstairs," Paula clarified.

"I'll check it out," the policewoman promised and jogged back down the hallway one more time, pulling her gun out of its holster as she went.

The Hispanic policeman turned back to us. He looked tired to me. There was red showing in the whites of his eyes, and the bags beneath them were too pronounced for a man of his age. Poor guy, I thought. He couldn't be over thirty. Then he began giving orders.

"Okay!" he barked, surveying us with hostile eyes. "We'll want everyone's names and addresses. Then we'll interview each of you separately. Do not talk among yourselves." He finished off by patting the gun in his holster.

I didn't feel sorry for him anymore. I felt sorry for us.

"Officer," said Iris, raising her hand for attention. "I'm concerned about those poor little girls—"

"No one talks!" he interrupted, drawing himself up to his full height and glaring menacingly at us. "Do you understand?"

I certainly understood. *Yes, sir!* I nodded emphatically. From the silence around me I figured we all understood.

After a few minutes of this silent treatment, someone new came through the door. She was a tall, rangy redhead, with an open, freckled face that might have been a teenager's but for the wrinkles that put her years past forty. Her copper-colored suit had a cut similar to Paula Pierce's navy blue one. The woman wasn't smiling, but her neutral expression was an improvement over the hostile gaze of the policeman who stood guard over us.

Trailing behind the redhead was an undistinguished, medium-sized white man. His only memorable feature was a rosy complexion—and a surly expression.

I sighed. It *was* going to be a long night.

The redheaded woman pulled the Hispanic policeman away for a quick conference, headed down the hallway, then returned, her face less open than it had been a few minutes ago.

"I'm Detective Sergeant Oakley," she said in a surprisingly melodic voice. "Who's in charge here?" Melodic, but firm. Very firm.

She got the same answer the policeman before her had received. Silence.

"Come on," she prompted, her voice ringing higher now, but still on key. "Someone talk to me."

I turned to look in Meg's direction. I wasn't the only one. Barbara was giving her the eye now too. So was Ken. And Alice. I guessed Alice didn't feel like taking charge anymore. I couldn't blame her.

"Um," said Meg in a tiny voice. "I suppose I might be the one in charge. I was teaching a vegetarian cooking class here this evening." She stopped to blow her nose in a tattered Kleenex. Her voice was even smaller when she spoke again. "But I don't really know anything about this place, or anything, really. Maybe Alice . . ."

Twenty minutes later, Sergeant Oakley, having ascertained that no one was in charge, and that the closest thing to being in charge was having found the body, was interrogating me in the kitchen at the chest-high butcher-block table. Detective Utzinger, the nondescript man with the rosy complexion, was taking notes.

Sergeant Oakley had an interesting interrogative technique. She was friendly, undemanding, even consoling—and as manipulative as a psychotherapist as she led me ever so gently through my story.

I told her everything I knew, in great detail. She would say "ah," "hmm" or sometimes, "That must have been upsetting," as I ended a sentence, and stare at me with warm, concerned hazel eyes. Then I'd tell her something else. I actually found myself telling her about Wayne's mother, Vesta. Oakley was a great listener. If I had been the murderer, I'm sure I would have confided that fact to her too. I actually felt a bit guilty that I wasn't the murderer as I left the kitchen to have my fingerprints taken by yet another police officer, blond and male this time, standing guard in the dining room. It would have been so nice to help Sergeant Oakley out with a confession.

The blond policeman introduced himself as Officer Tate, rolled my fingers in ink and pressed them to a card, then told me I could go. He was the only policeman left in the dining room. The original two officers were nowhere to be seen. I would have taken Tate's advice and left the Good Thyme, but I had to wait for Barbara. She was in the kitchen with Sergeant Oakley now, presumably undergoing the same gentle grilling I had. I hoped she would be all right.

I took a seat near the front of the dining room where I could watch everyone else. God, I was exhausted. My body felt unnaturally heavy, and my head ached with the effort to think clearly. Was one of the cooking-class members a murderer?

Not necessarily, I told myself as I surveyed those members with exhaustion-blurred eyes. Meg was sitting with Paula and Gary now. She looked even more tired than I felt, her pale face slack, eyes staring into space. Gary leaned against Paula's sturdy shoulder, his dark face relaxed, his eyes closed. Was he actually napping? I shook my head. If he could sleep at a time like this, he was a lot more relaxed than I was. Maybe I needed a crystal to rub. In any case, Paula was tense enough for both of them, her face tight and twitching. Was hers the face of a murderer?

Someone else might have come in and killed Sheila, I reminded myself. I looked at Leo, slumped in his chair. I would have loved to believe he was the killer, but he looked too shaken to me. Or maybe he just needed a drink. Ken, on the other hand—

The front door of the restaurant swung open, interrupting my thoughts. Two men strolled in. Were these more policemen?

The first man was big and burly in a Hawaiian shirt and jeans. A diamond stud glistened in his left earlobe. He might have been good-looking with his curly black hair, mustache and strong jaw, but his eyes squinted. They looked mean. The second guy was tall and thin, except for his pot belly. His face was friendlier, clean-shaven with protuberant eyeballs and a big smile. A big stoned smile. I smelled the not-so-faint odor of marijuana wafting from their direction. Policemen?

"Whoa," said the man in the Hawaiian shirt jovially. "What's happening?"

The thin man's eyes drifted to Officer Tate in his police uniform, and he nudged the burly guy.

"Who are—" the policeman began.

"Dan!" interrupted Alice. She ran to the husky man, her arms outstretched. "Oh, Dan," she wailed. "Sheila's dead. She was killed, murdered—"

"You, sit down!" commanded Officer Tate, glaring at Alice. "Sir," he said, bringing his gaze back to the burly man. "If you will identify yourself . . ."

The man didn't so much as glance at Tate. After a moment of slack-jawed blankness, he grabbed Alice by her shoulders and pulled her toward him. "What do you mean, Sheila's dead!" he shouted.

Officer Tate tapped the man on the back. The man took his hands away from Alice's shoulders and whirled around.

"What the fuck is going on here!" he demanded of the officer. Tate winced. I didn't blame him. The question had blasted my ears, a couple of yards away.

"Who are you?" the policeman demanded in turn, his voice quiet but firm, and reinforced by his hand on his gun.

The big man stared at him for a moment, looked down at the gun, then answered. "Dan Snyder," he said. "This is my restaurant. Who the fuck are *you*?"

Dan Snyder. My stomach lurched as I realized this was Sheila's husband.

"I'm Officer Tate of the San Ricardo Police Department. I'm going to have to ask you to—"

"Where's Sheila?" Dan asked, his voice lower now, fearful.

"Listen," said Tate. "If you'll just follow me—"

"Where's Sheila!" Dan roared.

Officer Tate gripped his gun and looked around for help. It came from an unexpected source. The thin man who had arrived with Dan put an arm around his friend.

"Hey, buddy," he said. "Everything's cool. Let's hear what the man has to say."

Dan's shoulders slumped. He looked at Tate. "Is Sheila really dead?"

Officer Tate looked him in the eye and nodded.

Dan screamed, "No!" as the door to the Good Thyme swung open again. "I don't buy it! What the fuck—"

This time it was a plump older woman with permed gray hair who walked through the door. Her soft, doughy face was stretched into contours of panic. Dan looked at her and went silent.

Officer Tate turned to the newcomer. "And who are you?" he asked. Good question.

The woman's eyes darted around the room, then came back to Officer Tate and Dan Snyder.

"I'm their grandmother," she answered. "Are Opal and Topaz okay? They called me. They said they were scared—"

"Who are Opal and Topaz?" Officer Tate asked mildly.

"Sheila and Dan's children," Alice answered when it became obvious that Topaz and Opal's grandmother wasn't going to.

"Are the children all right?" the older woman asked again. "Where are they?"

"I'll find out, ma'am," promised Officer Tate.

"Where's Sheila?" growled Dan ominously.

I hoped no one would tell him. He didn't need to see her body.

"Where's Sheila!" he shouted.

Detective Utzinger and Sergeant Oakley emerged from the hallway just as the echoes of Dan's shout died away. Barbara trailed behind them, her eyes wide with curiosity.

"Husband," Tate mouthed and Oakley took over.

She laid a gentle hand on Dan's arm. "Let me help you," she said and led him unprotesting down the hall to the kitchen, with Utzinger taking up the rear.

By the time Barbara and I walked out the door of the Good Thyme Cafe five minutes later, everything was calm. Relatively calm, anyway. Topaz and Opal's grandmother had eventually identified herself as Rose Snyder and had been allowed to join her grandchildren and the police officer babysitting them. Zach, the thin man who had arrived with Dan Snyder, was excitedly telling Officer Tate how he had spent the evening. Sergeant Oakley and Dan Snyder himself were still in the kitchen. And the cooking-class murder suspects were all sitting quietly at their tables. I took one glance back, then let the door swing closed. I resisted the urge to run to my Toyota, keeping pace with Barbara's slow steps instead.

Not all of the suspects were left in the dining room, I reminded myself as I unlocked my car door for Barbara. My stomach churned unhappily as I stared at my friend's beautiful Asian face. Damn. I wished I could wipe the memory of her yelling at Sheila out of my mind. I wished she hadn't left me for an ice cream cone. I wished—

"Don't worry, kiddo," she assured me as she slid into the car. "It wasn't me."

A wave of relief calmed my churning stomach. Of course it wasn't Barbara. I felt light with new energy as I climbed into the driver's seat. How could I have even imagined her a murderer?

"But Sergeant Oakley thinks it might have been me," Barbara added cheerfully. "So we'll just have to find out who really killed Sheila. Then everything will be fine."

We argued all the way home. I said I wasn't going to investigate. She said if I didn't want to help, she'd do it herself. I said that could be dangerous to her health. She said it would be more dangerous to her health to be convicted of murder. I said I didn't believe that Sergeant Oakley thought she was any more likely a murderer than the rest of us. Barbara reminded me that she was a psychic. She knew Oakley suspected her. I asked her why she didn't just figure out who the killer was with her psychic powers.

She turned to me, her eyes pinched with unhappiness.

"Kate, I think I've lost them," she whispered.

"Your psychic powers?" I asked.

She nodded, then took a deep breath and went on. "I tried to tune in to the murderer, to anyone really. And all I got was a garble of voices that didn't connect to the people in the room." Her voice grew fainter as she put a hand over her face. "Kate, I'm worried. I don't think I've lost the ability completely, but it's all screwed up. It's not working."

"Maybe the voices were spirit guides," I suggested glibly. I wouldn't have recognized a spirit guide if one had shaken my hand, but Barbara had mentioned them often enough. In fact, I was never quite sure if Barbara was actually psychic, or just very sensitive to nonverbal cues. But Barbara's belief in her own psychic powers was at her core. The belief in their loss had to have shaken her.

"Maybe they were spirit guides," she repeated slowly, but her face was still troubled. "No, it won't wash," she said after a moment. "Something is seriously out of whack. Maybe the body . . ." Her voice trailed off.

Poor Barbara. I had to distract her somehow.

"I guess we could talk to some of the people from the class," I offered. "Find out what they saw—"

I stopped myself as I heard my own words. What was I saying?

Barbara grinned at me and I remembered that I had wanted to distract her. Well, I had.

"When we call them," she said eagerly, "we can find out who knew who, and how they feel—"

"Actually, I don't think we can contact the people in the class," I interrupted, backpedaling as fast as I could. "We don't know most of these guys' last names, much less their addresses and phone numbers. How could we even find them?"

"Easy," she said, her grin deepening. She drew a folded, lined sheet of paper from her jumpsuit pocket. "I've got the sign-up list," she told me.

Damn.

By the time we arrived at Barbara's apartment building, I had uneasily agreed to make a few calls. Nothing more, I told her. She laughed and planted a kiss on my cheek before departing. Then she was gone in a blur of hot pink.

I felt a hundred years older, but not any wiser, when I walked into my dark house five minutes later. My hands were shaking as I shut the door behind me. I leaned up against it, my forehead pressed to its wooden surface as my mind played reruns of Sheila's dead body.

Then I heard a faint sound close behind me in the dark. It was the sound of someone breathing very quietly. I listened for movement. There was none. Only the sinister, quiet breathing. I slid my hand toward the doorknob, then turned it slowly. The squeaking of the doorknob as it turned sounded like a scream in the quiet. I yanked at the door, pulling it open all of six inches before I felt the hand on my shoulder.

"Gotcha," a voice whispered.

- Four -

TAI CHI MOVES came to me instantly. I centered myself, then whirled around to face the whisperer, my knees bent, my arms positioned to protect my body.

It took me a moment to recognize the malicious face smiling in the dark. Vesta Caruso. Of course, it was Vesta. Reluctantly, I let my arms drop. My body was still tingling. When I took the time to think, I realized it couldn't have been anyone else. But my head had been too full of images of Sheila's dead body to think. I had forgotten all about Wayne's mother. I had been prepared to fight.

"What's the matter, little Miss High-and-Mighty?" hissed Vesta, clearly pleased with the sensation she had created. "Got a guilty conscience?"

My body was still ready to fight. Fueled by leftover adrenaline, my arms rose again without permission. I stared at Vesta's tall, skinny body. Just one little shove, my arms pleaded, and she'd topple right over.

I forced my arms back down, horrified at my own thoughts, my hands suddenly cold and shaking.

A light blazed on, momentarily blinding me. As my vision returned, I saw Wayne at the light switch.

I took one look at his homely, scarred face and felt a surge of warmth rising from my abdomen and spreading through my torso and down my arms toward my cold fingertips. I had grown conditioned to his heavy eyebrows, cauliflower nose, and curly brown hair. Conditioned to his tall, muscular body. The sight of

Wayne stimulated a response of love in me as instantly as the sound of an electric can opener stimulates hunger in a cat.

"Everything okay?" he asked, his voice low and gruff. I could see only the bottom halves of his eyes under the low, heavy brows, and they looked worried.

Why was he worried? Was I late? I looked down at my watch. It was a little after nine-thirty, not much later than the time I would have come home if the class had proceeded normally. Past nine-thirty, and time to tell all.

"Something happened at the class tonight—" I began in a whisper.

"Look at her," Vesta cut in, her tone high and triumphant. She squinted her eyes at me. "She's acting funny. You ask me, she's hiding something."

I shut my mouth abruptly. I wanted to tell Wayne every detail of my evening, and then weep in his arms. But I wasn't going to make a move until Vesta left us alone.

I stared at the woman, with the absurd hope that she'd take the hint. Her face was a fairy-tale witch's, with small navy blue eyes under low brows, a long, crooked nose and a thin, malicious mouth, all topped by a long tangle of dyed black hair. The only thing that was missing was the pointed hat. Wayne's homeliness filled me with love. Vesta's didn't. Not that I have anything against witches. Glinda, the Good Witch of the North, had been my personal hero when I was a child. Unfortunately, Vesta had more in common with the Wicked Witch of the West.

"Ask her what she's been doing," she commanded Wayne. She pointed an accusing finger in my direction.

"Mom, don't," Wayne begged softly. He held out a hand. Was it for me?

Vesta strode toward him and laid claim to the hand before I had a chance. Wayne gazed at me over her shoulder, his rough face a study in frustration. Maybe I wouldn't wait for Vesta to leave.

"The woman who owned the restaurant—" I began again.

"Waynie," interrupted Vesta, her voice suddenly quavering. "I had a chest pain just now. Do you think it was a heart attack?"

He looked into her face. "Are you serious, Mom?"

"Oh, yes," she answered. "I hate to trouble you, but it scared me a little."

"I'll call the doctor," he said brusquely.

"No, no," she whispered. "I'll talk to a doctor tomorrow . . ."

Wayne sighed, then put an arm around his mother and led her down the hall to the back room, now her bedroom. Another round to Vesta. I believed her report of chest pain about as much as I believed politicians who said they just wanted to be of service.

I waited for a few minutes, still standing there in the entryway, hoping that Wayne would be back. Then I stomped into the bedroom alone, changed into a bathing suit and stomped out onto the back deck to soak in the hot tub.

My cat, C.C., joined me after I had climbed into the tub. She sat in a chair a safe foot away and complained. I slid in deeper, letting the hot water boil away the tension in my muscles. If C.C. was meowing about Vesta Caruso, I was in complete agreement.

Vesta hadn't been born a Caruso, or even married one. She had been born Vesta Skeritt, but had changed her name to Mrs. Caruso when Wayne was born, listing the father as Enrico Caruso. Wayne didn't know exactly why she had chosen the opera singer's name. A joke? Defiance? Wishful thinking? I had felt such pity for Vesta, starting off at eighteen as a single mother in the days when single mothers were identified by far less positive descriptions. I still felt for her occasionally, at least when I wasn't in her malign presence.

Maybe his illegitimacy was the reason that Wayne had wanted to marry me so badly. Whatever his reasons, I was glad he had finally settled for living with me. My first, and last, marriage had left me gun-shy. And up to the time of Vesta's arrival, Wayne and I had been happy together, fixing our separate vegetarian and meat meals, but sharing our lives and a bed.

Sweat dripped down my forehead. I closed my eyes. That wasn't a good move. Sheila's strangled body flashed into my mind instantly. My eyes popped open and I wondered how much time would have to pass before that image would fade from my mind's eye. I splashed my way out of the tub much to C.C.'s loud disapproval. *Wayne*, I thought, *I've got to tell Wayne*.

He was waiting for me in the bedroom, sitting on my velour-draped Goodwill couch. His face was creased by lines of misery.

"Kate," he greeted me as I walked in, the lines in his face softening.

He was with me in three long steps. He scooped me up in his arms and held me to him, soaking the front of his flannel shirt. If he noticed I was wet, he didn't say so.

By the time he set me back down, he was apologizing about Vesta, about himself, about everything. Two hours later, he was still apologizing and making plans to move Vesta out of my house. I never did get a chance to tell him about Sheila Snyder's murder. I fell asleep with my head on his chest and dreamed of strangled bodies rising like Lazarus.

I didn't get a chance to tell him the next morning either. Wayne got up, cooked Vesta breakfast and told her she would have to leave. Vesta began to cry in long heart-rending sobs.

I sat at my desk, paying Jest Gifts bills, and listened to Wayne's gruff voice get progressively higher and more defensive in the kitchen. He didn't look me in the eye when he kissed me goodbye. He growled "business downtown," and left.

Vesta looked me in the eye, though. I was lucky she didn't spit in it. She flounced into my ex-dining room, now my home office, and gave me a big smile.

"You'll never win," she told me.

I wondered if she was right. If this was a game, the score was about forty-five to zero, her favor. But I smiled back steadily until she left my office to sit in the living room, where she complained loudly that I had to be crazy not to own a television set.

Once she was gone, I grabbed my Safeguard check ledger, a calculator and the stack of bills on my desk and threw them all into a box. I added payroll cards and some tax forms. I knew Wayne probably did have business downtown at one of the string of restaurants he owned and managed. But if he wasn't going to stick around, I wasn't going to either. I didn't have to work at home today. I didn't have any designing to do, only paperwork. I could visit the Jest Gifts warehouse across the bay and work in that closet we called the office. Or I could go to the library and work there. I could even go to Barbara's if she was home today. As a free-lance electrician, she made her own hours. I dialed her apartment number, betting she'd be there.

"Hey, kiddo, I was waiting for your call," Barbara told me as she picked up the phone. Maybe her psychic powers had returned. "You can work over here if you like," she added, confirming my guess.

I was halfway out the door when the phone rang. Vesta pounced on it. I heard her talking in a low voice. Wayne? I wondered. Or maybe a pesky salesman?

Shrugging, I picked up my box of paperwork and started down the stairs.

"Oh, Kate," Vesta called out cheerily.

Why was her voice so friendly? I dropped the box and walked back up the stairs.

"Your husband, Craig, is on the phone," she said.

"My ex-husband!" I snapped and reached for the receiver, remembering how Vesta's eyes had lit up when she had met Craig. My ex-husband would have liked to be my husband again. He wasn't pushy about it, but his desire was obvious. Vesta was only too delighted to encourage him.

"What do you want?" I greeted him curtly.

"Just to see how things are with you," Craig answered cheerfully. "Vesta tells me you and Wayne aren't getting along."

"Goddamm it!" I shouted. "That is not true!" I saw Vesta's rapt face watching me and modulated my tone.

It took me another ten minutes to convince Craig that Wayne and I were doing fine. Just fine, thank you. Then I left for Barbara's, wishing it were true.

Barbara met me at her apartment door wearing a ratty turquoise T-shirt under farmer's overalls. She still looked like a fashion model. But it was the piece of paper in her hand that caught my attention, the sign-up sheet for last night's class.

"Hey!" she greeted me, smiling into my worried face. "Don't worry. We're just gonna talk to a few folks."

"Barbara," I said, holding my box of paperwork out in front of me. "I've got work to do."

Her face grew more serious. "So do I," she told me. "I turned down two possible gigs today. But settling this murder is far more important."

She motioned me through the doorway. I sighed and walked in. Barbara's living room was furnished with a couple of blue futons folded into couch position, an old arcade fortune-teller machine featuring a woman's head in a gypsy scarf that lit up and nodded and cackled when you put in your nickel, a few stacks of books, and a dozen crystal balls. They were real quartz-crystal balls, mounted on carved stands all over the room.

"We don't know that it even *was* one of the people in the class who murdered Sheila," I argued as I set my box down. "How about letting the police handle it?"

"It was someone in the class," Barbara told me, her eyes serious. "I'll bet it was because she hit her little girl."

I pushed a pile of tarot cards to the side of the nearest futon and took a seat. "If people went around killing everyone they saw hitting children," I replied, equally serious, "there would be a helluva lot more dead bodies around."

None of my arguments made a dent in Barbara's resolve. Half an hour later, we were making phone calls. Barbara was in her bedroom using her personal phone line. I was in the living room using her business line. And worse, I was setting up appointments to see potential murderers in person. I'd agreed to the plan only when Barbara had promised me that we would visit any suspects as a team. Her capitulation had been all too swift. I rubbed my throbbing temples. I had been suckered again.

I got Alice Frazier the first try, on duty at the reception desk of the Stanton-Reneau Insurance Agency in downtown San Francisco. And Meg was there too, Alice told me, doing temp work. I invited them to lunch. Alice put me on hold for a minute or two, then returned to accept the invitation. Barbara and I could meet them at their office, she told me. She sounded perfectly happy about the arrangement, unafraid. That made one of us.

I called Iris Neville next. She was breathless with excitement at the prospect of being interviewed.

"So glad to be included," she assured me.

I told her we'd see her within the hour, and wondered what was wrong with these people. I could be the killer. They should be nervous.

I was on my way into Barbara's bedroom to tell her the news when she yelled my name. I ran the last few steps, visions of murder, even kidnapping, flooding my brain. But Barbara was only held captive by the screen of her television set.

"Look," she said pointing. "Our murder's on TV."

"—deeply upset by this recent act of violence," a well-dressed, olive-skinned man with large mournful eyes was saying to a microphone-wielding reporter. "The members of the San Ricardo Police Department are working around the clock to discover the identity of the perpetrator."

"Lieutenant Madrid, do you have any suspects yet?" the reporter asked.

"I cannot say at this time," the man answered.

As the reporter turned back to the screen, Barbara touched a button on her remote control and the picture disappeared.

"Jeez-Louise," she said. "If that's the head of the detective bureau, we're in trouble."

I shrugged my shoulders. However politic his words, Lieutenant Madrid had a better chance of solving this murder than we did.

"Okay," Barbara said, all business now. She picked up a notebook. "There's no one at Ken Hermann's but an answering machine. I left a message. Leo didn't write down his last name, but his phone number is connected to an art gallery. The woman who answered said Leo'd be in most of the day. Paula Pierce and Gary Powell wrote down the same number, but it's busy." She paused to scribble down some notes, then looked up at me. "So what'd you get?" she asked.

Barbara was impressed when I told her about our two appointments. She leapt off her bed and gave me a big hug in celebration, then changed into a pair of beige slacks and a conservative silk print blouse in a matter of seconds.

I looked down at my own MY CAT WALKS ALL OVER ME shirt, complete with paw prints. My mother had given it to me for my birthday.

Barbara saw the look and tossed me a lavender silk blouse. Luckily she wore her clothes loose. I changed into the silk blouse and tucked it into my jeans. I wondered if she'd let me keep it.

I was glad I was wearing the silk blouse when we got to Iris's house in the San Ricardo hills. Iris was in silk too, an embroidered, cream-colored silk tunic over matching pants. She opened the door and her wide blue eyes took in our outfits approvingly.

"Oh, my," she said, "you both look so nice."

I imagined that she was comparing *my* blouse to the zoo

T-shirt I had worn the night before. I'm often subject to these flashes of style paranoia.

"What a beautiful tunic," purred Barbara.

That got us into the living room, a large, beautifully decorated room in tones of gray, mauve and cream. A group of couches in muted floral patterns formed a conversation area at one end of the room. A grand piano dominated the other end.

"Do you play?" I asked politely. I figured it wouldn't be socially correct to ask her outright if she had murdered Sheila.

"Yes, I do," she trilled. She toyed with what looked like a chopstick stuck into her silver French twist. "Are you musical, yourself?" she inquired.

I shook my head violently. The closest I'd ever been to music was an old boyfriend who had strummed the guitar far more lovingly than he had me.

"You could play piano with those fingers," she said, looking at my hands.

She reached toward me. "May I?" she asked and clamped her cool fingers around my wrist, pulling my hand up in front of her intent face. "Such nice, long fingers. Such a good spread," she said, stroking the fingers in question.

"Uh, thanks," I replied, feeling vaguely embarrassed, as if she'd peeked at my underwear. She let go of my hand.

"My fingers, alas, were never long enough to be a true concert pianist's," she confessed, holding out her small hand as evidence. "I practiced and practiced when I was a girl. I had the ear, but not the hands."

She sighed and put her inadequate hand to her chest. Tragedy became her. Her strong features were noble in their sadness, her straight back unbowed.

How in the world was I going to segue into murder? I checked for Barbara at my side. But she was gone, looking at a series of photographs on the wall behind the piano.

"Ah, you've found my little collection," said Iris, her voice cheery again.

I stepped past the piano and looked more closely at the rows of framed black-and-white photographs. They were all pictures of pairs of hands. Nothing else, just rows and rows of disembodied hands. An image of Iris's small hands wrapping electric cord around Sheila's neck superimposed itself onto the wall of photos. I swallowed hard and it disappeared.

"These hands are Liberace's," she told us, pointing to a pair at the bottom. "Can't you just see the music in them?"

I nodded insincerely.

"And these are Van Cliburn's," she continued.

She pointed out the hands of some two dozen musicians, then went on to other celebrities: Saddam Hussein's—"so evil," Albert Schweitzer's—"such kindness in them," Richard Nixon's, John F. Kennedy's, and on. And on. Finally, she reached the top row.

"Let's see if you can guess whose hands these are," she challenged us, her finger on a photo at the far end of the row.

They looked like everyday hands to me, four fingers and a thumb each. I glanced in Barbara's direction. It was going to take a psychic to come up with a reasonable guess.

"I'll give you a clue," Iris said. She smiled broadly. "Murder."

"Murder?" I repeated, my voice squeaking.

"Speaking of murder," said Barbara calmly, "did you see anything suspicious last night?" Not the most graceful segue, but certainly better than I had accomplished.

Unfortunately, Iris hadn't seen anything suspicious. She hadn't known Sheila Snyder, nor anyone else in the class previously. She couldn't imagine who had done such a thing. And she was very sorry she couldn't be of more help.

We did learn that she had been a nurse before she married her late husband, Norris, a dear man who had also played the piano. They had owned a lovely little music store in San Francisco for many years, such a joy. Now she volunteered her time at hospices and shelters for abused women. So many good causes.

She asked us if we'd like some tea. She had herbal, she assured us, and some delicious little cookies from the health food store. I felt a pang of guilt as we refused. This woman was a different breed of social creature than I, but she was intelligent, lively, and good-humored. And she was lonely. You could see it in her eyes, especially when she spoke of her late husband.

"Maybe another time," I said, not sure if I meant it.

"Yes, perhaps we could have lunch someday," Iris suggested as she walked us to her front door.

"That would be great," I told her.

Iris squeezed our respective hands goodbye and we turned to leave.

We were all the way out the doorway when Barbara suddenly turned back.

"So whose *were* those last hands?" she asked Iris.

Iris chuckled. "Are you sure you don't want to guess?"

We both shook our heads.

She brought her face closer to ours and whispered, "Ted Bundy's."

- Five -

I SWALLOWED, THEN forced my face into a strained smile. Some-how, I didn't think I would enjoy lunching with Iris now, unless we had a chaperon—preferably an armed one.

"Gee, that's really interesting," said Barbara, her voice a little too high to be sincere.

But Iris didn't seem to notice the effect that her identification of Ted Bundy's hands was having on us.

"I'm so glad you think so. So few people understand," she said, her speech quickening with enthusiasm. Her wide blue eyes gleamed as she went on. "You can see the cruelty in his finger-tips, can't you? And his extraordinary ability to plan in the way he holds his hands." She brought her own small hands together, clasping them in front of her chest. "So fascinating really, when you think of the use that he put his hands to."

Goose bumps formed on my arms. I swallowed again.

"Fascinating," Barbara echoed.

Iris dropped her hands and smiled apologetically. "But I mustn't ride my favorite hobbyhorse any longer," she said briskly. "You two have things to do. It was so good of you to drop by."

When Iris shut her door, Barbara and I practically ran to my Toyota.

"Jeez-Louise," whispered Barbara once we were locked in the car.

That about summed it up. I turned the engine on and drove to-ward the highway without speaking. Before we got there, Bar-bara broke the silence.

"Let's go downtown," she directed. "I want to see the Good Thyme Cafe again."

I followed her direction without thought. My mind was too busy with Iris to think about anything else.

I parked a block away from the Good Thyme, turned off the engine and looked at Barbara.

"Do you think Iris is our murderer?" I asked softly.

"I don't know," Barbara answered. She rubbed her forehead with the palm of her hand. "I don't get anything weird from her psychically. She seems friendly, harmless." She shook her head. "No, it can't be Iris."

"Then who?" I demanded, suddenly angry with Barbara, angry with myself for going along with her. I didn't want to visit any more murder suspects. "I can't imagine any of the people from last night's class as a murderer," I said. It wasn't really true. If I allowed myself to, I could imagine each and every one of them strangling Sheila.

"How about Paula Pierce?" Barbara countered, her voice rising. "She's an attorney. And she was angry when Sheila came on to Gary—"

"Just because she's an attorney, doesn't mean she's a murderer," I interrupted, holding my sore stomach. "Ruthless, maybe. But not a murderer."

"Then what about her husband, Gary?" Barbara demanded, her voice even louder. "He's too quiet. And the way he fondles that crystal. Jeez-Louise! I like crystals, but enough is enough."

I didn't answer. I was remembering Gary's warm smile.

"And Meg, the cooking teacher!" Barbara pressed on. "It was her SaladShooter. And she knows how to use it."

"Sheila was not shredded to death," I said evenly.

Barbara let out a quick snort of laughter. Then she frowned and paled. Was she remembering just how Sheila *had* been killed?

"Sorry about that, kiddo," Barbara apologized softly. "I guess I'm just searching for an easy answer." She reached out and put her hand on mine. "Are we still friends?" she asked.

"Of course," I answered, and my stomach relaxed instantly. I looked into her all-too scrutable Asian face and saw real concern there. How could I have been mad at Barbara?

She smiled back at me. "I'll bet it's that lecherous creep, Leo," she said cheerfully.

Damn. Now I remembered why I was mad. I opened my mouth to argue.

"Or his friend, Ken," she added quickly.

I closed my mouth and thought about Ken Hermann. I remembered the way he had goggled from behind his glasses. And the half-smile on his face after Sheila's body had been discovered. Sheila had cut him off while he was ranting about poisons in our food. Maybe that had made him angry. I shivered.

"He could be—" I began.

"Alice!" Barbara yelped abruptly. She hit the dashboard with her fist. "Alice knew the Snyders ahead of time!" She turned to me, her beautiful face made more beautiful by the intensity that clarified it. "And Alice set the class up," she breathed.

Alice Frazier: plump, pretty, friendly and energetic. I had liked her, liked her a lot. I put my head into my hands. I didn't want to think about it anymore.

"Let's go check out the Good Thyme," Barbara said eagerly. She opened the car door and hopped out.

I groaned. Barbara came around to my side and pulled me from the womb of my Toyota.

Luckily, the Good Thyme Cafe was closed. But Barbara dragged me around to canvass the other businesses on the block, hoping for gossip about the Snyders. The boy scooping ice cream at the shop on the corner had never heard of them, but Barbara enjoyed her pre-lunch, double-chocolate cone. The owner of the bike shop knew them, but only because they dumped their extra garbage in his bins. He'd seen them do it, he assured us indignantly. The folks at the book store, the variety store and the barber shop didn't want to say anything about the Snyders, but the man tending bar two blocks down let us know that the Synders were too "stuck-up" to put Christmas decorations in their windows like the rest of the local businesses.

Barbara stopped to make some phone calls on the bar's pay phone while I sipped a Virgin Mary—Bloody Mary, hold the vodka—and worried about my undone Jest Gifts paperwork. Barbara was grinning with excitement when she got back from the phone. She had reached Paula and arranged a five o'clock appointment at her law office in San Francisco. At least Paula was working today, I thought miserably.

Barbara hustled me out to the car before I had a chance to finish my drink. We had forty minutes to drive from San Ricardo to downtown San Francisco to meet Alice and Meg for lunch.

It took me forty-five minutes. I was searching desperately for a parking space, knowing I would never find one, when I saw them waiting in the shadow of a tall office building. I couldn't miss Alice, her ample body elegant in a well-cut electric-blue suit and high heels. But I would have never seen Meg if I hadn't been looking for her. She wore a gray pantsuit that blended into the gray stonework behind her. Her pale face was visible though, and staring in our direction. She lifted her hand in a tentative wave.

I pulled the steering wheel to the right and skidded into a bus zone. Meg and Alice piled into the car and the whole thing got easier.

"Go up four blocks and take a right," ordered Alice. "There'll be an underground parking lot on your left."

"Yes, ma'am," I replied thankfully.

I still liked Alice. She gave great directions. I'd worry about her being a killer after I got out of traffic.

The restaurant she took us to served salad, soup, and a few hot entrees and sandwiches cafeteria style, a necessity for office workers who had only an hour for lunch. Meg, Alice and I all got garden salads with whole-wheat rolls. Barbara asked for lasagna. I eyed her tray enviously as we paid for our meals and carried them to a laminated wood table.

We ate in silence for a few minutes. The salad was limp, the Italian dressing too oily. Barbara squinted her eyes and stared at Alice. Alice stared back at Barbara. Meg sniffled and kept her eyes on her salad.

"So, Alice," I said finally. I tried to keep my voice friendly, conversational. "You knew the Snyders before, didn't you?"

Alice's eyebrows went up. Wasn't she expecting this kind of question? Why did she think we were meeting her for lunch? After a moment, her eyebrows came back down and she answered.

"Sheila and Dan and I all lived in the same commune," she told us. Her eyes went out of focus as she remembered. "This was years ago, way before their kids. When I was still thin," she added, laughing. "So was Dan. God, he was a hunk. There were twelve of us originally. We all put in a little money and leased this huge old farmhouse out in Granville. Called it Heartsong. It was really neat, at least for a while.

"We all shared chores. Sheila cooked vegetarian meals. Maybe that's why I was so thin. She never could cook worth a damn." Alice laughed again. Then her eyes came back into focus. She shook her head sadly.

"Did you keep in touch?" asked Barbara.

"No," Alice answered. She took a bite of salad and mumbled through it "I left the commune in '73. Stopped making macrame and went back out into the real world. Got a real job. I didn't see Dan and Sheila again till a few months ago at a farmers market. What a trip! After all these years. We got together a few times. I ate at their restaurant." Alice smiled.

"Sheila still doesn't cook very well," she said. But then her smile disappeared. "I guess I should say, she *didn't* cook very well. It's hard to believe she's dead." She bent her head over her salad and took another bite.

"How did Dan and Sheila get along?" I asked through a mouthful of my own salad.

Alice's head jerked up at the question. Her eyes narrowed, her good-natured face no longer good-natured.

"I mean—" I began.

"I know what you mean," she snapped. "Dan loved his wife, loved her absolutely, without reservation. Even when she hit the kids, he would just ask her to stop. He loved her more than anything, more than . . ." Her eyes went out of focus again as her words trailed off.

Was she thinking that Dan had loved Sheila more than her? I remembered the way she had run to Dan the night before, her arms outstretched. She was in love with Dan. Suddenly, I was sure of it. Alice had a motive. I stared at her heart-shaped face for a moment, my head buzzing with adrenaline. I barely heard her as she began to speak again.

"—terrible the way Sheila hit those kids," she was saying indignantly as I tuned in. She turned to Meg. "Remember when we visited Sheila to set up the class? She hit the little one so hard she fell over."

Meg nodded, her green eyes round in her pale face.

"Parents shouldn't do that to their kids," Barbara muttered.

I stared down at what was left of my salad.

"They shouldn't, but they do," I muttered back, thinking of what Wayne had told me about the beatings Vesta used to give him. He still had scars on his back from the belt she had used. And worse scars on his psyche, I was sure. My hands automatically bunched into fists as I thought about her.

"You've got my sympathy, kiddo," Barbara told me, patting my shoulder. "It can't be any picnic living with that witch."

I looked up. Meg and Alice were staring at me, wide-eyed with apparent curiosity. Of course they weren't psychic like Barbara.

"Kate's boyfriend's mother is living with them," Barbara explained. "She beat on Wayne—"

"So, did either of you see anything suspicious last night?" I asked Meg and Alice, changing the subject abruptly.

Alice pointedly shifted her gaze to Barbara. Damn. I guess the sight of Barbara kneeling next to a recently killed corpse might have seemed suspicious.

"I didn't kill Sheila," Barbara stated for the record, returning Alice's gaze. "But I know it looks like I might have." Alice's face began to soften. "And I'm scared," Barbara added. "That's why we're trying to figure this thing out." She waited a beat, then asked, "Won't you guys help us?"

Alice and Meg both nodded solemnly. Barbara could be persuasive. There was no doubt about it. My insides knotted up. She had persuaded me too, persuaded me that she hadn't killed Sheila. Was it true?

Of course it was true, I chided myself. I ate my whole-wheat roll and listened absently as Barbara asked questions to which Meg and Alice seemed to have no good answers. The reason Barbara was so persuasive, I reassured myself, was that she was telling the truth.

"I just didn't notice anything else," Alice summed up. "Did you, Meg?"

Meg shook her head.

Barbara sighed. "Are you guys going to hold a class next Monday?" she asked.

Meg and Alice looked at each other. I guessed that they hadn't talked about the possibility of further classes yet.

"I know it sounds weird," Barbara continued. "But I think it would be a good idea to hold the second cooking class as originally scheduled. Assuming this whole thing isn't over with by then." She paused for a moment, her eyes half-closed in thought. "Maybe we could learn something important if everyone who was there the first night would come again on Monday."

"Maybe," agreed Alice quietly. She tapped her fingers on the table. "Maybe if we pretended we already knew who did it, like in the movies—"

"Wait a minute, you guys—" I began.

But Alice kept talking, her voice rising with enthusiasm. "We'd have to set it up now, make sure everyone would come." She turned to Meg. "How about it?" she asked.

"Um," said Meg, her voice as thin as she was. "I don't know." She sniffed. "I mean, I don't even have the sign-up sheet anymore. I think the police took it."

I saw the blush that started in Barbara's neck and rose through her cheeks. I sighed in relief. If she was this obviously guilty over taking the sign-up sheet, I would have to have noticed a larger sign of guilt if she had really killed Sheila.

"I think I can get everyone's phone numbers," Barbara said, her voice too high.

"Really?" asked Alice. She looked at Barbara, her head tilted quizzically.

"I have a friend with connections to the police," Barbara explained.

I raised an eyebrow at her myself.

"Felix," she specified.

Damn. I had forgotten about Felix, Barbara's reporter boyfriend. He was going to be ravenous for information once he found out about the murder.

Meg and Alice were looking at each other again. "Okay?" asked Alice.

Meg nodded slowly. "Okay," she agreed.

"We'll do it," Alice announced. She grinned widely, reminding me suddenly of Barbara, and raised a glass of Calistoga water.

"I propose a toast," she said. "To success."

* * *

Meg and Alice had to leave soon after the toast. I dropped them off in front of their building, then turned to Barbara before driving back into traffic.

"Well?" I prompted.

"I don't know," she whispered sadly. "I didn't get anything psychic on either of them." She rubbed her forehead roughly. "Just more garble."

I pulled out into traffic, thinking about Alice and her relationship with Dan, grateful that Barbara's psychic powers were down for the moment. I didn't want to share my current thoughts with Barbara. She didn't need any more reasons to suspect Alice of murder.

We were already across the Golden Gate Bridge when I remembered our five o'clock appointment with Paula Pierce. I'd just have time to do a couple hours of work; then we'd have to return to the city.

My box of paperwork was still waiting for me when we got to Barbara's apartment. Too bad no one had stolen it. I picked it up off the blue futon and carried it into her kitchen to work at the black-lacquered table there. Barbara withdrew to her bedroom to make more phone calls. Ten minutes later I had written enough checks to keep my major creditors happy for a week, and was starting on the minor ones. I felt a hand on my shoulder.

I turned, expecting to see Barbara, but saw instead a small, slender man with a luxurious mustache and soulful eyes. He was Barbara's boyfriend, Felix. And he wasn't smiling. I tensed up, waiting for his harangue. It wasn't long in coming.

"So, you and Barbara find a stiff, and don't bother to tell me," he snarled. "Me, a friggin' crime reporter! Not a word. No way, José—"

Barbara cut him off mid-sentence with a kiss. I began packing up.

"No howdy-hi?" she asked Felix with a Cheshire cat grin.

He glared at her. "You!" he shouted. "Benedict Arnold Chu! My own sweetie and you don't even tell me about the murder! Holy Moly, Barbara, I'm a reporter. I'm your old man . . ."

I threw the rest of my paperwork into the box in a hurry, dropping an eraser on the way. It fell between Felix's sock-and-sandal-clad feet. I fumbled for it, knocking against Felix's big toe in the process.

"Yow!" he yelped.

I straightened up and looked into his eyes curiously. I had barely touched him. What was the matter? He fell into a chair, howling.

I looked at Barbara. "Gout," she mouthed.

I took the coward's way out. I picked up my box and ran.

Vesta was waiting for me at the door when I got home.

"There's a call for you on your machine," she said, smiling.

I smiled back tentatively. Maybe she was trying to be nice. Everyone deserves a second chance. Right?

Vesta followed me to the answering machine. I pushed the re-play button.

"Are you the one who killed her, bitch?" a husky voice exploded from the machine. "Huh? Because, if you are, I'm gonna get you!" The voice lowered to a whisper. "That's a promise," it said. Then all I heard was the dial tone.

- Six -

VESTA CACKLED GAILY behind me. I turned to her, wondering for
one wild, heart-thumping moment if she was the one responsible
for the message. No, not Vesta, I decided. I turned back to the
answering machine, then took three long deep breaths. Who had
left the message? I rewound the tape, then played it again.

"Are you the one who killed her, bitch?" it began. I turned it
off before I got to the part where the voice promised to "get me"
if I was the one.

Was that Dan Snyder's voice? I tried to recall the sound of his
voice from the night before, but all I could remember was the
way he'd looked, big and burly in his Hawaiian shirt, his eyes
squinting angrily. It had to be him, I told myself. Or maybe his
friend Zach.

"Where'd you get the blouse?" came Vesta's voice from behind me.

I flinched, startled. I had almost forgotten her.

"Doesn't look like your regular stuff," she added.

I looked down and recognized the lavender silk blouse I had
borrowed from Barbara. "My friend lent—" I began.

"Didja steal the blouse when you murdered the lady?" Vesta
asked conversationally.

I swiveled my head around to look into her dark, malevolent
eyes.

"I didn't murder anyone," I said firmly.

Vesta put a hand to her mouth and giggled. Then she asked me
if I had stolen the blouse to impress my new lover.

* * *

I left my house within five minutes of having arrived. With my box of paperwork in my arms, I headed toward Barbara's again. If Felix was still there, so be it. I could handle his harangue better than Vesta's Alice-in-Wonderland questions. Malice-in-Wonderland, I corrected myself.

But Felix was nowhere in sight when Barbara opened her apartment door.

"I told him to take off," she explained with a sigh.

Then her eyes flashed with indignation. "He was driving me bananas with his questions. Jeez-Louise, Kate, he's a vampire! He wanted to know everything. What the body looked like, what I felt like, who I thought did it . . ."

She ranted for a full five minutes. I didn't blame her. I had been at the receiving end of Felix's inquisitions before. She hadn't. And he was her boyfriend. That had to be worse.

"Sic him on Iris," I suggested once Barbara ran out of words.

"Maybe I'll just do that, kiddo," she said, smiling.

She wrapped her arms around me and laughter vibrated through both of our bodies as we hugged. Then she let go and motioned me into her apartment. I took a seat on one of the blue futons and looked up at her.

"I got a call on my answering machine . . ." I said slowly, hating to spoil the mood. "I think it was Dan Snyder—"

"He called me too," Barbara interrupted cheerfully. She sat down next to me. "He thinks the two of us killed his wife."

"He what?" I yelped.

She reached over and patted my hand. "He's in pain, Kate," she said earnestly. "He wants to blame someone. And we're it. He has this theory that we were in it together. Someone must have told him that we found Sheila's body."

"Aren't you scared?" I demanded, fastening my eyes on Barbara's lovely, serene face.

"I don't think he's really dangerous," she said with an easy wave of her hand.

And that was that. I wanted to call the police. She didn't. I wanted to quit investigating. She didn't. I wanted to move to Alaska. She didn't. She had some paperwork to do. She advised me to do the same.

It was good advice. After an hour of meaningful interaction with the Jest Gifts payroll account, I wasn't in a gibbering panic anymore. So what if this maniac thought we killed his wife? What was he going to do about it? Now I was only frightened. Very frightened.

Barbara tapped me on the shoulder as I was reaching for my accounts payable file. My rear end levitated a full inch above my chair, then landed again with a *whump*. "It's time to visit Paula Pierce," she said and dragged me down the stairs to the apartment parking lot before I could formulate an objection. She offered to drive. I refused the offer. Barbara's driving style—eyes on her passenger instead of the road—scared me almost as much as Dan Snyder.

We were on the Golden Gate Bridge when Barbara drew a sheet of newsprint from her purse and unfolded it to its full three-foot length. This was the "paperwork" she had been working on for the last hour, a chart of murder suspects that included columns with the scrawled headings of "opportunity," "motive" and "psychological profile." She read pieces of it all the way into San Francisco, occasionally flashing the sheet between my eyes and the windshield when she wanted me to see something important. She had read almost to the bottom of the chart when we reached Paula's office in the Mission District.

As I circled the block looking for a parking space, Barbara told me her conclusions. Boiled down, her chart seemed to prove that anyone could have done it. Alice, Meg, Ken, Leo, Iris, Gary, or Paula. Or the family members. Or Dan's friend Zach. According to Barbara's chart, they all had opportunity. They all had motives. Lots of motives.

I prayed to the goddess of parking spaces as Barbara expounded. I was instantly rewarded. A Honda pulled out of a legal parking space in front of me. I slid into the space thankfully.

"Well?" prompted Barbara as we got out of the Toyota. She looked into my face eagerly.

"You've got a great imagination, that's for sure," I told her, smiling to take the sting from my words. "I especially liked the theory about Sheila really being Iris and/or Leo's illegitimate daughter."

Barbara frowned for a moment, then grinned as we crossed the street at the light.

"We'll do it, Kate!" she shouted over the noise of traffic. She waved her fist in the air jubilantly. "We'll find the murderer. It's only a matter of time."

The sound of my groan was lost in the street noise.

Paula's law office was up a flight of red-carpeted stairs, above a bakery. The black-and-gold lettering on the glass door read "Pierce and Nakhuda Law offices, Specializing in Women's Law."

Barbara opened the door and the two of us walked in. The offices were furnished more luxuriously than one might expect to find over a bakery. Plush cream-colored carpeting, two camel-colored sofas, and rosewood shelves filled with law books gave the room a professional look. The young Hispanic woman behind the rosewood reception desk detracted somewhat from the businesslike image. Not that she wasn't well dressed. Her open cotton blouse looked fine. It was the baby nursing at her breast that didn't match the rest of the room.

"Can I help you?" she asked, smiling politely.

"Kate Jasper and Barbara Chu," I said briskly. "Here to see Paula Pierce."

She shifted the baby to her other breast, picked up the telephone with her spare hand and murmured a few words, then asked us to take a seat. I sat down on a sofa as ordered. Barbara didn't.

"What an absolutely adorable baby," she cooed, walking closer to the desk.

From where I sat, the baby didn't look extraordinarily adorable, just a small lavender bundle with a few dark hairs on its head. I would have bet Barbara was trying to make points before she launched into the questions she really wanted answered.

"Have you been with Ms. Pierce long?" she asked.

The young mother shrugged gently, not enough to disturb the baby. Barbara moved quickly to her next question.

"What exactly is 'women's law'?" she asked.

"Oh, lots of stuff," the young woman answered. "They do divorce, custody battles, employment discrimination, wrongful termination, child-support collection—stuff like that." She shrugged her shoulders again.

"How do you like Ms. Pierce?" Barbara pressed on.

A genuine smile lit up the young woman's face. "She's wonderful!" she said enthusiastically. "I wouldn't have custody of my baby now if it weren't for her—"

A door opened to her side and the wonderful attorney in question walked through. Paula Pierce looked much as she had the night before, stocky in today's gray business suit, her cropped salt-and-pepper hair as uncompromising as ever. The circles under her eyes might have been a little darker, her mouth a little tighter, but other than that, she looked unaffected by Sheila Snyder's death. She jerked her hand, motioning us through her door.

"Please, come in," she said brusquely.

As we entered Paula's office, I looked back over my shoulder at the young woman nursing her baby. I wanted to hear the end of her story.

"I have twenty minutes," Paula announced.

I closed the door regretfully and sat with Barbara on yet another camel-colored sofa. Paula Pierce took a chair behind her rosewood desk and looked at us expectantly. I could hear the sound of traffic through her open window, even smell the paired scents of yeast and sugar drifting up from the bakery below.

"Well?" Paula prodded impatiently.

"We wanted to get your thoughts on the murder," Barbara said, smiling.

Paula didn't return the smile. "I don't have any more knowledge concerning last night's events than you do yourselves," she stated categorically.

"But you might," I argued, appealing to her sense of fairness. "You don't really know unless we compare notes."

"Perhaps," she answered, her eyes thoughtful. "But I've already told the police everything I consider relevant."

I thought for a moment. The woman was a cause attorney. What would it take to move her? "The police think Barbara was the murderer," I said.

Bingo. Paula sat upright in her chair, her face now filled with concern.

"Have the police harassed you?" she asked Barbara.

Barbara shrugged her shoulders. "Not really," she said softly, looking down at her lap. "But I'm scared. They don't like me. They don't know what to make of an assertive Asian woman. I don't fit their stereotypes." I knew that Barbara wasn't just making this up from whole cloth. I had seen it in people's eyes before, the confusion and affront over this rowdy Chinese-American woman. She had more in common with Bette Midler, even Madonna, than Susie Wong.

Barbara raised her eyes to Paula's. "Will you help me find the real murderer?"

Paula nodded. She was hooked.

"What did you and your husband do on the break?" Barbara asked.

Paula pursed her lips more tightly. For a moment I thought that Barbara had lost her. But then she spoke.

"We chatted with Meg Quilter for probably one or two minutes. Meg is an old friend." Paula paused, her eyes looking past us, remembering. "Then I went to the bathroom. Gary waited for me in the dining room. The two of us left the restaurant and walked to the park across the street. We saw you there, lying on the grass," she said with a nod in my direction. "And that woman, Iris. Though I think she left fairly soon afterwards. I don't know where she went."

She squinted her eyes. "Later, Leo and Ken came down the block. Leo had been drinking, apparently. He made crude remarks to a young woman walking by."

I nodded. I remembered the young woman in the halter top.

"Then Leo and Ken returned to the restaurant. I'm afraid I can't vouch for anyone else," Paula said with a little sigh. "Gary and I walked inside again. I wanted to speak to Leo, but I couldn't find him. Ken said he was in the bathroom. Gary and I wandered back into the kitchen. A few minutes later we heard your cry from the pantry."

She shrugged her shoulders and her eyes focused on us again. "You know the rest," she said.

"Had you ever met Sheila Snyder before last night?" Barbara asked, her eyes on Paula's face.

"Not to the best of my knowledge," Paula answered with a change in expression.

"How about Gary?" Barbara pressed.

"My husband has nothing to do with this mess," the attorney rapped out, jutting her chin forward. *So, Gary is the sore spot*, I thought.

"Could we arrange a time to speak to him?" Barbara asked, lowering her voice a bit. "He might have noticed something."

"Or he might *not* have," Paula pointed out. She sighed and leaned back in her chair. "I'm sorry to be so brusque," she said after a moment. "I'm concerned about my husband. Mr. Snyder, the dead woman's husband, has been making phone calls to Gary, accusing Gary of murdering his wife."

"Dan Snyder called Gary?" Barbara and I cried together.

Paula nodded, her eyes perplexed.

"He called each of us too, and accused us of murder," I explained. "Maybe he's calling everyone."

The information flowed more freely after we told Paula about our own troubles with Dan Snyder. She expanded on his phone calls to her husband. First he had accused Gary of being Sheila's lover, then he moved on to an accusation of murder. Using a string of racial epithets, he had threatened to kill Gary, and to kill Paula just to "even the score."

No wonder Paula was sensitive about her husband.

Finally, Paula said that she and Gary were usually home together on Thursday afternoons. I could see the reluctance in her face when she gave us her home address. We might still be the murderers for all she knew. But she gave it to us, then showed us out. She was a fair woman.

The reception area was empty when we left. The young mother had gone home, along with her baby and her baby's story.

It was almost seven by the time I got home. I had left Barbara at her apartment, still clutching her chart, then driven the last few miles to my house in a state of exhaustion. Wayne's car was conspicuously absent when I pulled into the driveway. Damn. I was going to have to face Vesta alone. I pulled my box of paperwork out of the car and took a deep breath.

She was waiting for me at the door.

"About time you were home, Little Miss Stuck-Up," she said.

"Did you miss me?" I asked sweetly.

I was gratified to see her jaw drop. I left her standing in the entryway and put my box down next to my desk, smiling a secret smile. One point for Kate. Finally.

Why had it taken me so long to score? Working in a mental

hospital some years earlier, I had learned that the personalities of the insane vary widely beyond their diagnoses. There were friendly schizophrenics, quiet schizophrenics, and spiteful ones. The same went for the manic-depressives and the alcoholics. Vesta was a spiteful one, whatever her diagnosis. And the only way to handle the spiteful ones was to ignore the spite, to act as if their words and gestures were benevolent. It always threw them. I had also learned never to turn my back on them. Another important lesson. How could I have forgotten?

The doorbell rang before I had a chance to ponder the question any further.

Vesta was at the door in a heartbeat, opening it an instant later. I wished she would show more restraint. There was still a murderer running loose.

"Does Kate Jasper live here?" came a high, trembling voice that seemed familiar.

"She asked us to visit if we were in town," added a deeper, gruffer voice.

I walked up behind Vesta, who seemed to have been struck mute, and I looked over her shoulder.

Two women, both older than Vesta, stood at my door. Two women I hadn't seen in two years. The first woman still looked like a geriatric schoolgirl, her frail body dressed in a bright yellow T-shirt, culottes and knee socks. Her tiny face was framed by wispy white hair. Thick glasses obscured her eyes. The second woman was larger, more substantial. Her solid body was packed into heavy jeans and a flannel shirt. Her cheeks were even jowlier now, and there was some white in the gray braid wrapped around her head. But her blue eyes were as bright and sharp as ever.

I pushed past Vesta with my arms extended. The twins! That was what the Delores locals had called these two lifelong companions. And that was how I remembered them. Arletta Ainsley and Edna Grimshaw, the twins. The women who had saved my life.

I hugged Arletta first, gently. I was always afraid I'd crush her frail body. Then I hugged Edna, hard.

I stepped back and looked at the two of them. Edna's jowly face grew flushed. Was she embarrassed? Living in Marin, it was easy to forget that some people didn't hug automatically. But

Arletta's face held a different emotion beneath her glasses. Curiosity.

"Introduce your friend," Edna ordered, with a jerk of her head in Vesta's direction.

I looked back at Vesta. Now I understood the looks on the twins' faces. Vesta had turned on a hundred-watt glare for the occasion.

"Vesta Caruso," I rattled off quickly. "Wayne's mother. You remember Wayne, don't you?"

"Of course we do," Arletta warbled. "A very kind man, as I recall."

She stepped forward and pumped Vesta's hand, introducing Edna and herself with the grace of a diplomat.

Even Vesta couldn't resist her. She mumbled an acknowledgment, then backed away from the doorway.

I motioned the twins into the living room. Edna's sharp eyes darted around the room and landed on the canvas chairs that hung from the ceiling beams. She smiled and lowered herself into the chair for two. Arletta fluttered down beside her.

"Good as a porch swing," Edna commented. She pushed off with her feet without being instructed.

"We read about last night's murder in San Ricardo," Arletta whispered. She leaned toward me, her voice soft but insistent. "Do you know anything about that one?"

My mouth dropped open. How did she know? Did she just figure I would be involved in any murder in the vicinity? Or was it was an inspired guess?

The silence grew longer. I looked behind me. Vesta still stood in the entryway watching us. And listening.

"No," I squeaked. I hated to lie to them. "Not really," I amended.

Arletta looked at Edna with triumph in her eyes.

The doorbell rang again. This time I beat Vesta to the door. When I opened it, I wished I hadn't.

"Okay, Kate," Felix snarled. "Give!"

I put a finger up to my lips, gesturing for silence. Felix ignored it.

"Barbara won't talk to me," he whined. "I can't friggin' believe it. I'm her old man and she won't give me diddly."

"Felix—" I tried.

"Well, there's more than one way to skin a cat," he said, his big brown eyes narrowing. "And you'd better tell me what you know. *Capeesh?* You were with her when she found the body. And now the two of you are bugging the suspects, asking questions. I know it!"

I looked behind me. Vesta was smiling again. Suddenly, I felt sick to my stomach.

"What are you two up to?" he demanded.

I did the only thing I could think of. I suggested dinner. Dinner out. My nausea would pass once we were out, I told myself. Edna, Arletta, Felix and I could share a friendly meal. The twins had met Felix a couple of years before in Delores. I even essayed a half-hearted invitation to Vesta. She declined. I almost kissed her. Almost.

The rest of us piled into Edna's rental car. I was so relieved that Vesta wasn't joining us that I didn't stop to ask what restaurant we were headed for.

Fifteen minutes later, we were parked a block from the Good Thyme Cafe. My stomach was doing high jumps, aiming for my throat.

"They won't be open," I kept saying as we walked up the block. Nobody seemed to hear me.

Edna, Felix and Arletta shared a smile when we got to the entrance. The sign on the Good Thyme door said "Welcome."

Edna pushed the door open. Then someone inside the restaurant screamed.

- Seven -

THE FOUR OF us rushed through the doorway of the Good Thyme Cafe as·the long, undulating scream came to an end.

It wasn't hard for me to spot the screamer over Arletta's shoulder. There weren't many patrons in the dining room, and they had all turned to look at a young, red-haired woman wearing a checked apron. She stood in the center of the sea of white, vinyl-covered tables with her eyes closed and her head thrown back.

"I can't take it anymore!" she howled. She let out another, shorter scream in confirmation, then shouted, "I quit!" and ripped off her apron.

"Maybe we can eat here another time," I whispered hopefully.

My whisper fell on deaf ears. Felix, Arletta and Edna stood transfixed as they watched the young woman. I walked in front of Felix and waved my hand in his face. It was useless.

"Earth to Felix—" I began.

"You can't quit!" shouted a new voice.

I spun back around just in time to see Dan Snyder stomping into the dining room. Kitchen whites clothed his burly body. Anger clothed his face.

"Oh, yeah?" said the redhead. "Watch me."

She strode to the cash register, grabbed her purse, then sauntered past us and out the door, without a backward glance.

Dan watched her exit with squinting eyes. As I watched him watch her, a thought occurred to me. Maybe his squint wasn't a sign of a cruel nature. Maybe he just needed glasses. He wasn't a bad-looking man otherwise. His jaw was strong, his features were even, and the combination of his curly black hair and mustache was appealing. His gaze shifted to the four of us near the doorway.

"You!" he roared.

Damn. Nearsighted or not, he had spotted me. I swallowed, then attempted a friendly smile.

"You've got some fuckin' nerve, showin' up here," he snarled. "Wanna see where she died again, huh? Wanna check that you didn't leave anything behind, maybe?"

I let my smile die.

Dan was within a foot of me in four long strides. He bent his head toward my face. He wasn't squinting anymore. But I still didn't like the look of his eyes, whites showing around dark hazel irises. I swallowed again.

"Was it you, bitch?" he hissed. "Was it you? Or maybe that lesbo friend of yours?"

Lesbo friend? I wouldn't even attempt to address that one.

"I didn't kill your wife," I said, taking a step backwards. I wished I could stop my voice from shaking. "Nor did my friend—"

"No!" he roared. "No more bullshit!"

I closed my eyes. No wonder the waitress had quit, I thought with sudden sympathy. My whole body was trembling now. I knew I shouldn't keep my eyes shut, but I didn't want to see Dan Snyder's face anymore.

"Young man, behave yourself!" came a high, trembling voice from my side.

I opened my eyes. Arletta was speaking, her index finger extended and shaking.

"Whatever grief you are experiencing, you have no right to take it out on Kate," she told him. "Kate is doing her best to help you."

I could see the confusion in Dan Snyder's face as he turned his eyes in Arletta's direction. How was I supposed to be helping him? Arletta gave him no time to rally.

"Come along," she said, leading the way out the door. "We'll go elsewhere."

I directed Edna to the Starship Cafe. Goofy as it was, the Starship had to be an improvement on the Good Thyme. Ten minutes later, the four of us stood at the Starship's entrance, which was designed to resemble the *Star Trek* transporter.

"Far friggin' out," breathed Felix.

"My," twittered Arletta. "They've made it very realistic."

Edna just chuckled, then led the way into the transporter.

Our host was dressed in silver tights and a navy blue tunic. He had great legs, but a surly expression. He seated us at a table decked out in a metallic silver tablecloth and handed us menus. The menus were new, different from the last time I had visited the Starship. These were large round disks of laminated cardboard that pictured "Star Station, Planet Earth" on one side in blue seas and green continents, and listed dishes from the Asteroid Appetizer Platter to a Zodiacal Light Linzertorte on the other side.

"Our specials tonight are fresh Solar Salmon in Dill Sauce and Heavenly Halibut with homemade chutney," the host rattled off in a monotone. I guess I wouldn't think it was very cute anymore either if I had to do it every night.

"Three soups," he continued. "Lunar Lentil, Klingon Clam Chowder and Jupiter Jambalaya."

He finished off with a list of drinks, and a little sigh.

"Look up," I ordered after our host had taken our drink orders and sullenly departed.

We all gazed up at the ceiling, painted in shades of midnight blue and purple with a universe full of pasted-on silver stars. What magic, I thought. I let my eyes wander among the heavenly constellations and forgot my troubles.

When I brought my eyes back down, Felix, Arletta and Edna were all staring in my direction.

"No more stalling, Kate," hissed Felix. "Give."

I gave.

I told them most of what I could remember of the events from the night before. Our drinks arrived midway. I sipped my Quantum Carrot Juice and told them the rest. I had just finished describing Dan Snyder's arrival, when our waitress appeared. She was a slender woman who didn't fill out her official tunic and tights as well as Lieutenant Uhura, but she was friendly.

"What'll it be, folks?" she asked cheerfully.

Arletta and Edna ordered fish. I asked for a Venusian Vegie Burger. Then the waitress turned to Felix.

"What's low fat and low protein?" he asked unhappily.

"We have Planetary Pasta with steamed vegetables—" she began.

"I'll have two orders," he cut in, stroking his mustache. "What else?"

The waitress let her mouth drop open for a moment, then continued.

Felix added a green salad with no dressing, a side order of rice and a fruit salad to his order. He was a small man but he still had a big appetite, gout or no gout.

"So what's the poop, Kate?" he asked as soon as the waitress had left. He bent forward and looked into my eyes. "Who did it?" he whispered.

I bent forward and whispered back three words: "I don't know."

"Kate!" he yelped.

"Now, now," chirped Arletta. She put a restraining hand on his arm. "We all need to work together if we're going to solve this mystery."

I turned to her. On the surface, she was a frail old woman with wispy white hair and thick glasses. But I knew that through those glasses she observed things I didn't see. And she had been anything but frail when she had joined Edna to save my life.

"What do *you* think?" I asked her.

"I think we haven't nearly enough information," she replied. "And there are a good many questions to be answered." She smiled encouragingly. "Have you asked yourself who benefits from this death?"

I looked up at the ceiling again and thought. "I suppose her husband inherits," I said slowly. "But I don't know what she had to leave."

"Diddly, besides her community property share of the restaurant and its building," Felix contributed with a smug smile. I kept forgetting that as a reporter he was a source of information as well as an information sucker.

"Her husband was the angry young man we met at the Good Thyme?" Arletta asked.

I nodded in confirmation.

"You said the woman hit one of her children," Arletta continued. "Do you suppose that was an isolated incident? Or was there, perhaps, a pattern of abuse?"

"A pattern, I think," I answered, remembering the incident Alice had described. "But the children couldn't have . . ." I faltered.

"You'd be surprised," Edna offered, her voice gruff.

I turned her way for a moment. Her jowly face was stern, her blue eyes sparkling cold. She had been a nurse for all of her working life. She must have seen things in that job I would never see in my lifetime. Goose bumps formed on my arms.

"I'd like to talk about the class members," Arletta said. Her high, wavering voice brought me back to the present. "Did any of them have a previous relationship with the murdered woman?"

"Alice did," I answered reluctantly. Should I tell them that I thought Alice was in love with Dan?

"And . . ." prodded Arletta.

I looked across the table and caught a glint of hungry curiosity in Felix's eyes. No, I decided. I wouldn't share any vague theories.

"And the cooking teacher, Meg Quilter, had met Sheila once," I said instead.

"Kate," rumbled Felix threateningly.

I tried to ignore him, a task about as easy as ignoring detonating nuclear warheads.

"What kind of chucklehead do you think I am?" he demanded shrilly. "I know what you're doing. You're sitting on something—"

"Solar Salmon," our waitress interrupted, setting the dish down in front of Arletta. I smiled up at her gratefully. I'd leave a good tip no matter what the food was like.

"And Heavenly Halibut," she continued, "Venusian Vegie Burger, two Planetary Pasta with steamed vegies, Sulu Salad, Far-Away Fruit Salad, and a side of rice."

She plopped the last five items down in front of Felix. "Thought you'd want them all at once," she said and left.

We discussed the vegetarian cooking class members as we ate. The Venusian Vegie Burger would have been tastier if I'd gotten a chance to swallow once in a while. But every time I took a bite someone asked me something. Arletta questioned me extensively about Leo's apparent alcoholism and lechery. I wasn't sure what she was hoping to learn. Edna was more interested in Paula's protective attitude toward her husband, Gary. And Felix almost drove me crazy with questions about Iris. I had made the mistake of telling him about her photo of Ted Bundy's hands.

By the time Edna dropped me back at my house I felt like

three separate vampires had taken turns at my neck, sucking me dry of information.

I walked into my house alone, hoping Wayne would make it all better.

One look at his face told me Wayne might make it all worse. His eyebrows had dropped so low, I couldn't see his eyes at all. His frown was as deep as the Grand Canyon, and just as stony. In an instant I remembered that I had never told Wayne about the murder. My stomach commenced churning.

"Wayne, I never got a chance to tell you—" I began.

"Where have you been?" he growled. It wasn't a friendly growl. It was a growl of a wounded bear.

I saw Vesta smiling behind Wayne. What had she told him?

"Can we talk about this privately?" I asked softly.

"No," he answered.

I blinked. Wayne didn't play the role of a heavy husband. At least he never had before. As he glared at me, I felt the blood rise in my face. How dare he treat me like a . . . like a wife?

"Fine," I said, keeping my voice even. "I'll talk to you later."

I walked past Wayne and Vesta into the bedroom. If anyone was going to sleep on the couch tonight, it wasn't going to be me. This was my house, goddammit.

I felt Wayne silently slide into bed around midnight. I pretended to be asleep. Then, after a couple of hours of tossing and turning, I really was. By the time I woke up on Wednesday morning he was gone.

At nine o'clock I was on the phone to Barbara again.

"We can't do any more snooping," I told her. "It's too dangerous." My late-night ruminations had convinced me that Wayne had a right to be worried about my investigating. Of course that assumed he *was* worried about my investigating. I still wasn't sure what Vesta had told him.

"Is Wayne giving you a hard time?" Barbara asked. She picked the damnedest times to exercise her psychic powers.

I grunted. I didn't want to say anything. Vesta was probably lurking nearby.

"Listen, kiddo," she said. "We've got to keep at it. The police have already been here this morning. They're on my case."

I sighed, then tried to think of an honorable way out.

"I've got to do a little electrical work," she continued briskly.

"I'll be done before noon. Then I'll pick you up and we can go visit Meg. She's going to be home today. She's expecting us."

"Barbara!" I objected.

My doorbell rang.

"You'd better get that," Barbara said. "I'll see you later." Then she hung up.

Sergeant Tom Feiffer of the Marin County Sheriff's Department was at my door, six feet of masculinity under curly blond hair. And he was smiling, that faintly leering smile that I never quite knew how to interpret. Was he really flirting? Or did he just know that the smile would rattle me? I heard C.C. meowing behind me. Did she have the answer?

"Hi there," Feiffer said, winking a clear blue eye at me. "I hear you got tangled up in another murder."

I opened my mouth. I wanted to tell him that he was wrong, that it was some other Kate Jasper who had stumbled over the body. But I couldn't. I let my mouth close.

"Can I come in?" Feiffer asked, still smiling.

"I guess so," I said unenthusiastically.

My tone didn't faze him. He strolled into the living room and stopped at the two pinball machines against the wall, a legacy from my former marriage. C.C. peered up at Sergeant Feiffer, then streaked across the room and out her cat door. Sometimes she was a pretty smart animal.

"Still got Hayburners and Texan," the sergeant commented approvingly. "Great games."

"Wanna play?" I asked slyly.

I knew that pinballs were his weak spot. He was an addict. If he was playing, I just might be able to get some information out of him. I switched on Hayburners, the machine I remembered as his favorite. The back glass and playfield lit up in an enticing glow. I hit the reset button. The score reels turned back to zero with a clunk, and the six metal cut-out horses in the back glass raced in reverse to the starting gate.

Sergeant Feiffer stepped up to the machine and hit the reset button again.

"Double play," he said. He looked at me, a challenge in his blue eyes.

"You first," I said, accepting his challenge.

Hayburners didn't have any bumpers, but it had back targets, high-point side lanes and jelly fish rollovers on its lime green, yellow, orange and red playfield. Hitting any of the six back targets moved a corresponding horse forward a notch along the back-glass race track. And with enough notches each horse came in, raising the stakes on the rollovers and the side lanes.

Feiffer pressed the center disk that launched the steel ball. The ball hit a back target, moving the number three horse up, and rolled lazily toward the top left flipper.

"So, how is the county sheriff's office involved?" I asked softly.

He hit the flipper button easily despite my question, and the ball glided over a jelly fish rollover, netting him ten points, then rolled back.

"San Ricardo P. D. asked for assistance," he answered briefly, slapping the flipper button again. The ball sailed up a side lane. Fifty points. It rolled back down toward the bottom right flipper.

"Who do they suspect?" I asked, not really expecting an answer.

"Your friend, Barbara Chu, looks kinda interesting," he told me, sending the ball to hit another back target.

Damn. I hadn't shaken him, but he had shaken me. I hadn't really believed Barbara when she'd said the police were on her case.

"But then, so do a couple of other people," Feiffer added.

"Who?" I asked eagerly.

He laughed as he hit the right-hand flipper button. "Why don't you tell me?" he said, smiling. "You're out there nosing around where you shouldn't be."

He glanced in my direction as the ball moseyed up a side lane. The smile left his face. He stared for a moment over my shoulder. It was a moment too long. The ball came rolling toward his left bottom flipper. Too late, he pressed the button. The ball skated on the flipper for an instant, then slid off the tip and down the drain hole.

I looked behind me. Vesta stood there in a low-cut black dress, her hand lifted in a coy wave. She was smiling at Sergeant Feiffer, a smile very much like his own faint leer. She cocked her head and blinked her eyes. I suppressed a giggle and turned back to the sergeant.

"Introduce me to your handsome friend," Vesta ordered, her voice as thick and sweet as honey.

My handsome friend was beginning to look a bit pale.

"Sergeant Tom Feiffer, Vesta Caruso," I said quickly. "Anyway," I went on, "you can take my word that Barbara is completely incapable of murder. If she was thinking of murder, she wouldn't have yelled at the woman beforehand—"

"Why don't we *all* sit down and talk," suggested Vesta, her tone implying activities other than sitting.

"This won't take long, ma'am," Feiffer said with a nervous glance in her direction. He turned his eyes on me. They were serious now.

"I've got two things to say," he rapped out. "One, keep out of this case. It could be dangerous. Two, tell everything you know to the San Ricardo police."

Then he gave me one last furtive smile and strode out the front door.

I turned to Vesta. Her homely face was downcast. I felt an instant of sympathy for her.

"Thank you," I said sincerely, glad she had driven Feiffer away.

She turned her back on me and stomped down the hall to her room.

I stepped up to Hayburners and launched the ball.

I had moved the four and six horses across the finish line and was aiming at the back target that would bring the number three horse in, when the phone rang.

Damn. I let the ball dribble down the drain hole and walked to the phone. I was too late. Vesta had already answered.

"Who is it?" I asked her.

I didn't like the way Vesta was taking over answering the phone. Suddenly I wondered how many phone calls she had taken, how many phone calls I had missed, how many friends and business associates she had alienated.

Vesta ignored me.

"Who is it?" I asked again, louder this time, hoping I wouldn't have to battle her physically for possession of the receiver.

I didn't. She turned and held the whole phone set out to me.

"It's Detective Utzinger from the San Ricardo Police Department," she said happily. She grinned and added, "It's for you."

- Eight -

VESTA WASN'T KIDDING me. Detective Utzinger was indeed on the line. In a monotone, he told me that Detective Sergeant Oakley wanted to see me. Today. My stomach gurgled an objection, then began serious churning.

I made an afternoon appointment and set the receiver back down gently. Vesta scrutinized me with curious eyes.

I turned on a big smile. "The police said they could use my help. Isn't that great?" I said enthusiastically.

Vesta squinted suspiciously. I kept my smile in place. She snorted, then turned and headed back down the hallway. Only then did I put my hand on my churning stomach.

A couple of Tums later, I took a seat at my desk and concentrated on Jest Gifts. As I processed orders, I wondered: What was Sheila Snyder really like? Had her husband loved her? Or hated her? Or both? I didn't want to think about Wayne. The Snyders were much more interesting.

I was still thinking about the Snyders two hours later when my stomach growled, this time demanding an early lunch. A tofu burger popped into my mind, the kind they sold at the health food store. Salivating, I considered the possible connection between health food stores and vegetarian restaurants. Would the people at the health food store have known the owners of the Good Thyme Cafe?

It was worth a shot.

It took me ten minutes to get to Life Foods. I hurried through the door and began loading a shopping basket. Oatios went in, then bok choy, a loaf of raisin-millet bread and soy milk. I made my way past the bins of grains toward the refrigerator cases. An oversized man in a navy blue suit held a mobile phone to his head as he walked down the aisle in front of me.

"I got basmati rice," he boomed. "Of course I got organic! What else do you want?"

Who was on the other end of the line? I wondered. His sick wife? Or maybe his boss?

"Amazake? What the hell is amazake?" he shouted into the phone. Probably not his boss.

I edged by him as unobtrusively as possible.

"I'm not yelling," he yelled.

I grabbed a tofu burger and some carrot juice and took another aisle back to the front counter. I could still hear the man yelling into his phone. Now he was looking for lentils.

I joined the line at the register. It was a good long line. For once, I was glad.

"Anyone here ever eat at the Good Thyme Cafe?" I asked conversationally.

A tanned woman in jogging shorts near the front of the line answered first. "I went there with a friend a couple of times last year," she told me. "Horrible place, bad vibes."

A tall, bearded man behind her disagreed. "I love the Good Thyme!" he exclaimed. "The prices are reasonable and they give you lots of food. Great burritos. They're huge."

"But the food's so yucky—" the tanned woman objected.

"Anyone know the owners?" I asked quickly before she could go on. I didn't really want to hear about the food.

"It's a husband and wife who own it," the man said. "The wife does the cooking. The husband runs the cash register. They have some college kids waiting the tables."

"I don't know how they stay in business," the tanned woman added, shaking her head. "My friend said she'd never once seen all the tables filled there. It's no surprise with that yucky food. And the man at the register is too damn surly if you ask me—"

"Wasn't the lady who just got murdered one of the owners?" asked a woman with a long black braid. Her eyes were wide and staring my way.

No one answered. More heads turned in my direction.

"Was she really?" I said innocently, hoping my rapidly reddening face didn't betray me. "How terrible."

"She was strangled," confirmed the young, well-muscled man behind the cash register. There was a hint of relish in his tone. "It was in the paper."

"I'll bet her husband did it," said the tanned woman. "The guy's got bad vibes."

"God, I hope they don't go out of business," whispered the bearded man.

Then the line went silent, all neighborliness suddenly gone. I could hear the man with the mobile phone again over the clicking of the cash register keys. He was shouting about aduki beans by the time I left the store.

I gobbled down my tofu burger as I drove home. It was a good thing I finished it, because Barbara was waiting for me when I pulled into my driveway. She gave me two minutes to put my groceries away, then dragged me back outside.

"I've got directions to Meg's house," she said, jumping in my Toyota.

I sighed and slid into the driver's seat.

"Where to, madam?" I asked in my best chauffeur's voice.

"Richmond District, San Francisco," she replied. She grinned widely. "And don't spare the horses, James."

Barbara didn't stop chortling until we were halfway across the bridge. Then her face got serious.

"I talked to a friend of mine at Berkeley," she announced. "She took calculus from Gary Powell. She says he's a damn smart guy, even if he does carry those goofy crystals around all the time."

"And ..." I prompted.

"That's it from her," Barbara told me, frowning. Then her face brightened. "But I talked to an artist friend of Felix's who knows Leo. He said that Leo owns an art gallery. In his opinion, Leo can be a real jerk, though he does give new artists a chance in his gallery. And he said that Leo has a drinking problem ..."

I had a nose. I had already smelled Leo's drinking problem. But I didn't interrupt Barbara as she took the tiny threads of information she had gleaned about Leo and wove them into multiple murder motives. Whatever the present state of her psychic powers, she still had a great imagination.

I spotted the Victorian building that housed Meg's flat just as

Barbara came up with motive theory number forty-seven, Sheila's inopportune discovery of Leo's impotence.

Meg's building stood across the street from Golden Gate Park. She buzzed us in when we rang the bell. Then we climbed the two flights of steep stairs to her door. No wonder the woman was so skinny. Climbing these stairs had to take the weight off.

"The living room's a mess," Meg whispered, greeting us at her front door. Her silky blond hair was in braids today, her sea-green eyes as round as ever. I looked into her pale face and wondered if she'd look any older if she wore makeup. In the dim lighting of the hallway she looked about twelve years old.

"That's okay," I told her. I tried a reassuring smile. "You should see my house.'

She shrugged her rounded shoulders and ushered us in.

A "mess" did not fully describe her living room. It wasn't really messy, just full. Very full. She had more stuff in there than I had ever seen in one person's house.

The volume of artwork alone was staggering. Stacked against one wall were abstracts in bold primary colors. One in blues and reds was in progress on an easel. A drafting table nearby held pen-and-ink drawings. I moved forward for a closer look. What had appeared to be a woman's silhouette at a distance resolved itself into a dark, hellish hive populated by hundreds of naked, misshapen human forms pressed together and writhing like earthworms. Ugh. Not my type. Not my type at all. I diverted my gaze to a nearby painting, an immense and lifelike representation of a sensuous four-foot carrot lounging against a background of lacy parsley. Better. Much better. This was my idea of art. I saw a refrigerator-sized eggplant behind it, and the corners of a dozen or more canvases behind the eggplant.

"Are these all your work?" Barbara asked. Her voice held an uncharacteristic note of awe.

"Nothing's really very good," Meg mumbled, shrugging her shoulders again.

"But they're wonderful!" I objected. "I love the carrot." Meg blushed. At least it put some color into her face.

"And these drawings are, uh . . . really interesting," Barbara added, holding up another pen-and-ink drawing, a sister hive to the one I had looked at earlier.

I stepped away from the drawing and tripped over an oscilloscope, then noticed the rest of the electronic equipment scattered around the room. And there were books. Rows and rows of books in shelves, and in piles on the floor.

"Do you live here alone?" I asked.

Meg looked down at her toes and nodded. Then she sniffled. If I had all her talent I wouldn't be so damn shy, I told myself, jealous for a moment. But then again, what if her shyness went hand and hand with her ability to focus on her work?

"Would you like some tea?" Meg asked diffidently.

"That would be wonderful," I said with the undue heartiness I usually save for children.

She led us into a kitchen that smelled of cinnamon and nutmeg. It was far tidier than the living room—no jumble of books and artwork here, just a lot of notes under magnets on the refrigerator. And a scattering of appliances on the gleaming, yellow-tiled counters. A canvas depicting over a yard of sliced purple cabbage hung on the wall next to the gas stove. Barbara and I sat down at an uncluttered yellow Formica table while Meg put on the teakettle.

"I made pumpkin bars," she said, her voice barely louder than a whisper. "No fat, no dairy."

"So, that's the wonderful smell!" Barbara warbled.

A few minutes later, I decided the pumpkin bars not only smelled good, they tasted good too. They were sweet and chewy, with currants and cloves as well as cinnamon and nutmeg. I had almost forgotten why we were there as I took a bite of my second one. But Barbara hadn't.

"So, have you worked with Alice for very long?" she asked Meg.

"Just off and on," Meg said quietly, her eyes lowered. "I just do temp work. The paintings bring in a little money."

I should hope so, I thought indignantly. I hoped she was being paid what they were worth. She couldn't be a very good saleswoman.

"But you're pretty close friends with Alice, aren't you?" Barbara pressed, leaning forward across the table.

"She likes me," Meg said, lifting her eyes. There was a lilt of wonder in her voice as if she couldn't quite understand why Alice might like her.

"Of course she does," I said encouragingly. Somehow Meg brought out the third-grade teacher in me.

"Do you think Alice is in love with Dan?" Barbara asked.

Meg tilted her head as she stared at Barbara, wide-eyed. "Dan?" she repeated.

"Dan Snyder," Barbara said impatiently. "You know, Sheila's husband."

"Oh," Meg said. She lowered her eyes again and sniffled. "Alice never mentioned it. Not that she'd confide in me necessarily." She wriggled in her chair. "I just don't know," she finished.

Barbara's interrogation of Meg was beginning to feel like child abuse to me. I shot her a cautionary look, and she settled back in her chair with a martyred sigh. She took a bite of her pumpkin bar. It was my turn.

"Have you known Gary and Paula long?" I asked.

"Oh, forever," said Meg, smiling at me now. "They've been really good to me over the years. Paula's helped me find work. And helped me sell the paintings. Gary's helped me build stuff. They're both really great people."

I smiled back, trying and failing to come up with a way to segue into Paula or Gary's possible motive for murder.

"Did Gary and Paula know the Snyders before?" Barbara asked.

The smile left Meg's face. "I don't think so," she said, shaking her head.

"Did *you* know them before?" Barbara demanded.

"I don't think so," Meg answered once more. She twisted her thin hands together. "I met Sheila before the class. With Alice, you know. But I don't think I ever met her before that."

Barbara looked at me. I shrugged my shoulders. We could always ask Meg if she killed Sheila. But she'd probably just say she "didn't think so."

"I've got an appointment," Meg announced suddenly, straightening her shoulders.

"What?" I squeaked, startled.

"I have to go to an appointment," she enunciated clearly. "I have approximately ten minutes left to get ready."

She stood and smiled graciously at us. Barbara and I rose from our seats as if we were on strings.

"I guess we'll be on our way, then," I said. "Thank you for your time."

"My pleasure," she replied.

As Meg walked us out of the kitchen, I read one of the notes on her refrigerator. CANDY, it said in scrawled block letters. I turned to ask her if she had a healthy, low-fat recipe for candy, but thought better of it when I saw the chill in her green eyes.

"Jeez-Louse," said Barbara once we were safe in the Toyota. "Was that the bum's rush or what?"

"She might really have an appointment," I said, putting the key in the ignition.

Then I remembered my own appointment. With the San Ricardo Police Department. My stomach turned over at the same time the engine did.

"Why did she throw us out?" Barbara asked quietly as we whizzed towards the Golden Gate Bridge. I thought for a while.

"Just because she's shy doesn't mean she's stupid," I answered finally. "Maybe we hit the limit of Meg's tolerance for nosy, personal questions. We weren't very subtle, you know."

"Maybe," Barbara said absently.

"She could be protecting Gary or Paula. Maybe asking about them triggered the reaction," I theorized. I glanced at Barbara. She was staring out the front window with unseeing eyes. "So, what did you get psychically?" I asked.

"Not a friggin' thing!" Barbara exploded.

Damn.

Barbara put her head in her hands. "I've lost it, Kate," she whispered. "I thought I was okay again, but I've lost it."

I spent the remainder of the trip home trying to convince Barbara she'd get her powers back. Powers I hadn't completely believed she had in the first place.

Barbara was limp when I gave her a goodbye hug at my house. She dragged herself out of the Toyota and into her Volkswagen bug like an old woman. Instead of her usual blast-off, she pulled slowly out of the driveway, signaled and drove carefully away. Poor Barbara.

I sped toward the San Ricardo Police Department wondering what to do for her. Another psychic might be able to help her, I thought as I parked in the police lot. I looked at my watch. I was five minutes late. I forgot all about psychics. Fear took over my mind.

The San Ricardo Police Department's waiting room was larger than Mill Valley's. Larger and shabbier. I checked in with the officer behind the bulletproof glass, then sat down on a molded fiberglass chair obviously made for an alien with a bowling-ball-shaped bottom rather than a human being. I wondered how many condemned men and women had sat here before me. I may not be psychic, but my imagination can be every bit as good as Barbara's.

There was only one other person in the room, a young woman with blond ringlets who was sobbing loudly into a shredded Kleenex. Victim, criminal or girlfriend? I wondered. I wanted to put my arm around her. I looked around for help. Didn't anyone care that this young woman was suffering?

I was so worried about her that it took a few minutes for the shouting to seep into my consciousness.

First it was just a dull roar. Then I heard a distinct "No!" And, "No, it's not enough!" The voice seemed to be getting closer.

I heard a buzzer and the door to the waiting room opened. A burly man with curly black hair emerged. My breathing stopped when I recognized him. Dan Snyder. He turned back to the doorway.

"Just keep the fuck outa my way!" he bellowed at someone I couldn't see.

Then he turned back and strode toward the front door. He was almost there when he noticed me.

"You!" he shouted.

I flattened myself against the chair, looking toward the bulletproof glass for help.

Snyder saw my look. He lowered his voice.

"I'll get you!" he hissed and walked out the door.

At least the young woman across from me had stopped crying. She was staring at me in apparent fascination when my name was called.

Detective Utzinger escorted me into the interrogation room.

Sergeant Oakley was still a good listener. I had forgotten that about her. I had forgotten about her warm, concerned, hazel eyes and her musical voice. I told her nearly everything: all about our investigations, every word I could remember anyone saying, including the words of Dan Snyder's threatening phone call. The only things I omitted were some of Barbara's more imaginative theories. And a few of my own. Once I had done a complete mind dump, I figured it was my turn. I leaned forward.

"Do you think Dan Snyder is actually dangerous?" I asked.

"Do you?" Oakley answered, her eyes crinkling at the corners.

I tried again. "Does he really have an alibi?"

Sergeant Oakley leaned back in her chair and laughed.

"Feiffer warned me about you," she said, shaking her red head.

I felt the blood rising in my cheeks.

"I need to know," I insisted.

Sergeant Oakley stood up. She was definitely a tall woman. She came around the table and looked down at me.

"All you need to do is to stay out of this," she told me in an even voice. "I mean it. Go home and do whatever it is you do. Leave the investigating to us."

Detective Utzinger escorted me out.

I climbed into my Toyota with mixed emotions. I was glad to be out of the police interrogation rooms, but I wished I hadn't made such a fool of myself. I turned the key in the ignition and pulled out of the parking lot. A black truck pulled out behind me.

I was on the highway entrance ramp when I felt the first bump. It wasn't very hard. For a moment I thought I had imagined it. I looked in my rearview mirror and saw the top of the grillwork on a Chevy truck and the bottom edge of its windshield. Suddenly, the edge of the windshield disappeared from my mirror. The grille grew larger. The truck rammed me again. Harder than the first time. Much harder. My body slammed against the car seat. My head smashed against the headrest.

What the hell was going on? I swiveled my head around to look as I steered my car forward. My neck screamed in pain.

But I recognized the angry face in the truck window. It was Dan Snyder's.

- Nine -

DAN SNYDER'S TRUCK rammed me again. This time I was ready. As ready as someone with incipient whiplash can be, anyway. I took a deep breath and told my body to relax and roll with the bump. I didn't slam into the seat as hard this time. But it still hurt.

Should I accelerate? Try to outrun him? I had a feeling my Toyota Corolla was no match for his Chevy truck in the long run. And if I went much faster, being rammed might make me lose control. Not now, I decided.

I was too busy, anyway, steering forward on the entrance ramp as the truck rammed me again and again. By the sixth collision we were both on the highway doing our bumping Chevy-Toyota dance in the slow lane. None of the people in the cars whizzing past seemed to notice what was going on. No one slowed down to look.

By the seventh bump I'd had it. I jammed my foot on the gas and zoomed forward until I'd put a few car lengths between my Toyota and Snyder's truck. Then I swerved into the emergency lane and braked, one hand firmly on my horn, hoping to attract attention. Still, none of the cars going past slowed down.

I held my breath and watched in my rearview mirror as Snyder's truck began to follow me into the emergency lane. Damn.

But then, as he was almost to me, he sheered off and moved back onto the main highway. He was past me and gone in seconds.

My legs and arms began to shake. My ears roared with adrenaline. But I was safe.

I rubbed my neck and swiveled my head experimentally. The pain wasn't excruciating. Not yet, anyway. I told myself I'd live. I realized then that Dan Snyder could have rammed me a lot harder. Or done worse. My shaking hands began to sweat.

I got out of my car on trembling legs and walked to its rear. I love the rubber bumpers on my Toyota. There were light gray smudges on the back bumper, but no dents. I bent over to kiss the rubber, then thought better of it as I noticed a white smear that had apparently been deposited some time ago by a low-flying bird.

I climbed back into my car. It was time to call the police.

I gave my dashboard an affectionate pat, then pulled back onto the highway. The next exit took me to downtown San Ricardo. I forced myself to breathe deeply and rhythmically as I drove slowly back through town to the police station.

I wasn't very relaxed when I got there, though. I leapt out of the car the instant I parked and ran into the police station. The waiting room was empty now. I hurried up to the round-faced officer seated behind the bulletproof glass.

"Dan Snyder rammed me," I told him without preamble.

He looked up at me uncomprehendingly.

I tried again. "The guy whose wife was murdered. He rammed my car with his truck."

"You've had an accident," the policeman said slowly, nodding now that he thought he had it figured out. "Did you get the license number of the other vehicle?"

"It wasn't an accident!" I shouted. "He rammed me!"

"Calm down, lady," the officer ordered with a frown.

"Look," I said, keeping my voice steady with an effort. "I need to talk to Sergeant Oakley. She knows what this is about."

"Sergeant Oakley's not here," the officer told me. He rummaged around in the trays on his desk and pulled out a printed form. "You'll have to fill out an accident report."

I looked into his round face and opened my mouth to argue. But his eyes were empty both of comprehension and compassion. I gave up.

"Never mind," I said quietly.

I turned around and left.

I rubbed my neck with one hand and steered with the other on my way home. My mind ran in circles. Had Dan Snyder murdered his wife? Did he ram my car as a warning to me to keep out of the investigation? That didn't really make much sense. I shook my head, then winced at the pain in my neck.

If not to discourage me from investigating, why did Snyder ram me? Grief? Maybe he *had* loved Sheila, I thought. Maybe he had loved her so much that he was striking out at anyone involved with her death. I shivered suddenly, wondering if I should try the police again. No. One try was enough, I decided. And I was almost home.

Wayne's Jaguar was in the driveway when I got there. As I pulled my Toyota in behind it, my mind whirled in even bigger circles. Should I tell Wayne about the accident? Would he even listen? Did he care anymore? Tears filled my eyes suddenly. All the fear and misery of the last few days came welling up with them. Damn. I didn't want Wayne to see me crying. Or Vesta.

I wiped my eyes with the back of my hand, then heard a *thunk* on the top of my car. I sat bolt upright. For one panicked instant, I thought Dan Snyder was still chasing me. But then a pair of paws appeared at the top of my windshield, followed by the tips of two cat ears, and finally by C.C.'s upside-down, yowling head.

I opened my car door and C.C. hopped lightly from the roof onto the front hood and down to the ground. She led me up the front stairs, nagging me all the way. She was hungry! What a surprise.

Wayne opened the front door.

"Kate," he said, then opened his arms. I peeked under his heavy brows and saw a moist expression in his eyes that looked an awful lot like the same fear and misery that I had been feeling.

I ran the last few steps, pressed my face against his chest and threw my arms around him. He reached around and gave me a bear hug in return. My neck bent back.

"Ow!" I yelped.

He released me, then stared down at my face, his brows dropping like curtains over the tops of his eyes.

"What's wrong?" he asked quietly.

"I hurt my neck," I mumbled, looking away.

"You okay?" He put a tentative hand to the back of my neck.

I nodded, then winced. I waited for him to ask me how I had hurt myself. He didn't.

He led me to my office chair in silence. Once I sat down, he began massaging the stiff muscles of my neck and shoulders with his big, gentle hands. When the muscles were warmed and loosened, he took my head in both his hands and pulled it up until my spine was stretched straight. I felt the pieces of my neck slipping back into place. Then he went back to kneading my muscles.

Ten more minutes of massage was all it took. I talked.

I told him about Sheila Snyder's death, about the people who were at the Good Thyme that night, about Barbara's fear of being a suspect, about our investigations, and finally, about Dan Snyder's ramming my Toyota. I was glad Wayne was behind me where I couldn't see his face. But I could still feel his hands tighten when I told him about Dan Snyder's assault.

"Wayne?" I whispered. "Are you angry?"

"Not at you," he growled softly, depositing a light kiss on the top of my head.

"Really?" I cried. Already my neck felt better. It barely twinged when I turned to look at him.

"Really," he assured me. He walked around my chair and knelt down in front of me. "I'm concerned about you," he said, looking up into my face. "Afraid for you. Worried to death about you. But not angry with you." He shook his head. "You helped me when I needed help. You have to help your friend Barbara. But . . ." He faltered.

"But . . ." I prodded.

"Be careful, Kate," he said. His eyes filled with tears. He looked down at the carpet. "Couldn't stand to lose you," he said, his voice thick with feeling.

I dropped to the floor and within seconds we were both hugging and crying, then rolling on the carpet and kissing, then—

"Made you an apple pie," someone said.

Through a blur of passion, I tried to make sense of the words.

"Mom," groaned Wayne.

I rolled away from him and looked up. Vesta stood above us, a flour-coated white apron over her black floor-length Addams Family dress.

I sat up.

"Just for Kate," she said, grinning. "Apple pie, natural as all get out."

"I—" I began, planning to tell her I didn't eat sugar.

Then it hit me. She had made me a pie. Hypoglycemia was a small price to pay for good family relations.

"I'd love some," I said with a smile.

Wayne and I followed Vesta into the kitchen. It was obvious she had been cooking. Flour was sprinkled all over the place like industrial strength fairy dust.

"Ta-da!" announced Vesta, pointing at the golden-crusted pie in the center of the kitchen table.

The three of us sat down and Vesta cut the pie. She put a good-sized piece on a plate and passed it to me.

Wayne held out a plate for his share.

"Kate first," Vesta fluted gaily. She handed me a fork.

Wayne shrugged his shoulders, his face troubled. Was he suffering from foreplay-interruptus, I wondered, or something else? I returned my attention to the apple pie on my plate.

Vesta watched as I cut myself a bite and put it in my mouth. Luckily, I didn't swallow.

Ugh! The apple filling tasted like salt. *Poison*! I thought and spit it out. I ran to the sink and washed my mouth out with water.

Vesta leaned back in her chair and cackled.

Wayne grabbed the plate of pie.

"Don't eat it!" I shouted. "It's poisoned!"

He didn't seem to hear me. He stuck a finger in the apple filling, brought it up to his nose and sniffed. Then he licked his finger and grimaced.

"Mom?" he growled.

"Salt," she said, gasping between cackles. "I made it with two cups of salt instead of two cups of sugar!"

"Why?" asked Wayne, his voice as deep and angry as a volcano.

Vesta stopped cackling. She turned to him, her eyes full of innocence now.

"I know Kate doesn't eat sugar," she said. "So I made it with salt. I was just trying to please her, Waynie."

"Oh, Mom," Wayne groaned. He put a hand over his eyes and shook his head.

Don't believe her, I pleaded silently. *She's not just crazy. She's malicious. Don't let her fool you.*

But Wayne just kept his eyes covered. It was up to me.

"Why didn't you eat any of the pie yourself?" I asked Vesta. I kept my voice calm.

"Oh, I prefer sugar in mine," she said smugly.

"I suppose that's why you told Wayne not to take any," I said angrily, my calm floating away on a cloud of steam. "I suppose—"

The doorbell rang before I could finish my sentence. As I walked to the door, I belatedly remembered my plan never to show Vesta how much she was getting to me.

The doorbell rang again.

"All right, all right," I muttered and opened the door.

Felix was on my doorstep. His big brown eyes were squinting angrily.

"Where is she?" he demanded as he pushed his way inside.

"Where is who?" I returned, closing the door behind him. Was he looking for Vesta?

"Barbara Chu, that's who," he barked. "Barbara Benedict Arnold Chu."

"I don't know where Barbara is, Felix." I sighed.

He looked into my eyes and stroked his mustache thoughtfully for a few moments. Then he looked beyond me to the living room, searching it with his eyes.

"Felix, I am not hiding Barbara behind a potted plant," I said evenly, pressing my fingernails into my palms to keep from screaming at him. I had lost my cool with Vesta. I wasn't going to lose it with Felix.

"Well, then where the Sam friggin' Hill is she?" he pressed. "I called her apartment. I've left messages on her bloody friggin' answering machine. She's not communicating with me, Kate," he whined to a finish.

I looked down at the sock-covered toes sticking out of Felix's sandals. Which one was the toe with gout? Maybe I'd just step on all of them.

"You're both holding out on me," he started up again. "A big bucks story like this and neither of you will give me diddly. You better talk to me or—"

"Or what, Felix?" came Wayne's deep voice from behind me.

Wayne walked to my side and crossed his arms over his mesomorphic chest. He scowled down at Felix, using the formidable scowl that had won him a job as a bodyguard, his eyes nearly invisible now under angrily furrowed eyebrows. Wayne was over six feet tall, and muscular. Felix's slight body couldn't have been over five feet five. For a moment I felt sorry for Felix. Then he opened his mouth again.

"Hey, Wayne," he said with a comradely wave. "My old lady won't give me poop for a pig farm. And Kate, here, is holding out too. And—"

The doorbell rang before either Wayne or I had a chance to throttle him.

I opened the door, and Barbara bounced in with a big smile on her face. Had her psychic powers returned?

"Hi, kiddo," she said cheerfully. "Ready to go for a ride? I talked to Alice and we—"

Then she noticed Felix. The smiled turned to a glare.

"Where the friggin', fraggin' hell have you been?" he demanded.

Barbara continued to glare without replying.

C.C. wandered in and interjected a pitiful yowl.

"Holy Moly, babe—" began Felix again.

"Don't start in," warned Barbara, her voice low and vibrating.

"Start in? Waddaya mean, start in? All I want to do is talk to you—"

"Interrogate me, you mean! Jeez-Louise, have you ever asked if I'm okay? I found a dead body!"

Felix opened his mouth to reply, then seemed to think better of it.

Vesta stepped up to our little group, smiling.

"Felix," she purred. "How about some apple pie?"

- Ten -

I GRINNED AT Vesta with a spark of genuine affection. My mother-in-common-law wasn't so bad, I decided. How does the saying go? "The enemy of my enemy is my friend"? Vesta's heart might not have been in the right place, but her spleen certainly was.

"The pie's homemade, Felix," I said seductively, telling myself I wouldn't *really* let him take a bite.

I heard Wayne try to suppress a snort of laughter. Felix heard it too. He peered at me suspiciously. Then his eyes traveled back to Vesta.

"I'm sorry, Mrs. Caruso," he said politely. "I'm on a restricted diet. I'm not allowed diddly." He let out a long, deep sigh, his face a study in martyrdom.

Barbara stared at him for a moment, then rolled her eyes heavenward.

"Listen, kiddo," she said to me impatiently. "We gotta get a move on."

"Where're we going?" asked Felix.

"I don't know where *you're* going," Barbara said, her tone cool enough to freeze summer. "*Kate* and I have a date."

I didn't remember any date, but I figured Barbara had probably made one for us with one of the murder suspects. It seemed to me she had mentioned Alice on the way in.

I turned to Wayne. "All right, sweetie?" I asked him softly.

His head nodded, but his eyes were worried.

"Barbara will be with me," I assured him. "I'll be fine."

"I know," he growled, then turned away.

I fed the cat, kissed Wayne and left with Barbara as Felix and Vesta watched.

"So, what was in the pie?" Barbara asked once we were in the car.

"Two cups of salt," I muttered, feeling suddenly ashamed of myself.

I had to wait a full minute for Barbara to stop laughing and give me directions.

At least we weren't going far. Alice lived a freeway exit away in Sausalito. We were parked in front of Alice's apartment building and on our way up the rickety stairs before Barbara thought to ask me how come I had a pie made with two cups of salt in the house.

"Vesta," I whispered and rang Alice's doorbell.

"Hi, you guys," Alice caroled as she opened the door.

For all her concern about her weight, her plump body managed to look far better in a fuchsia sweatshirt and sweatpants than mine would have in a designer business suit.

I said "Hi" back and gazed at her, wondering what it was exactly that gave her that elegant look. Was it her posture? Or maybe her personable, heart-shaped face? Or was it her well-cut black hair?

Barbara gave me a little shove and I remembered myself. I stumbled into Alice's apartment with a smile on my face.

Barbara followed me in, gushing. "I love your place," she told Alice. "The colors are just gorgeous!"

Alice's living room was as elegant as she was. It had probably started off with a beige rug and white walls, the same way my living room had. But the resemblance ended there. Alice had added white wicker furnishings with pillows in blue-greens, pinks and lavenders. The curtains and paintings reflected the same clear colors. There was nothing jarring here, nothing that clashed. Even Alice's fuchsia sweatshirt looked right for the room.

"Gee, thanks," Alice was saying to Barbara. She smiled broadly, evidently pleased by Barbara's praise. "I love these bright colors. I couldn't stand a room filled with yucky browns or something." She waved her hand at a wicker couch for two. "So, siddown, you guys."

We did. The wicker was easier on the eyes than it was on the body. The pillow under me didn't extend to the knobby edge of the seat. I could feel the contours of bent twigs poking into the backs of my knees as I squirmed around trying to get comfortable.

Alice sat across from us, apparently at ease in her wicker chair. "So," she said, bending forward eagerly. "Are you guys still investigating?"

I didn't really want to answer that question. "Bumbling" was a closer description of our activities so far than investigating. Dangerous bumbling at that, I thought, rubbing my neck. Luckily, Barbara spoke first.

"We're still trying to figure things out," she said, her voice low and sincere. "And we need your help. You knew Sheila Snyder. You know Dan Snyder. What can you tell us about them?"

"Well . . ." Alice faltered. She ran her hand through her black hair and thought for a moment.

"I gotta be honest," she said finally. "Sheila could be a bitch. Back at the commune she was on everybody's case all the time about better organization. She made all these crazy lists. And schedules and stuff. Tried to get us to follow orders. Then she'd get drunk and forget her own rules. What chutzpah!"

"Was she an alcoholic?" Barbara asked quietly.

"Maybe," said Alice, staring over our heads with eyes that were out of focus, lost in memory. "The rest of us were more into weed than alcohol in those days. But whiskey was definitely Sheila's drug of choice. Though I think she stopped drinking recently. At least that's what she said when I visited her to set up the class. She was in A.A. or something. But . . ."

"But . . ." Barbara repeated encouragingly.

"Well, the way she hit those kids," Alice said, shaking her head and frowning. "It was obvious she still had some kind of problem."

"How about Dan?" Barbara slipped in quietly.

"Dan was different," Alice replied. She smiled and her eyes went out of focus again. "He was always easygoing. Mellow . . ."

Mellow! He hadn't been mellow when he rammed my car, I thought angrily. My neck and shoulders stiffened as I remembered. I realized then that I hadn't ever told Barbara about the incident. I'd better warn her soon, I thought, and tuned back in to Alice.

". . . made flutes out of bamboo and sold them. He's a real good musician, you know. Dan can play anything. He might have had a good music career if Sheila hadn't dragged him down so bad." Alice shook her head again. "Maybe now he'll get back to his music again."

I resisted looking at Barbara. Did Alice realize she had just handed us a possible motive for Dan? Or for herself?

"What's Dan got to say about Sheila's death?" I asked.

Alice's eyes came back into focus. She frowned as she shrugged her shoulders. I tried again.

"Has he accused you or threatened you—?"

Alice sat up straight in her chair. "Of course not!" she interrupted indignantly. "Dan's not like that." She paused and ran her hand through her hair again. "He's just a little upset right now, you know?"

I nodded. I knew. I knew.

Barbara tried for a while after that. Was Dan violent? Was Dan a drug abuser? Had Dan hated his wife? Alice answered no, no and no, her voice growing tighter on each negative. It wasn't any use. In Alice's eyes Dan was just a nice guy caught up in terrible circumstances. If she saw another side to him, she wasn't talking about it. And now she was angry at Barbara, angry at what Barbara's question implied.

"How about your friend Meg?" Barbara asked, switching gears abruptly.

"What about her?" Alice demanded. So much for a friendly, willing informant.

"Oh, we were just curious," I interjected quickly. "She's such a talented artist."

Alice looked from me to Barbara and back again. I held my breath. Alice's features softened. I let my breath out.

"She's unbelievable, isn't she?" Alice said, her friendly smile back in place. She pointed to the wall in back of us. "Look, that's one of hers," she said.

I turned and saw a bold abstract in sea-green, lavender and hot pink. It was Meg's style, all right. My neck twinged. I turned back to Alice.

"Meg is so smart, you wouldn't believe it," Alice rattled on

enthusiastically. "She does all kinds of art, types a hundred
words a minute and invents these dynamite vegetarian recipes. I
keep telling her she ought to do a cookbook." She shook her
head slowly. "The things that woman can do with tofu—"

At the word *tofu*, my stomach emitted a long, loud growl. I
blushed as I glared down at it.

"Whoa," Barbara said, laughing. "That beast ought to be in a
cage."

Alice giggled along with her, then suddenly cried, "You must
be hungry!" and jumped out of her chair.

"What a doof I am," she said. "I didn't even think to offer you
guys food." She waved her hands. "Up, up!" she ordered and led
us protesting into the kitchen.

Her kitchen was as elegant as her living room. Clean and
white, it was furnished with a wicker-and-glass table surrounded
by more wicker chairs with turquoise pillows. A four-by-six
painting of pale green and dark purple grapes, which had to have
been done by Meg Quilter, hung on the far wall.

"Let's see," Alice said, peering into the refrigerator. "I've got
carrot sticks, apples, yogurt, low-fat cottage cheese—"

"Please, you don't have to feed us," I objected. Now I was really embarrassed.

"Sit, sit," she said, waving one hand at the wicker chairs, her
eyes still on the contents of the refrigerator. "And whole-wheat
bread." She closed the door. "I've even got peanut butter hidden," she finished in a whisper.

She stared at us inquiringly as we sat down. Was she waiting
for permission to break out the peanut butter?

"Sounds great," said Barbara.

I sneaked a quick glance at my friend's weakly smiling face.
Barbara's idea of "great" was barbecued pork ribs, onion rings
and beer, not whole-wheat and peanut butter. Carrots with nothing on them were her idea of cruel and unusual punishment. She
must have had more questions she wanted to ask.

"Okay," said Alice, opening the refrigerator again. "Let's
party!"

She set carrot and celery sticks, fruit, bottled Calistoga water
and bread on the table, all the while telling us about the diets
she'd been on.

"... Weight Watchers, Kemper Rice Diet, Nutri/System, Bev-

erly Hills, Jenny Craig, Oprah's diet." She crunched a celery
stick. "For all the good it did Oprah," she said and pulled a tiny
jar of peanut butter from a lavender bin beneath the sink.

"Only for you guys," she said wistfully as she added the jar
to the pile of food on the table.

"I've been going to Overeaters Anonymous for six years," she
added, taking a seat. "Right now I'm about forty or fifty pounds
over my ideal weight—"

"But you're gorgeous!" I burst out. Already, I couldn't stand
all this dieting. And I was only hearing about it.

"Huh," she snorted. "I'm a card-carrying chubbo. At least I
am now. But I won't be for long! I'm gonna do Pritikin. Meg's
gonna help me. Low fat, high fiber, whatever. She knows how to
cook it." Alice smiled at us. "Dig in," she said.

We dug in. And talked. But no amount of talking could convince Alice that she was beautiful the way she was. As I spread
peanut butter on whole-wheat, I thought about sending Wayne
over. He loved fat bottoms. At least he loved mine. I took a bite.
On second thought, I decided to keep him just where he was.

Barbara nibbled on a piece of bread without enthusiasm as she
led the conversation back from weight-loss to Dan and Sheila
Snyder. Alice was good-natured enough to answer Barbara's
questions, but she didn't say anything we hadn't heard before.
Barbara fidgeted in her wicker chair for a while, then stood up
just as I had taken my last bite of apple.

"Oh, Jeez!" she cried, looking at her watch. "I'm late for an
appointment."

I played along, although I was pretty sure that her appointment was with her idea of dinner, something far more tasty and
fattening than Alice had to offer.

"We owe you a meal," Barbara told Alice on the way out.

"I'll hold you to it," Alice answered cheerfully. She waved a
quick goodbye and closed the door behind us.

"So, why'd Vesta make a salt pie?" Barbara asked as we
climbed down the rickety stairs. Damn. I had forgotten all about
the pie.

But I did my best to explain it on the way home. Then I told
her how Dan Snyder had rammed my car.

"Jeez-Louise," she murmured. "Maybe he *is* nuts."

"Alice thinks he's a nice guy," I said sarcastically.

"Yeah, but Alice is nuts herself," Barbara argued, apparently missing my sarcasm. "Anybody who spends that much time thinking about food has gotta be."

I scanned Barbara's petite body with a sideways glance. "People who can wear anything less than a size ten aren't allowed opinions on diets," I informed her. "They're lucky they're allowed to live."

She leaned back in her seat and laughed. Then she complained about Felix until I dropped her off at her car.

It wasn't until I opened the door to my own dark house that I thought seriously about Alice's obsession. If there was a way murder could have lost Alice forty pounds without dieting, I would have been the first to suspect her. But killing Sheila couldn't have done that. Still, it had freed Dan from his marriage, I reflected. Freed him to get to know Alice again.

As I reached for the light switch in the entryway, I heard a noise from the living room. A faint, whistling sound. I left the lights off and tiptoed in. Wayne was curled up in a fetal position on the couch, snoring softly. A surge of affection warmed my body as I looked down at his sleeping face. Sometimes I felt that I would do anything to protect him, anything to protect our relationship. The rapture of love was a powerful motivator. The warmth dissipated as my mind turned back to Alice. What would she do for the relationship she wanted?

I shook off the thought. I liked Alice. I didn't want to suspect her. And there were plenty of others to suspect. Dan, Meg, Iris . . .

I blew Wayne a quiet kiss and tiptoed from the living room into my office. The stack of Jest Gifts paperwork was still waiting for me. I sighed and dug in.

It was almost midnight when I heard Wayne's footsteps behind me. Then I felt his warm hands on my shoulders.

"Love you, Kate," he growled softly. "Sorry I've blown it."

I swiveled my chair around to look at him. Under his heavy eyebrows, his eyes were filled with something that might have been sadness. Or maybe defeat. His broad shoulders drooped.

"Mom's . . ." he began. He faltered, dropping his gaze.

"I love you, too," I said softly as I stood up. He needed to know that before he went any further.

He lifted his eyes. "She's difficult," he said, his voice rising slightly in pitch. "I know she can't stay here. But I can't just abandon her."

I could feel my own shoulders droop. He was right. He couldn't just abandon her. But she had to leave.

"What about getting an apartment for her, like you said before?" I suggested. "Or a house . . ." There was no response.

"She wants me to go with her," he said softly.

I stiffened. Of course, that was what she wanted. My fists clenched. I wasn't going to let her. I wanted to scream "No!" But I just clamped my jaw down and nodded.

"Thought she was well enough to take care of herself," he continued brusquely. "Not so sure anymore."

"How about a nurse?" I tried. "Maybe a paid companion."

"Maybe," he said thoughtfully. His shoulders straightened a little. "There's got to be a way."

I put my arms around him. He embraced me tightly, his chin resting on the top of my head.

"We'll figure it out, together," I whispered into his chest.

We held each other for a few more heartbeats. The intimacy was worth the strain on my sore neck. Wayne must have sensed that strain, because he broke away. Then he bent over to look into my eyes.

"I'll do something," he promised, his voice deep and gravelly. "Soon."

That was good enough for me. I took a deep breath.

"Race you to the bedroom," I whispered. I winked lasciviously.

His face softened into a smile. Then he began running.

He won the race. But I jumped him once he made it to the bed. Wayne was ticklish. A surprising trait in a man who was a karate black belt and a former bodyguard, but true nevertheless. I stripped off his socks before he had time to stop me and tickled the undersides of his feet. Instantly, he was giggling and flailing helplessly.

Than I attacked, pulling off the rest of his clothes. Despite his heavy breathing, I had a feeling he wasn't fighting me very hard. His warm mouth landed on mine and I gave up the struggle, offering him all the resistance of a vat of warm Jell-O. I sighed happily as he unbuttoned my shirt. He kissed my bare shoulder gently, and at that moment I knew how C.C. felt when she purred. His mouth moved downward and I heard a thumping sound. My heart?

No. It wasn't my heart.

I heard more thumps. Wayne's head jerked up.

"Keep it down in there! I'm trying to sleep!" came Vesta's voice from the other side of the wall.

Wayne and I groaned simultaneously.

At least we did something simultaneously, I thought as Wayne rolled away from me. I turned on my side and watched his muscular body deflate.

"Meet you at the Holiday Inn?" I suggested.

Wayne groaned. Or laughed. Actually, I think he did something between the two.

Vesta thumped the wall again.

I pulled off the rest of my clothes and snuggled up to Wayne under the covers.

Two hours later I awoke, cold and shivering. The covers were crumpled at the bottom of the bed. I crossed my arms over my chest and rubbed them, watching the almost full moon through the skylight, thinking about murder. Who had killed Sheila Snyder? Dan? Alice? I looked over at Wayne, his body silvery-white and beautiful in the soft moonlight. Would I kill for love? I considered Vesta, sleeping in the next room. It was a thought.

A bad thought, I lectured myself. Violence didn't solve anything, et cetera, et cetera. I looked back at Wayne. He sighed in his sleep.

I smiled and kissed his forehead gently, then his mouth. His eyes popped open.

"Ka—" he began.

"Shhh," I warned. I put my finger across my lips, then across his. He kissed my finger. It wasn't long before we were back where we had left off.

We made love in an exquisite agony of silence, then lay together, whispering in the moonlight.

Then he told me that he'd sold his first short story.

I threw my arms around him and squeezed, murmuring congratulations wildly, trying not to shout.

"When?" I asked finally.

"Last Wednesday," he whispered.

"Why didn't you tell me before?"

"I couldn't," he said quietly. "Not with Mom here, not with this issue between us."

"Oh, sweetie," I sighed and kissed him again.

Vesta didn't wake up the second time either.

My alarm rang at eight the next morning. I stretched and instantly regretted it. My neck and shoulders were still sore. There was a note on the pillow next to me.

"I had to go," it read in Wayne's nearly illegible handwriting. "I made you oatmeal. I love you."

A hot shower helped my poor body. I dressed and walked into the kitchen, feeling good. Vesta sat at the kitchen table, stirring a cup of black coffee. She looked up at me and glowered.

I smiled and sat down across from her. A pot of oatmeal was at my place. I lifted the lid and a wisp of steam escaped. Wayne couldn't have left too long ago. Maybe he was checking out apartments for Vesta, I thought happily.

"You'll burn, you know," Vesta hissed at me.

"What?" I asked, startled. Was she talking about the hot oatmeal?

"You'll burn," she repeated. "In hell." She leaned forward and grinned triumphantly. "Wanna know why?"

– Eleven –

I SHOOK MY head. I most definitely did *not* want to hear why I would burn in hell. At least not at breakfast. Shaking my head didn't stop Vesta, though.

"Because adultery is a sin!" she proclaimed, pointing her long, skinny finger at me for emphasis. Then she leaned back in her chair, a smug smile on her face.

"That's nice," I replied and returned her smile for a few heart-beats before standing back up.

I stepped up to the refrigerator and opened it, wondering in spite of myself. Why would I burn in hell for adultery? I wasn't even married. I found some soy milk and brought it back to the table. I knew I should just ignore Vesta's proclamation, but . . . I sat back down.

"All right, what do you mean, 'adultery is a sin'?" I asked.

Vesta just winked at me, happy to have caught my attention.

"I'm not married, nor is Wayne," I pointed out.

"If you're not married, how come you have a husband?" she demanded happily.

"I don't have a husband," I told her, keeping my voice even. "I have an *ex*-husband."

"Have it your way," she said sweetly. "But God knows. And the Devil." She rubbed her hands together. "You'll fry for sure."

"Thank you for sharing," I said, and ate my oatmeal.

I had plenty of time to mentally replay the interaction with Vesta as I drove over the Richmond Bridge and down the highway to

Jest Gifts' Oakland warehouse. Ad nauseam. Next time I'd ignore her, I promised myself as I handed out paychecks.

On the return trip, however, my thoughts drifted back to Sheila Snyder's death. Dan and Alice. Alice and Dan. Their names rolled through my mind and connected again and again as I traveled up Highway 580 toward the bridge. But they weren't the only suspects, I reminded myself as I pawed through my purse, searching for the bridge toll.

There was Iris, for instance, with her creepy photo collection. I dropped a dollar bill into the toll collector's outstretched hand, then rattled out of the toll booth onto the bridge. Had Iris hung the photo of Ted Bundy's hands with the others because his hands were interesting or because he was her personal role model?

I drove across the bridge and down 101, my neck and shoulders aching all the way. Maybe it was the weight of the multiple suspicions crowding into my head. Paula Pierce was another formidable woman, I thought, seeing her stocky, business-suited body in my mind's eyes. How far would Paula go to protect her husband? To defend anyone she believed was oppressed, for that matter? And Meg Quilter, pale, talented and quiet. Too damn quiet, actually. Maybe she was repressed. Maybe she was raging inside! Then again, maybe not. I sighed as I took the Stinson Beach turnoff.

And how about the three I hadn't seen since the night of the murder? Paula's husband, Gary: the mathematics professor with the fondness for crystals. He was another quiet one. Then there was Leo. Ugh. He certainly wasn't quiet. He was a loud, leering drunk. Could I add violence to the list of his faults? And Ken. I had almost forgotten Ken, almost forgotten the way he had giggled in the wake of Sheila's murder.

I pulled into my driveway and climbed the stairs to my house, feeling both sore from driving and crabby to boot.

The phone rang on cue the instant I opened the door. I charged ahead, beating Vesta to it by a hand's length. She snorted and headed back down the hallway as I picked the receiver up.

"Hey, kiddo," Barbara greeted me.

"How do you do that?" I asked her impatiently. "How do you know when I'm walking in the door?"

"Practice," she answered. "Hey, I went up to Leo's gallery today—"

"We're supposed to visit these people together," I interrupted her. "The buddy system, remember?"

"Oh, Leo's harmless—"

"Barbara!" I shouted, picturing a drunken Leo with his plump hands wrapped around my friend's slim neck. In my current mood, it wasn't a totally unattractive picture.

"Okay, okay," she capitulated cheerfully. "We'll go together this afternoon, right after we visit Paula and Gary."

I opened my mouth to object, then closed it again, hoist by my own buddy system.

"I'll see you around three," Barbara caroled and hung up.

I sat down at my desk to stare at the piles of paper that covered it. I looked at my watch. I had less than four hours to do twelve hours' worth of work. I sharpened a pencil and began filling in forms.

I had barely worked an hour when the phone rang. If that was Barbara again, I thought, I'd murder her myself. I had work to do, damn it.

"Hello!" I barked into the phone.

"Hi, this is Ann," a concerned voice said. "Are you mad about something?"

"I'm fine," I lied as my mind shifted gears. I hadn't seen my friend Ann Rivera in at least a month. Something began to itch at the back of my consciousness

"Did you forget our lunch date?" she asked. That was it. Lunch! I pushed a pile of papers aside and saw it written there on my desk calendar, "Ann—Miranda's—12:00."

"Right, lunch," I said, trying to put some enthusiasm into my tone. I looked at my watch. It was after twelve. "I'm on my way," I told her.

It took me seven minutes to get to Miranda's in downtown Mill Valley. I burst through the doors, startling a doe-eyed waitress clutching two menus to her breast. Mozart murmured from the sound system in a quiet rebuke to my noisy entrance. Even the pastel decor and tastefully arranged flowers seemed offended.

"One for lunch?" squeaked the waitress.

"I'm meeting a friend," I told her, peering around her slight form.

I saw Ann in a booth near the windows. I semaphored frantically. Ann smiled and waved. The waitress jumped back as I rushed by.

"You look great," I told Ann, panting as I slid into the booth across from her.

And she did. Her black hair hung in a new, sleek pageboy. Her brown skin glowed. Even her gray pinstripe suit looked good against the mauve upholstery of the booth. Ann's chocolate-brown eyes look worried, though.

"You seem awfully anxious, Kate," she said quietly, pulling a yellow marigold from the flower arrangement in the center of the table. "Is something bothering you?"

"Who, me?" I protested, resisting the urge to get up and run around the table a few times to calm down.

She smiled her toothy smile and stuck the flower behind her ear. Suddenly, she didn't look very businesslike anymore.

"Yes, you," she said. "What's wrong?"

"Murder!" I blurted out.

I heard a gasp to my side. I turned and saw the doe-eyed waitress. Her head was pulled back, her arm extended full-length, holding out a menu as if she were feeding a snarling lion. Should I explain myself?

"I'll have the chevre-walnut salad," interjected Ann, wisely cutting off any explanation on my part. "And iced herbal tea."

I followed suit, ordering the soba noodle salad with grilled tofu. And carrot juice. I didn't need to see a menu. I had memorized the precious few vegetarian entrees at Miranda's in the first three times I'd visited.

The waitress didn't write our orders down. They never did at Miranda's, part of their general atmosphere of good taste. They averaged about one mistake an order. I wondered what it would be this time.

"So," said Ann once the waitress had left. She looked me in the eye. "Are you talking about the murder of the woman who owned the Good Thyme Cafe?"

I nodded, wondering if all my friends were psychic now.

"The Good Thyme's an awful place," Ann drawled. "Are you sure she wasn't killed because of the cooking?"

I thought about it for a moment. The cooking had been pretty bad. But who had eaten there before? I had. Alice, probably—

"I was joking, Kate," Ann enunciated carefully. She waved a hand in front of my face. "Joke? Ha-ha?"

"Sorry," I mumbled. Now I was feeling foolish as well as nervous. I leaned across the table to explain. "I guess I'm a little spooked. See, I was there. I saw Sheila Snyder's dead body. There was an electrical cord twisted around her neck—"

I heard another gasp beside me. The waitress had returned to confirm our drink order.

"Did you say carrot juice?" she asked in a high, fluttering voice.

I nodded.

She looked at Ann. "Then you're having the apple juice?"

"No, I'm having herbal iced tea," Ann corrected her slowly and clearly. Ann Rivera was the administrator of a mental hospital. She was good at directions.

"Oh, of course," the waitress whispered, nodding her head vigorously at Ann, while her eyeballs traveled surreptitiously back to me.

I wondered if the service would be better or worse, now that I had apparently terrified the waitress. What was wrong with her? Had she heard about the Good Thyme murder? Was she afraid her days were numbered as a restaurant employee? She turned and left, with a backwards look over her shoulder. Maybe she was just naturally timid.

Once we were alone again, Ann got serious. "Have you ever asked yourself why you keep getting involved in these things?" she said.

"Of course I ask myself," I shot back, my shoulders tightening. "But I don't get an answer. And if you mention karma, I'll kill you!"

I looked quickly to my side. Luckily, the waitress had missed that one. I turned back to Ann with an apologetic smile.

"So, tell me about it," she ordered.

I did. Ann was a good listener as well as a good director. By the time the juice and tea arrived, Ann had a pretty good idea who all the players were. By the time our salads arrived, Ann knew just about everything I did.

"There's a murderer on the residential ward at our facility," she said thoughtfully as she stuck her fork into her salad. "Killed his wife about forty years ago." She took a big bite of greens, nuts and goat cheese. "Apologetic little guy," she mumbled through the salad. "Though he claims to be Attila the Hun. It's the only name he'll answer to."

"Claiming to be Attila the Hun probably kept him away from the electric chair," I pointed out.

I took a bite of my own salad. The soba noodles and crisp vegetables were as good as ever in a light, tangy dressing, the tofu marinated in the same dressing and charcoal-grilled. Tasty, as well as tasteful. That's why we came to Miranda's.

"Maybe he would have gone to Death Row," she conceded with a shrug. "But maybe not. The way it is, he's been warehoused for forty years. And he'd get out if he'd only knock off the Attila story."

"Wayne's mother, the woman who's living with us now, spent twenty years on a psych ward," I told Ann through a mouthful of noodles. "Overmedicated."

"What was wrong with her originally?" Ann was looking at me with new concern in her eyes. I could tell she didn't like the idea of a former mental patient living with us. Well, neither did I.

"I think she was diagnosed as a schizophrenic," I answered. "But she's really just . . ." A number of words went through my mind, none of them genteel enough to utter at Miranda's. "She's mean," I said finally.

"What do you mean, 'mean'?" Ann prodded.

It took me fifteen minutes to tell her, between mouthfuls. Ann shook her head sympathetically as I finished the tale.

"I'm sure glad we don't have her at our facility," she told me. She plucked the marigold from behind her ear and put it back in the vase, looking like a hospital administrator again.

"God knows how we'd diagnose the woman," she added, her voice taking on weight as she spoke. "Just plain 'schizophrenic' doesn't cut it anymore for most of them." She shook her head. "We have to be specific, very specific. Or else we get sued for malpractice. You wouldn't believe it. There're about a million psychoses and conditions and disorders."

"Like what?" I asked. I was curious. When I had worked on a psych ward, we had used three basic categories: schizophrenic, manic-depressive and alcoholic.

Ann took a sip of tea before answering. "Okay," she said, her voice a little lighter. "Say someone comes in with amnesia—"

"Hit 'em over the head again," I advised.

She laughed. "I only wish it was that easy," she drawled. "If someone has amnesia, it might be from prolonged alcohol abuse, or delirium, or brain damage, or MPD—"

"What's MPD?" I asked.

"Multiple Personality Disorder," she answered. She took another sip of tea.

"You mean like *The Three Faces of Eve*? And *Sybil*?"

"You got it," she told me. "God, these MPD patients are bizarre. Flipping in and out of personalities like they're changing the channel on a TV set."

Someone cleared a throat next to me. I jumped, startled. It was our waitress. I wondered how long she'd been standing there.

"How about dessert?" she proposed, a weak smile on her face. Her eyes took on a glazed look as she began to recite. "We have homemade lemon cheesecake, chocolate brownies with ice cream, fresh fruit compote, guava-mango sorbet—"

"Stop right there," Ann ordered, holding out her hand like a traffic cop. "I'll have a decaf espresso."

"Is there any sugar in the fruit compote?" I asked. My stomach gave a little churn in favor of dessert.

"Only a tiny bit of honey," she whispered.

"I'll take it," I said, hoping it wasn't anything like Vesta's apple pie.

"Go on," I told Ann after our waitress had departed.

She leaned forward across the table. "I've seen these MPD patients, Kate," she said earnestly. "They really do seem to be more than one person, at least more than one personality. And some of their personalities don't know what the other personalities have done, so they look like amnesiacs. But then, another one of their personalties may know exactly what the rest are doing. It's like talking to totally different people, with totally different memories." She threw up her hands. "God, what a mess! You practically need a different diagnosis for each one."

"Why are they like that?" I asked.,

"Usually terrible abuse as children," she answered, her chocolate-brown eyes suddenly sad. "The theory is that they divide into separate personalities in order to split off the memories of the abuse." She leaned back and began twirling a black curl around her finger, a sure sign she was upset.

"But then, most of the mental disorders we see begin with childhood abuse," she said, her voice high and vibrating with tension. "God, some of the alcoholics we get in. It makes me sick to think they have kids! Violent sons of bitches, some of them."

I just nodded, knowing that Ann's parents had been abusive alcoholics. Every once in a while she talked about them. She usually kept the subject in the abstract, speaking of patterns in dysfunctional families or Adult Children of Alcoholics meetings. She got too upset when she talked about real people. I wondered, not for the first time, why she chose to do work that was bound to expose her to the kind of abusive alcoholics she'd been raised by. I opened my mouth to ask.

"There was this man we had for a while last year," she said, cutting me off before I had a chance. "He killed a guy in a bar, drove home, and didn't remember any of it the next day. He's a perfectly nice man. When he's not drinking." She laughed. It wasn't a happy laugh.

"And then, there're the sociopaths," she went on angrily. "They're the hardest to spot. Sometimes they're charming, real charming." She reached to twirl her hair again. "We have this old man on the residential ward. He's helpful and friendly, a real doll. You wonder what he's doing locked up. Then you take a look at his chart. He's a three-time child molester!"

She leaned forward and spoke in a hushed voice. "The Girl Scouts visited last Christmas. A nurse walked in and there he was, with one of them in his lap!"

"Decaf espresso," came a whisper to our side.

This time, Ann and I both jumped. Our waitress handed Ann the decaf. "Guava-mango sorbet," she said to me.

"Didn't I . . ." I faltered. In between multiple personalities, alcoholics and sociopaths, I couldn't remember exactly what I'd asked for.

"She ordered the fruit compote," Ann said.

Our waitress sighed. Her doe-eyes moistened.

"Any sugar in the sorbet?" I asked.

"Sweetened with fruit juice only," she recited hopefully.

"Good," I said. "I'll take it."

She handed the sorbet over and whispered, "They won't let us write down the orders."

I nodded sympathetically. Ann rolled her eyes.

"When are you going to stop being such a caretaker?" she asked once the waitress was out of sight. Her affectionate smile took the sting out of her words.

"Caretaker? Is that a diagnosis?" I asked her back.

She laughed. I took a bite of sorbet. It was tart and cold on my tongue. And sweet. Sighing, I closed my eyes and let it melt into my mouth. I've never been convinced that sex is the only orgasmic pleasure around. My stomach gurgled happily in agreement.

I swallowed and opened my eyes again, looking across at Ann. "Why do you work in a mental hospital if it upsets you so much?" I asked seriously.

Her head jerked up and her eyes narrowed. Damn. Maybe I shouldn't have asked.

"Join the crowd," she snapped. She crossed her arms. "My therapist wants to know why, too. I don't work with the patients directly, for God's sake! I'm in the front office. But—"

She stopped mid-tirade, uncrossing her arms, then raising them as if she were under arrest.

"Sorry, Kate," she whispered. "The answer is probably, 'because of my childhood.' I didn't mean to rant and rave."

"I was just curious," I told her, embarrassed to have upset her.

"Me, too," she said with a toothy smile. "You tell me if you figure it out first. Okay?"

"Sure," I agreed, reaching out to shake her hand. "It's a deal. All you have to do now is tell me how to get rid of Wayne's mother."

She shook my hand and laughed.

"Permanently?" she purred, her eyes glinting with mischief.

"Don't tempt me," I muttered.

"Well, I don't know how to get rid of her," Ann told me, "but I know what her diagnosis is."

"What?" I asked.

"JPND," she whispered.

– Twelve –

"WHAT THE HELL is JPND?" I demanded.

Ann bent forward and whispered, "Just Plain Nasty Disorder."

We both laughed far harder than the diagnosis warranted. We were still laughing when our waitress arrived with our check. She dropped it on the table and scurried away with one last, nervous, backward glance.

Ann and I paid up and walked out together. We shared a hug in the parking lot.

"Let me know what happens with your murder," Ann said. "And don't worry, everything will be okay."

I started to object to her characterization of the murder as mine, but a look at her smiling face stopped me. I hugged her again instead.

I drove home feeling warmed by the friendship we shared. I could never be a complete hermit. My friendships with other women meant too much to me. They were the staples of my life, the brown rice and tofu I needed to survive. Wayne was the dessert. I smiled, thinking of him with a scoop of sorbet strategically placed on his naked body. Never mind, I told myself. You've had enough dessert.

But the smile was still tugging at the corners of my mouth as I opened the front door and walked into my house.

"We have a guest, Kate," Vesta sang out gaily from the living room.

Cheered by her happy tone, I turned to see who was visiting. The cheer turned to chill instantly.

A burly man was sharing the living room couch with Vesta. I

recognized him instantly. Dan Snyder. My hands went icy. He rose from the couch and strode toward me. My neck and shoulders seized up in memory of the last time I had seen his face. Only this time he wasn't staring down from the windshield of his truck. There were no rubber bumpers between us.

"I wanna talk to you," he growled.

I started toward the phone an instant too late. Dan stepped in front of me. God, he was a big man! As tall as Wayne, but bulkier.

Maybe Vesta could call the police, I thought, appealing to her with my eyes. But she only smiled, clearly pleased with the situation. I cursed to myself over the sound of my heart thudding in my ears and turned back to Dan Snyder.

I studied his face. I was close enough to see the black stubble on his cheeks, the red webs in the whites of his squinting eyes, and the dark circles beneath them. My heart eased a bit. He looked in worse shape than me. He must be grieving for his wife, I thought with a momentary surge of compassion. But then another possibility entered my mind. What if he was really in a panic, afraid he would go to prison for her murder?

"Who killed my wife?" he demanded. His voice was hoarse with anger. My heart jumped into my ears again.

"I don't know," I answered softly.

His hands formed into fists. "Don't give me that bullshit!" he shouted, thrusting his face closer to mine. "I wanna know who killed her!"

I took a deep breath and tried to center myself. In tai chi the person who is the most relaxed, the most flexible, wins. I'd pushed guys nearly his size off balance in push-hands exercises. But they weren't angry, I reminded myself. They weren't possible murderers. I didn't want to fight with this guy. I took a slow step backwards instead, keeping my eyes on his glaring face.

"I don't know who killed your wife," I repeated in a quiet, level voice. I took another slow back step. "I'm trying to find out."

He narrowed his eyes further. "Why?" he asked.

That was a good question. I couldn't tell him Barbara was under suspicion. Or that I had found bodies before—

He moved closer to me, closing the gap between us in one stride. Damn.

"Why?" he repeated, louder this time.

"Murder is a terrible thing," I whispered. Cold sweat dampened my shirt. "It shouldn't go unpunished."

He tilted his head as if considering my words. Then he nodded, his face softening.

I took a breath, and another backward step for good measure.

"Ask her why the police wanted to talk to her!" Vesta shouted from the couch.

Dan jerked his head in her direction, startled. Then he turned his renewed glare on me.

"Ask her about her friend, too," Vesta added. "They're up to something."

Dan grunted and reached for me. I took a few more quick backsteps and his hands closed on air. But not for long.

"Hey!" he bellowed and strode toward me, arms outstretched. I knew he could go forward faster than I could go backward, but I kept stepping away.

I was almost to the doorway. Should I run for it? Or use his momentum against him? He'd go over pretty easily with that forward tilt.

"What are you two—" he began.

"Young man!" shrilled a voice from behind me.

Dan looked past me, his eyes open with surprise. His arms dropped to his sides.

I chanced a quick backward glance and saw Arletta and Edna standing there. The twins! Arletta's frail body was rigid with disapproval as she peered through her thick glasses at Dan Snyder. Edna stood like a rock next to her, arms crossed over her chest.

"What do you think you're doing?" Edna demanded in a voice nearly as menacing as Dan's own.

Dan's shoulders slumped. He hung his head and muttered something I couldn't make out.

"May we come in, Kate?" chirped Arletta politely.

"Of course you can," I answered without turning my head. I still didn't want to take my eyes off Dan Snyder.

Two long strides took Edna to the left of me. Arletta took a few shorter steps to my right. I was surrounded, safe. My body let go and began to shake with relief and leftover adrenaline.

"You must be Dan Snyder," Arletta said, her high voice more gentle now.

Dan nodded, his eyes on her face.

"Kate has been trying to solve the mystery of your wife's death," she told him. "You might want to thank her for her efforts."

"Thank you," he muttered, dropping his gaze to the tops of his shoes.

"You're welcome," I replied quietly, suppressing a terrible urge to giggle. I rubbed my cold hands together instead.

"You're not going to let her get away with that!" shrieked Vesta. She leapt from the couch and ran the short distance to join our little group. "She's hiding something! Her and that friend of hers."

Dan squinted in her direction for a moment. Then he looked back at me. Damn.

"What are you hiding—" he began.

"Young man," Arletta interrupted him. "Kate is not hiding anything from you." Then she turned to Vesta. "I cannot imagine what your reason is for inciting this poor young man to suspect Kate, but your behavior is inexcusable."

"But—" squeaked Vesta.

"There is no excuse," Arletta repeated, her gaze unwavering. Vesta glared back defiantly for a moment, then turned and stomped away.

"Now," chirped Arletta, peering at Dan benevolently through her glasses. "Perhaps we can discuss this in a more congenial atmosphere. There is a very nice lounge in the lobby of our hotel. Would you be so good as to accompany us there?"

Dan stared at her, wide-eyed. To me, his bloodshot eyes seemed to cry out "No!" But his mouth mumbled "Okay," and he followed Edna and Arletta out the front door.

I watched from the porch as Arletta climbed into Dan's truck. Then Edna got into her rental car and the two vehicles drove in procession down the road until they were out of sight.

Once they were gone, I collapsed. I was shivering and shaking as I curled up in my comfy chair, asking myself over and over again what would have happened if the twins hadn't rescued me. I felt so cold. I considered calling the police. But what would I tell them? That Dan Snyder had shouted at me? That wasn't against the law. And he hadn't broken into my house. Vesta had invited him inside. Vesta!

I climbed out of my chair and marched down the hallway. I knocked on her door.

"Go away!" she shouted.

I looked down at the doorknob. There was no lock on this door. I could just walk in. But . . .

I thought of the years Vesta had spent in a psychiatric facility. There were no locks on the doors of the patients' rooms there either. They had no privacy, not even in the bathroom. I shook my head. I couldn't do it. Opening that door would be like putting her in an institution all over again. I sighed and walked back down the hall.

Minutes later, I was at my desk again, still feeling weak but a little warmer. As I picked up the State Board of Equalization's Sales and Use Tax form I wondered why the twins had come to my house in the first place. Had I missed another appointment? I looked at my calender. It was blank for the day except for my date with Ann—and a note about the taxes that were due. I turned my calculator on and began jabbing the keys.

Barbara showed up an hour later, looking perfect in turquoise linen.

"Hey, kiddo," she sang as she breezed in. "You look terrible."

"Barbara!" I objected.

"What happened?" she asked, her tiny body quivering like a pointer on a scent.

"Dan Snyder visited," I answered briefly.

"And . . ." she prodded.

I knew from experience that it was no use trying to avoid her questions. I told her the whole story, standing there in the entryway. Then I waited for her reaction. She scrunched up her beautiful face and nodded slowly.

"You're not in any shape to drive to Gary and Paula's," she said finally. "I'll drive." Then she led the way out the door to her Volkswagen bug.

I was so dazed, I followed her.

We had just pulled onto the freeway when I suddenly remembered why I usually refused Barbara's offers to drive. She turned to me, explaining why she now thought that Ken was our murderer, while she guided her Volkswagen into the next lane, two feet in front of a barreling lumber truck's front bumper.

"Look out!" I yelped to the sound of squealing brakes.

"Kate, you know they never hit me," she said and continued with her theory.

I couldn't say what that theory was. It was wiped from my memory banks by the near collision with a Mercedes when Barbara switched lanes again. I closed my eyes for the rest of the trip across the Richmond Bridge and into the Berkeley hills. But I could still hear the squeals, honks and curses from the other cars.

When we arrived at Paula and Gary's house I got out of the car and knelt on their blacktop driveway.

"What are you doing?" asked Barbara.

"I'm kissing the ground," I told her. "I thought I'd never see it again."

"Get up, you wacko!" she ordered, laughing. She dragged me to the front door.

Paula and Gary lived in a two-story stucco house perched on the side of a steep hill. There was a small garden in front with yellow and orange nasturtiums running riot. Potted red geraniums lined the walkway.

Barbara rang the bell, but we'd barely heard its chime before barking and yipping ensued from inside the house.

"Did you tell them we were coming?" I asked anxiously.

Barbara nodded. Something thumped against the door. I wasn't sure if I wanted to be there when the door opened.

"Get down!" came a disembodied voice. There were more assorted thumps and yips and barks. "Down!" shouted the voice. "Down!"

The door opened a crack. Paula Pierce peeked out. "Back, get back!" she shouted over her shoulder as she waved us in.

I followed Barbara in reluctantly. Paula shut the door quickly behind us and the dogs exploded again.

A graying Labrador retriever almost knocked Barbara over as it jumped up to lick her face. I was glad she was in front.

"Down!" Paula shouted again. She wasn't in a business suit today. Blue jeans and an "Oil Isn't Worth Dying For" T-shirt clothed her stocky body.

A small, yipping, unshaved poodle scurried around in back of me and leapt with military precision to shove its nose into the center of my buttocks. Luckily, my yelp was inaudible over the general din. One of a matched set of two beagles sauntered over and leaned against my leg, looking sad. I bent over to pet him. The poodle took its opportunity to leap again. I jerked straight up as its nose goosed me the second time.

"Down, Emma! Down, Cesare! Down, Joe! Down, Joan!" Paula commanded. The animals were still for a moment.

Paula quickly ushered us into an adjoining room equipped with glass doors, telling the animals to "stay," in no uncertain terms. And they did, whining and begging the whole time, but remaining miraculously in place until the doors were shut. Then they lined up to stare at us through the glass, their eyes beseeching.

"Sorry about that welcoming committee," came a rich baritone from beside us.

I turned my head and saw Gary Powell. I had forgotten how attractive the man was. The smile he greeted us with stretched all the way across his good-natured face. His brown eyes exuded warmth and serenity.

"A seat?" he offered, indicating a long beige couch.

Barbara and I sat down and were swallowed up by the plush cushions. I tried to think of something to say. Barbara beat me to it.

"What a nice room!" she gushed.

I ran my eyes around the room. It *was* nice. There were plenty of windows and skylights illuminating the beige-and-white interior. And they were all filled with crystals, which reflected random rainbow fragments of light onto the carpet, bookcases and walls, even across the bottom of a Martin Luther King poster on one wall and the edge of Picasso's "Guernica" on the other.

Gary flopped into a cocoa-colored lounger across from us. Paula pulled up a straight-back wooden chair next to him. Colored lights danced merrily off her salt-and-pepper hair as she sat down. But her face was serious, her mouth pursed tight. She stared at us unblinkingly.

"Nice," I echoed Barbara weakly. I forced my face into a friendly smile.

"I've advised my husband to speak to you about the night of the murder," Paula said briskly. "But under no circumstances will he—"

"It's okay, honey," Gary interrupted, his voice soft but firm.

He looked into her eyes. "I didn't kill the woman. Nobody thinks I did."

"Well . . ." said Paula doubtfully.

"Everything's fine," Gary assured her. He reached a long arm out and squeezed her shoulder gently, then turned his gaze back in our direction. "What did you want to know?"

I turned to Barbara. I didn't want to be the one to ask the questions. I was already embarrassed to be here, intruding on Paula and Gary's time together.

"Can you tell us what you did during the class break?" Barbara asked cheerfully. Apparently, she wasn't embarrassed. "It might help us figure out where everyone was."

"Let's see," Gary rumbled, leaning back in his chair, his eyes staring up at the ceiling. He pulled his arm from around Paula's shoulders and stuck his hand in his pocket.

"Paula and I talked to Meg for a very short time—probably two or three minutes. I'm sorry I can't be more exact," he said. His hand came out of his pocket with something in it. A crystal? "Then Paula had to go to the john. I waited for her. Then we went outside—to the little park across the street."

"Who else did you see?" Barbara pressed.

He looked at her for a moment, then back up at the ceiling. As he rolled the contents of one hand to the other, I saw that I had guessed correctly. It was a crystal.

"I think everyone else was gone from the restaurant by the time we finished talking to Meg," he answered slowly. "When we went to the park we saw your friend Kate." He nodded toward me and smiled. "And the silver-haired woman, I can't remember her name—"

"Iris," Paula supplied.

He nodded. "Later, we saw the man in the linen suit—"

"Leo," said Paula.

"And his friend," Gary finished.

Paula didn't give Ken a name. Maybe she had forgotten.

"That lunatic interrupted Gary's class," she said instead, her face and voice both tight with anger.

"Ken?" asked Barbara.

"No, no!" Paula said impatiently. "Dan Snyder. He came to Gary's class and started raving. Racial epithets, accusations that

Gary had been sleeping with his wife!" She shook her head. "They had to call campus security to remove him."

"It's okay," soothed Gary, putting his arm around her shoulder again. "No one believed what he said. He didn't attack me physically."

"No, it's not okay," Paula insisted. "I don't like knowing there's a madman out there." She crossed her arms. "It's like those murders when we were in Oregon. A woman we knew was one of the victims. Only an acquaintance, but still. And they never found the killer—"

Paula stopped speaking abruptly. Her eyes narrowed. God, I wished I could read minds. Did she suspect Gary? He looked calm enough. I glanced at Barbara, hoping her psychic powers were working.

"Anyway," Paula continued briskly. "Something needs to be done about that man."

"Dan's harassed me too," I offered. "He came—"

The sound of the dogs exploding into renewed barks, yips and thumps cut me off.

"Paloma must be home," said Gary with a smile. "Our daughter," he explained.

We heard a new, higher voice crying, "Down! Down!"

Then a beautiful young woman burst in through the glass doors. She had Gary's warm brown eyes, and his height and slender build. But the firmness of her mouth belonged to Paula. Her skin was a flawless blend of both parents' genes. She looked old enough to be finishing high school, maybe starting college.

"Mom," she rapped out. "Have you been smoking again?"

I turned back to Paula in time to see her face redden. She recovered quickly, making introductions all around and telling Paloma that we were there to discuss Sheila Snyder's death. Paloma flopped down on the couch next to me.

"Are you guys real detectives?" she asked eagerly.

I shook my head. Barbara just chuckled.

It didn't take long for Barbara to get back to interrogating Gary, but the results were disappointing. Gary didn't seem to know any more than we did. Actually, he seemed to know a lot less.

"Do you have *any* idea who killed her?"' she asked Gary finally, a hint of desperation in her tone.

"No," he answered thoughtfully. "But it's probably only a matter of time. Once the police know all the variables—"

"Daddy!" Paloma objected. "Life isn't just an equation, you know,"

"I stand corrected," Gary replied with a bow of his head. "Actually, life is more like a series of simultaneous equations, which must be solved simultaneously. If they're to be solved at all."

Paloma groaned loudly and rolled her beautiful eyes. Then she got up and gave her father a kiss on the cheek.

"No more cigarettes," she told her mother sternly, then exited the room to the joyous barks and yips of the four family dogs.

"She's a beautiful girl," Barbara said once she was gone.

Paula and Gary smiled together for a change.

"We love her," Gary said simply.

Then Paula's face tightened again. "I worry about the two Snyder children," she said. "The fact that Sheila Snyder would hit a child in front of witnesses indicates an even worse pattern of abuse behind closed doors." She sighed. "The children are bound to be further traumatized by their mother's death. And the father is probably abusive himself."

"You don't know any of that for sure," Gary admonished gently.

"I can recognize the signs of child abuse," she argued. "Remember, I was abused myself."

- Thirteen -

THE ROOM WAS quiet for a few moments. I could hear Paloma and the dogs knocking around in some other part of the house as I stared down at a rainbow shimmering across the toes of my sneakers. I didn't know what to say. Barbara did, though.

"I know about abuse, too," she blurted out. "My father used to hit me all the time." Lines of anger creased her face. "Hard," she added.

Paula leaned forward in a mirror reflection of Barbara's posture. "My mother was the one who beat me," she revealed. "For anything. For nothing. It didn't matter."

They both shook their heads indignantly. Barbara couldn't have created more rapport with Paula if she had tried. For a moment I wondered if she *had* tried, if her revelations had been meant to manipulate Paula. But a look at the stiff set of her shoulders convinced me otherwise. After a few more moments of angry silence, Gary cleared his throat.

"Well, my dear," he said to Paula in an exaggerated upper-class accent. "You most certainly have had your revenge." His warm brown eyes were twinkling. "You married a black man."

Paula leaned back in her chair and laughed. It was a great laugh. Full-bodied and unrestrained. I was surprised she had it in her. She laughed until there were tears in her eyes.

"I did indeed get my revenge," she agreed, wiping the edge of her eye with her index finger. She put a loving hand on Gary's arm. "And it was worth it. In more ways than one."

She turned back to Barbara and me, smiling. "My mother would have probably joined the KKK if it weren't for the sort of 'riffraff' they allow in their membership. When I married Gary I effectively divorced Mother. A two-for-one deal. The best deal I ever made."

"Hmm," muttered Barbara, pretending to think. "It has possibilities."

As everyone laughed, my mind went back to Paula's act of revenge. Killing a parent caught in the act of hitting a child might be an even greater revenge for an adult who had survived her own abuse. Was this a motive? I remembered what Ann had said about most mental disorders arising from childhood abuse—

The glass doors burst open before I could finish the thought. Paloma swept into the room, her eyebrows raised in what looked like surprise.

"Dad, did you leave food out on the counter?" she demanded. Uh-oh. Maybe the look was anger.

"I didn't think they'd eat tofu, for God's sake," Gary muttered as he rose from his lounger and sprinted out the door. "That was for dinner, a recipe of Meg's . . ."

Paloma followed him out. His voice died away as he disappeared from view.

"Dogs," Paula explained, rolling her eyes. "My kids adopt them." She stood up. "I guess I'd better untangle the mess."

Barbara and I stood too. The interview was clearly over.

"I wish you luck on your investigation," Paula said as she led us back to the front door. Her voice was considerably warmer than it had been when she'd showed us in. "Keep in touch," she added and opened the door to let us out.

I was bursting with questions as we headed toward the car. What had stopped Paula Pierce mid-sentence when she was talking about the murders in Oregon? And Gary—why had he needed to assure her that he hadn't killed Sheila? Then there was the child abuse issue. Could that be—

Barbara opened the door to the Volkswagen. All the questions left my mind as thirty pounds of compressed dread sank to the bottom of my stomach. Barbara was driving. How could I have forgotten!

I got in the car and placed my hands over my eyes. Barbara revved the engine and took off.

We made it across the bridge without getting hit. But there were a few near misses. At least that's what they sounded like.

"Leo's gallery is just above San Ricardo," Barbara announced cheerfully as she took 101 north. "I hope they're open late. It's almost five."

"Fine," I mumbled.

"I haven't been able to get hold of Ken on the phone," she continued. "All I get is his answering machine. I've left messages, but he hasn't returned them. Don't you think that's suspicious?"

A horn blared somewhere close by. I shuddered.

"Well?" prodded Barbara. "What do you think?"

"I think you should keep your eyes on the road," I answered.

She laughed merrily. I was glad that somebody was happy.

We parked in front of Leo's gallery two squeals and three honks later. I didn't bother to kiss the ground after I got out of the Volkswagen. I knew I'd just have to get back in and let Barbara drive some more once we were finished here.

The gallery was located in a storefront, sandwiched between Ed's Hardware and Jeanne's Art Supplies. That was certainly convenient for the exhibiting artists, I thought. But I wasn't sure how good a location it was for drawing the kind of people who would *buy* art.

The turquoise neon script in the window read "Conn-Tempo Gallery." As Barbara pushed the door open I wondered what the name meant. It was probably a stylish way to say contemporary, but the words "contempt" and "con" as in conning someone into buying expensive artwork did enter my mind.

"Wow," I whispered once we were inside.

The small room was stuffed with artwork. It couldn't have been much larger than my living room, though it did have a high, accommodating ceiling. It had to. It was filled to the brim with paintings, sculptures, ceramics and twisted neon. Naked ladies, abstracts and heavy metal predominated. Heavy metal sculpture, that is. A ten-foot monstrosity in the center of the crowded room combined all three themes. It was definitely metal, definitely abstract, and I could tell it was female by the seven steel breasts that ran diagonally up its flank. The other sculptures clustered around it were harder to place. Altogether, the room looked like a mad scientist's storeroom. An artistic mad scientist, of course.

"Look at this," Barbara hissed from the nearest wall.

I made my way past a few more metal monstrosities and a

twisted neon object that reminded me of those things people used
to make out of balloons at county fairs. Barbara was pointing at
the corner of an oil painting depicting a woman naked to the
waist, holding a whip. The proportions were off, giving it an un-
pleasant, skewed perspective. The name painted boldly in the
corner was "Leo."

"Do you think he did that perspective on purpose—?" I began.

"Shhh," warned Barbara, nudging me in the ribs. She pointed
across the room.

Leo's short, plump behind was facing us. He was in a black
sweatshirt and tight black jeans today. Not a pretty sight. He was
pressed up against a young blond woman almost a head taller
than he was.

"Come on, baby," he said, aiming a kiss toward her lips.
"Give me some tongue."

She turned her head to the side and pushed him away.

"Chill out, Leo," she snapped. Then her voice softened.
"Okay?" she asked.

Leo shrugged. "Later, baby," he said amiably.

He turned and spotted Barbara and me standing in front of his
painting. He stroked his beard, then tossed his long black hair
out of his face with a flick of his head. It was a strangely co-
quettish movement.

"Interested in the painting?" he inquired as he stepped in our
direction.

"No—" I began.

"Yes," Barbara contradicted.

I smelled Leo when he was within a yard of us. Eau-de-vino,
his usual scent. He stepped nearer, his closely spaced eyes intent
on Barbara's face. The smell of partially metabolized alcohol
was overpowering.

"That's my work," he announced proudly.

"Is it really?" Barbara trilled. "It's so . . ."

Even Barbara couldn't finish that one.

"Interesting," I supplied.

His glance landed on my face, then continued down my body.
"Haven't I met you somewhere before?" he asked with a sugges-
tive wink.

"Of course you have," I answered impatiently. "The vegetarian cooking class."

His face paled, highlighting the cerise tracings of broken blood vessels on his nose and cheeks. For a moment I wondered if he was going to pass out. But he recovered quickly.

"I couldn't possibly forget a beautiful face like yours," he cooed, his skin color evening out to a uniform red once more. "Or yours," he added, turning to Barbara. He stroked his beard slowly.

Ugh. Neither his words nor his odor were doing my now queasy stomach any favors.

"What can you tell us about the night of the murder?" Barbara asked without further preamble. I had a feeling she wanted to get this interview over with as quickly as I did.

Leo flinched but answered, "It was an awful night, wasn't it? It all seems like a blur now . . ."

If you drink that much, everything probably *is* a blur, I thought uncharitably as he rambled on. Nothing he said was particularly enlightening. He claimed to have walked to a liquor store at the break. He said he'd never met Sheila Snyder before. And the sight of the body had made him sick.

"How about your friend Ken?" Barbara asked as he paused for air.

"What about him?" Leo shot back. His small eyes narrowed. "Why are you asking all these questions, anyway?"

"We're helping the police," I interjected. Barbara smiled. It wasn't a complete lie. If we happened to find a murderer for them, that would be a help.

"Ken was with me the whole time," Leo said. He was cooperating again, but there was a new wariness in his tone. He wasn't smiling anymore.

"Where does Ken work?" Barbara pressed.

"You'll have to ask him," Leo told us. "I've got work to do." He turned and began to walk away.

"Wait!" Barbara shouted.

Leo swiveled his head around toward us impatiently. His face was stiff.

"Has Dan Snyder been to see you?" she asked.

"Never heard of him," Leo mumbled and accelerated his pace toward the back of the gallery. He disappeared through a door partially hidden behind a stone carving easily identified as yet another naked lady.

"Nobody's watching," I whispered to Barbara. "Shall we rob the joint?"

She took a quick look around, then shook her head no emphatically.

We both giggled and turned to leave. We were almost out the door when I heard the sound of running footsteps behind us. I turned and saw the tall young woman Leo had been coming on to earlier. She couldn't have been much older than twenty. Her face was freckled and friendly, her legs long and conspicuous beneath her miniskirt.

She must have noticed my look. "He makes us wear this kinda stuff," she said apologetically.

"Leo?" I asked.

She nodded. My body stiffened with anger. The gallery wasn't a cocktail lounge. There was no reason to insist that she wear that short skirt. Except for Leo's pleasure, of course.

"So what's wrong with the old guy?" she whispered.

I looked at Barbara. She looked back at me, her eyes seeming to nod. I straightened my shoulders.

"Have you read about the murder at the Good Thyme Cafe?" I asked.

The young woman's eyes widened.

"Leo did that?" she yelped shrilly. "Is that what that looney tunes was screaming about this morning?"

"No, no—" I began.

"What looney tunes?" Barbara asked.

"—I wasn't accusing Leo of murder," I finished.

The young woman looked into my face, then into Barbara's and then back to mine. Her eyes were still wide. And now her mouth was gaping.

"Listen, we'd like to talk to you, to explain," I told her. Her mouth closed slowly. "When do you get off?"

She turned her head to look over her shoulder. Leo was still out of sight.

"I get a dinner break once you guys are outa here," she whispered. "Leo won't come out till you leave. So I gotta cover for him."

"All right," I whispered back. "Here's what we'll do. We'll go outside and wait for you. You tell Leo that we're going and you're going on break. Then—"

"I dunno," she said softly. She swallowed nervously.

"We'll buy you dinner," I proposed.

"Really?" she said, brightening. "Can we go to the sushi place?"

"Sure," I agreed, forcing a smile. Raw fish had never been my favorite even before I was a vegetarian. And I was betting it was still expensive.

"That'd be cool," the young woman said in a normal tone of voice. "By the way, I'm Ophelia."

"I'm Kate. This is Barbara." I made the introductions quickly and quietly.

"I'll be back in a sec," Ophelia promised. Then she turned and trotted to the back of the gallery.

Barbara and I hurried outside. We leaned up against the Volkswagen uncomfortably.

"I hope this doesn't get Ophelia in trouble," I said to Barbara.

"Job trouble or murder trouble?" Barbara asked, her own eyes worried.

Ophelia came racing out the door before I could answer.

She led us down the block to the Sushi la Rue. I wondered if my credit card was in trouble as we walked in. Dozens of Japanese and French flags that must have measured nine by six feet were hung on the walls and suspended from the ceiling between the tables. There was a man in a tuxedo playing piano in the corner. And even at this early hour, I could hear the clinking of glasses at the bar and the hum of muted conversation. It all sounded expensive to me.

"Three for dinner," I squeaked to a slender woman also dressed in a tuxedo.

"Reservations?" she asked with a severe look.

I shook my head, really worried now. She led us to our seats at a table covered in white linen. As we sat down I saw that the top layer was actually paper. That was good. She handed us menus, recited the daily specials, then turned on her heel and left.

"So," said Barbara, leaning across the table toward Ophelia. "Tell us about the 'looney tunes' who came in and screamed at Leo."

My eyes scanned the menu as I listened for Ophelia's answer. Franco-Nippon cuisine? I suppose the prices could have been worse. I saw sushi, coq au vin, omelets, sashimi, crepes, tempura and coquilles St. Jacques. There was even a vegetarian plate under ten dollars.

"He was this great big guy, you know," Ophelia told us, her voice shrill with excitement.

"Diamond stud earring?" asked Barbara.

"Yeah!" confirmed Ophelia, a smile on her freckled face. "You know the guy?"

"Dan Snyder," Barbara and I groaned together.

"He's bad news," I added. "Stay out of his way if you can."

"Fat chance!" Ophelia yelped indignantly. "Leo went and hid in the back room this morning. Told *me* to take care of the guy!"

I could feel angry blood rising in my cheeks. How could Leo do that to her?

"Why do you work for that—" I censored myself. "For Leo?" I finished.

"I'm an artist," she said diffidently. A blush crept up beneath her freckles. "He said he'd give me a show if I worked there for six months. And he pays me. Min wage, but it's worth it if he'll come through with the show."

Barbara and I shared a look.

"He's not that bad, really," mumbled Ophelia. "He acts like a big lech, but his wife would kill him if he really did anything, you know, serious. And she's the real boss at the gallery."

"Well, if Dan Snyder comes in again, call the police," I advised her. I would have liked to advise her to quit her job too, but I doubted that she'd listen. Leo had her where he wanted her. I hoped she got her show.

"So what's the deal, anyway?" she asked, excitement back in her voice. "How's Leo mixed up in this murder?"

"He was in a class at the restaurant the night the woman was killed," I told her. "So were we. And Dan Snyder is the dead woman's husband."

"Oh," said Ophelia in a small voice. She looked down at the table, subdued. "Do you think Leo really might've killed her?"

I shrugged my shoulders, wishing I could give her an answer. I didn't want to scare her. But if Leo *was* a murderer, I wanted her to be on guard.

"He's one possibility," Barbara said gently. "What do you think?"

She tapped her fingers on the table as she considered the question. "He drinks like a fish," she said finally.

"And . . ." Barbara prompted.

"He doesn't always remember what he's done when he's been drinking." Ophelia looked up at us, her eyes wide with doubt.

"Listen—" I began.

"Are you ladies ready to order?" boomed a voice from behind me. I jumped in my seat. "Or do you need more time?"

I turned and saw an Occidental man in a short, belted kimono over blue jeans. Who thinks up these outfits? I wondered.

"Well, *I'm* ready," said Barbara. "I'll have the coquilles St. Jacques."

"Excellent choice," our waiter told her.

"Sushi combo for me," Ophelia ordered happily.

"Very good," he commented.

"Vegetarian plate," I said.

He just grunted.

As he took our salad and drink orders a question occurred to me. A number of questions actually, one being how much this dinner was going to cost me. I hoped Barbara was planning on sharing the cost of Ophelia's sushi combo.

"Is Leo a vegetarian?" I asked Ophelia once the waiter had gone.

"Uh-uh," she replied, shaking her head. "But Ken is."

"Ken?"

"Ken is Leo's son," she said. "He's a real dweeb, you know, an accountant. He's got glasses and this real weird body kinda like Leo's, you know, short with a big butt."

"Does he talk about growth hormones and pesticides a lot?" I asked.

She nodded. It sounded like our Ken.

"But I thought Ken was his buddy," Barbara objected.

"Leo doesn't want people to know he's old enough to have a grown kid," Ophelia explained. She shook her head. "Weird, huh?"

"Jeez-Louise," muttered Barbara. "Who does he think he's going to fool? He looks old enough to have grown grandsons!"

"If Leo's not a vegetarian, why did he go to the class?" I asked, returning to my original thought.

"He's got some kinda heart problem," offered Ophelia. "He's supposed to eat low-cholesterol stuff. But he doesn't."

"Maybe he went to hang out with Ken," said Barbara.

"He probably wants a chance to hit on some new women," Ophelia sighed. "He's such a . . ."

"Jerk?" I suggested.

" 'Jerk' is much too kind," murmured Barbara with a grin. "I'd call him a grade A asshole."

Ophelia giggled at that one. Once again, Barbara had established rapport with an interviewee.

The vegetarian plate was okay. A minuscule bowl of miso soup, a small scoop of cucumber salad and a few tiny pieces of teriyaki-grilled tofu and broccoli. Only $9.95. I had a feeling this was the last time I'd visit Sushi la Rue.

On the other hand, Ophelia supplied us with the name and address of Ken's accounting firm. And Barbara split the fifty-dollar bill with me. I felt lucky.

We walked Ophelia back to the gallery and got in the Volkswagen again. The sky was just beginning to shimmer with early twilight. I put my hands over my eyes and we took off.

Halfway home, Barbara was still sounding off about Leo as I grunted agreement. Suddenly she stopped.

I dropped my hands from my eyes.

"Kate," she whispered urgently. "Look in the rearview mirror."

I craned my head around instead.

Dan Snyder's truck was right behind us.

- Fourteen -

THIS TIME MY field of vision wasn't limited by a rearview mirror. I could see the blur that was Dan Snyder's angry face through the Volkswagen's back window and the windshield of his Chevy truck. I could even read the lettering on the truck's grille. And the letters were getting clearer and larger. Much larger.

"Watch out!" I warned Barbara. "He's gonna ram—"

But she was way ahead of me. She veered off into the emergency lane and screeched to a halt before I could even finish my sentence.

I stared at her, my mouth still gaping open. My wrist was aching from bracing myself against the dashboard. My heart was thumping like a marching band in my ears.

"Why are you so surprised?" demanded Barbara with a weak smile. "I keep telling you no one ever hits me."

Suddenly, I believed her. But I didn't have time to tell her so.

"Uh-oh," she whispered, pointing.

Dan Snyder had pulled off the road too, about fifteen car lengths ahead of us. He jumped out of the cab of his truck and took a step in our direction.

Barbara looked at me, a hint of fear in her eyes now.

"Lock your door," I told her as I locked my own. "We can always take off again if it looks like he's getting violent."

Just then another car pulled off the road in front of us and slowed to a halt close behind Snyder's truck. It was a rental car and it looked familiar. Both doors opened at once. Edna stepped out of one side and Arletta out of the other.

Dan Snyder stopped dead in his tracks.

"Who the hell are they?" asked Barbara, her voice hushed with awe.

"The twins," I answered. "You can unlock your door now."

We watched from the Volkswagen as Edna, Arletta and Dan talked. We couldn't hear them, but we could see the pantomime. Dan waved his hands around for a minute or two. Arletta shook her thin white finger at him. Edna folded her arms across her solid chest and glared. Heads bobbed. Mouths wiggled. Finally, Dan seemed to give in. He hung his head as Arletta continued speaking, then turned and followed her back to his truck. She gave his hand a little pat and he climbed into the cab.

Meanwhile Edna was heading our way. Barbara rolled down her window.

"All taken care of," Edna told us gruffly, squatting down next to the car. "You can go on home now."

It was a measure of Barbara's awe that she did as she was told without question. We pulled back on the highway a few car lengths behind Dan Snyder. Somewhere behind us brakes squealed. I put my now cold and shaking hands over my eyes.

"Jeez-Louise," breathed Barbara as she switched lanes. I heard a honk close by. "Those are some far-out ladies. Tell me about them. I want to hear everything."

I did the best I could, telling her how I had met the twins at the health spa from hell. And telling her how they had saved my life. It wasn't easy to talk. I was feeling sick with adrenaline overload. Or maybe it was the Sushi la Rue vegetarian plate.

It wasn't until Barbara had left me off at the house that I began to wonder what the twins had been doing so conveniently nearby to us on the highway. It couldn't have been luck, I decided as I walked up the stairs. They must have been following someone. But who? Dan Snyder? Or Barbara and me?

I opened my front door and fumbled for the light switch with a cold hand. Another, warmer hand was already there. I jerked back, startled for a moment.

"Kate?" whispered Wayne and the light went on.

I grabbed him around the waist and pulled him to me, then laid my head against his chest, absorbing his warmth.

"Been looking at condos for Vesta, today," he whispered to the top of my head.

I looked up into his kind, unhandsome face and forgot all about Dan Snyder. "Yeah?" I said eagerly.

"Talked to some people about private nursing care, too," he added.

"That's great!" I shouted, then looked around guiltily for Vesta. She was nowhere in sight.

"Have you told her yet?" I asked more quietly.

Wayne shook her head. His brows came down, obscuring his eyes. I knew it was going to be hard for him to tell Vesta she had to leave. I just hoped he could do it. I wanted to beg him to tell her right now, but I restrained myself.

"Thank you," I whispered instead.

We made love to the Celtic jigs and airs of The Chieftains that night. Vesta didn't bang on the wall. Afterwards, I wondered why. Either she was asleep, I thought dreamily, or she knew something was up. Then *I* was asleep.

"Does your husband know you're an adulteress?" Vesta demanded the next morning as I crunched seven-grain flakes with soy milk. Maybe she hadn't been asleep after all.

"I don't have a husband," I muttered sleepily, not bothering to look up.

"How about your customers?" she went on. "How about your friends?" She leaned forward, her voice deepening along with her smile. "How about your mother?"

My stomach clenched. "How about giving it a rest?" I suggested and took my cereal out onto the back porch.

After I had finished breakfast I did a little paperwork, then got back to designing my new eyeball mug for ophthalmologists. The nose mugs for the ear-nose-throat specialists had been a big success, the feet mugs for the podiatrists a lesser one. I was planning mugs, neckties and scarves for all specialities. Almost all of them anyway. I hadn't been able to think of a pleasant image for the dermatologists, and the ones I had thought up for the gynecologists were probably X-rated.

By noontime I was working on the matching ophthalmologist necktie, which would feature staggered rows of wide-open eyeballs on a navy blue background. C.C. was yowling in the background for lunch. Vesta was pacing up and down the hallway, ranting to herself. My stomach tightened another notch with each shrill word she uttered. I thought about going to that claustrophobic little room I called my office at the Jest Gifts warehouse. I wished I had a bigger one. Wayne managed his restaurants from a regular office. Maybe I should rent one, too.

The doorbell rang, interrupting my thoughts. I leapt out of my chair gratefully.

I was even more grateful when I opened the door and saw the twins standing there.

"I hope we're not intruding," Arletta warbled. "We thought we might take you to lunch."

"Don't want to be in the way," Edna added brusquely.

"Are you kidding!" I cried and gave them each a warm hug. "Come in, come in. I called your motel earlier, but they said you were out."

Twenty minutes later we were at the Starship Cafe, looking at "Star Station, Planet Earth" menus again. I had offered to cook lunch, but the glance that Edna and Arletta had exchanged had told me they weren't up for vegetarian food. On the way to the cafe they had quietly interrogated me about Vesta. I was surprised. I had expected more questions about Sheila Snyder's murder.

"Who were you guys following last night?" I asked finally, setting my menu down on the silvery tablecloth.

Arletta peered at Edna through her thick glasses. Edna shrugged her sturdy shoulders.

"Dan Snyder," she growled.

I nodded eagerly. "And . . . ?" I prodded.

"We picked up Snyder's trail around five o'clock at the Good Thyme," Arletta chirped. I had a feeling she'd been reading more hardboiled mysteries lately. "He proceeded to the Conn-Tempo Gallery in a black Chevrolet truck. You and your friend . . ." She peered at me inquiringly.

"Barbara Chu," I supplied.

"Thank you, dear," she said thoughtfully, then continued. "You and your friend Barbara were proceeding on foot down the street with a tall young woman . . ."

"That's Ophelia. She works for Leo at the Conn-Tempo," I told Arletta.

"Thank you," Arletta repeated with a smile. In the guise of answering my question, she seemed to have asked a couple of her own.

Edna took over. "Snyder noticed the three of you. He whipped into a parking space and waited. When you and your friend got into the Volkswagen and took off, he was on your tail." She paused for a moment and tilted her head quizzically. "Why'd you put your hands over your eyes?" she asked.

Our waiter arrived a few minutes of explanation later, dressed in silver tights and a maroon tunic. His legs weren't perfect, but his face was pleasant and smiling.

I ordered the Planetoid Pasta Salad. Arletta got the Martian Chicken Marinade. And Edna asked for a Halley Burger, named for the English astronomer.

Then we got back to business.

"So, what have you found out about the Snyders?" I asked, leaning forward eagerly.

"Aren't well liked by the locals," Edna replied.

"They apparently made no effort to mingle," Arletta explained. She clicked her tongue. "And the neighboring business owners complain that they spent their money elsewhere."

"Cheap," Edna put in.

"Dan Snyder is a problem drinker and a drug user, according to our informants," Arletta added. "His wife didn't drink—"

"But people thought she beat the kids," Edna finished, her voice deep with disapproval.

"Their grandmother, Rose Snyder, is good to the children, though—"

"According to the neighbors," Edna clarified.

Our waiter brought our drinks before they could go on. It was just as well. I was getting a headache from swiveling my head back and forth as they took turns speaking.

I took a sip of carrot juice. It was cool and sweet. They hadn't used any tops when they'd made it.

Edna loaded cream and sugar into her coffee. "The cops don't know who did it," she said, stirring the mixture.

"They talked to you?" I yelped in surprise. Surprise and jealousy. The police wouldn't talk to me.

"We *are* concerned citizens," Arletta reminded me.

"Can't say as we know who did it, though," Edna continued, her rough voice disappointed. "Iris Neville seems okay—"

"But I thought the photograph of Jim Jones's hands was in poor taste," Arletta finished.

"No worse than Charles Manson's hands. Or Jeffrey Dahmer's. Or Ted Bundy's. She had those too," Edna pointed out.

My stomach did a tuck and roll. I had only noticed Bundy's hands.

Edna and Arletta went on to tell me about their visits to Leo, Meg, Alice, Gary and Paula. As far as I could tell, they hadn't discovered any important clues that Barbara and I had missed. They hadn't talked to Ken yet, either. But I was still impressed. Very impressed.

"How the hell did you find everyone?" I asked.

Edna and Arletta both smiled widely and identically. Despite the fact that Edna's face was jowly while Arletta's was delicate and bespectacled, the look was the same.

"Felix," they answered together.

I coughed as I swallowed a laugh. Felix grilled by the twins! I took a gulp of carrot juice and pictured the scene in my head. Delicious.

Once our meals came, it was my turn for revelations. I told them everything I could remember in between bites of pasta and vegetables. Then we argued over the check. We finally agreed to split it three ways.

They dropped me off at the foot of my driveway. Arletta rolled down the window.

"We're having an absolutely wonderful vacation," she warbled.

"Best ever," Edna confirmed and they drove away.

I turned to walk up the driveway, happy that they were happy. One woman's murder is another's vacation, I decided. Then I saw Barbara's Volkswagen.

All the fear of the last few days congealed into a hard cold lump beneath my rib cage. I could barely breathe. Talking about murder to the twins had been fun. Going to intrude on another suspect was not. Riding in Barbara's car was not.

"Hey, kiddo," Barbara greeted me, coming down the stairs. "Hop in. We're going to visit Ken Hermann at his office."

"I'll drive," I mumbled automatically.

Rutherford, Rutherford and Kent, the accounting firm Ken

worked for, was located in a six-story building in downtown San Ricardo, a skyscraper by Marin's standards. Barbara and I took the elevator up and walked down a silent, plushly carpeted hallway to the office. Barbara opened the door.

"Good afternoon," warbled the receptionist in a pleasant soprano. She was a young woman, well-dressed and smiling if not beautiful. She sat behind a mahogany desk that could have seated a party of ten for dinner.

"We're here to see Ken Hermann," Barbara announced briskly as we entered.

The receptionist's smile flickered. I took a closer look at her, wondering what the flicker signified. Her face was pear-shaped, her eyes small and pale despite makeup.

"Mr. Hermann is out on an audit," she told us, her voice less pleasant than a moment before. "Is this a personal matter?"

"Yes, it is," admitted Barbara. "But we need to talk to him. We've been trying since Tuesday. And we can't reach him at home."

The receptionist shrugged stiffly, her smile entirely gone now. I considered claiming we were his cousins from out of town, but a look at Barbara's Asian features told me the family relationship probably wouldn't fly. We'd have to settle for the truth.

"It's about the cooking class Mr. Hermann attended on Monday night," I explained. "A woman was murdered."

"Oh, dear," whispered the receptionist. All the stiffness left her body. She leaned forward, looking up earnestly. "Ken told me about it. He's not in trouble, is he?"

"No, no," I assured her, wondering if she thought we were from the police. "But we'd still like to talk to him."

"He really is out on an audit," she said, her voice raising defensively. "He's putting in sixteen-hour days until it's done. It's for a big case."

"Then why did he go to the class on Monday?" I asked. It sounded to me like Ken was using the audit as an excuse to hide out.

"The audit started on Tuesday," she answered. She lowered her voice again. "Listen, these guys *have* to put in sixteen hours a day if they ever want to make partner," she explained. "That's the way it is here at Rutherford, Rutherford and Kent."

That said, she crossed her arms and leaned back in her chair.

Barbara and I looked at each other.

"Well, I'd appreciate it if you'd tell Ken we'd like to talk to him," Barbara requested formally and handed the receptionist a business card.

We left before she read the card. I wondered if she would be surprised that Barbara was an electrician and not a policewoman.

I waited to talk until we were safe in the Toyota.

"Do you think the receptionist is in love with Ken?" I asked.

"Of course she is," Barbara told me, smiling smugly.

I wanted to ask her if she had her psychic powers back, but I didn't. It was too sensitive a subject.

"Well, that's it for the suspects," I said after a few moments, sighing. I was tired, physically as well as emotionally. My whole body felt heavy. "Do you have any idea who our murderer is?"

"That's *not* it," Barbara contradicted me. She turned her head to look into my eyes. "We've still got three suspects to go."

"Who?" I demanded. I couldn't think of anyone we'd missed.

"Dan Snyder's mother and his two little girls."

"The girls are too young," I objected automatically, but even as the words left my mouth I remembered Sheila's oldest daughter rhythmically clenching and unclenching her fists as Sheila berated her on Monday night. My body felt even heavier. It had been spooky then. It was even spookier in view of Sheila Snyder's murder.

"That's right," agreed Barbara.

"Your psychic powers *are* back!" I cried.

"So far, so good," she said softly. "Keep your fingers crossed for me."

I reached around her shoulders with one arm and squeezed.

"Let's go see Grandma Snyder and the little girls," she suggested, her voice vibrating with life again. "At the flat above the Good Thyme."

I groaned. "They're probably not even there," I argued. "Worse yet, Dan Snyder could be there instead."

"Trust me," she ordered with a grin.

I turned the key in the ignition reluctantly and drove to the Good Thyme Cafe, mentally cursing the obligations of friendship all the way.

The sign in the restaurant window said CLOSED UNTIL FURTHER NOTICE in hand-drawn block letters.

"Well, that's it," I said, my voice high and squeaky with relief.

"Nope," said Barbara, pointing. "Look at this."

"This" was a set of buzzers to the side of the door, one labeled A and the other labeled B. There was a small grille above them.

"Must be B," Barbara said and pushed the buzzer before I could ask her how she could tell.

"Hello?" came a female voice through the intercom. It sounded as tired as I felt.

"Good afternoon, Mrs. Snyder," Barbara boomed cheerfully. "My name's Barbara Chu. My friend Kate and I would like to talk to you about your son Dan."

There was a long silence from the intercom and then a single word, "Why?"

"We were there Monday night when Sheila died," Barbara shouted into the grille. "Your son has been harassing us and—"

"I'll be down in a minute," the voice said unenthusiastically.

It was more like two or three minutes before the restaurant door finally opened. Rose Snyder stood in the doorway looking like Mrs. Claus on a bad day. Her body was soft and round under an old-fashioned floral print dress, her face doughy with pink circles of color on each cheek. Her permed silver hair stuck out on one side. She stared at us bleakly through gold wire-rimmed glasses.

"I'm sorry if Danny has been bothering you," she said, her voice barely above a whisper. She looked down at her feet. "He's been . . . he's been upset."

"Grandma, Grandma!" shrieked a child's voice from somewhere inside the building. "Topaz hurt me! She twisted my arm!"

Rose Snyder's eyes blinked wide open. She turned and took a few steps into the restaurant. Barbara was in on her heels. I followed Barbara with a sigh and we were all inside. The Good Thyme dining room looked about like it had the last time, except that most of the wooden chairs were turned upside down on the tables as if someone had been going to sweep up.

"Opal, come down here to Grandma," Mrs. Snyder called out. She turned back to us, rubbing her hands together nervously. "I'm terribly sorry," she said.

'That's okay, Mrs. Snyder," Barbara told her.

"Please, call me Rose," she offered absently.

The smaller of the Snyders' two children came running down the hall, her face streaked with tears. Her brown eyes went round when she saw us, and she turned away shyly, chewing on the end of one of her braids.

"Opal, say hello to the ladies," Rose instructed.

"Hello," Opal muttered and sidled up to her grandma. Rose put her plump arm around the girl.

Opal's older sister wasn't far behind. The ten-year-old came slinking down the hall, her hands balled into fists. She had dark curly hair and haggard eyes. She stared at us without expression. The skin on my arms prickled into goose bumps.

"Topaz, say hello—" Rose began.

"You were there the night my mom died," Topaz interrupted, never taking her eyes away from us. "Did one of you kill my mom?"

- Fifteen -

"TOPAZ!" ROSE PROTESTED shrilly. "How could you say such a thing?"

Topaz kept her expressionless gaze fixed in our direction, not seeming to hear her grandmother.

"It's all right," I said quietly. It was more than all right. It was a good question. "I didn't kill your mother."

"I didn't either," Barbara chipped in, her voice deep and solemn.

Topaz stared for a few moments more, then nodded as if satisfied. She turned and walked away, her small, curly head held high.

"Excuse me for a moment," Rose said, then trotted after Topaz with Opal trailing in her wake.

"Topaz, honey," she called. "Wait."

Topaz stopped and turned back to her grandmother. Her fists were no longer clenched, but her face was still stiff. Rose knelt down in front of her, putting both her plump hands on the girl's thin shoulders.

"Honey, you've got to stop hurting your sister," she said, her voice high and strained. "No one hurts anyone anymore. No one. It's against the rules."

"Okay, okay," Topaz muttered, squirming impatiently.

Rose squinted pleadingly into the girl's unresponsive eyes for a few more heartbeats, then sighed and pulled herself to her feet. Had she gotten through to Topaz? Somehow, I doubted it.

"Why don't you take Opal upstairs now?" she suggested gently. "I'll be up in a minute."

"Can we watch TV?" asked Opal.

"For a little while, sweetheart," Rose agreed.

She gave each of the sisters a peck on the cheek. Then Topaz led the way back down the hall with Opal taking up the rear. Rose turned back to us.

"May I get you coffee or tea?" she asked politely, a tentative smile on her round face. Had she forgotten why we were here? Or was she hoping we would be equally polite.

"No thanks," Barbara declined for both of us. "But I would like to talk to you about your son Dan."

Rose's smile faded, leaving only the spots of pink rouge to brighten her face. Her shoulders slumped. I felt my own face grow hot in response. I didn't want to intrude on this poor woman. But I kept my embarrassment to myself. At the least, Rose Snyder was a valuable source of information. At the most, she might convince her son to stop harassing people.

"Would you like a seat?" she asked finally.

Barbara pulled three of the upended chairs from the nearest table and set them around it before Rose could retract her offer.

"I'm keeping the children home this week," Rose told us once we were seated. She looked down at the table as she spoke, her hands compulsively patting her silver hair. "I know I'm not their mother, but I do love them. I think . . . I hope it's better for them to be home."

Barbara and I nodded.

"I do worry about Topaz," Rose confided abruptly. She looked up at us, her eyes unhappy behind the wire-rimmed glasses. "She's violent. She got it from her mother, I guess." A natural blush bloomed beneath the artificial color on her cheeks. "Though Danny can be pretty explosive too. His father was the same way." She shook her head. "They say it runs in families."

We made sympathetic "uh-huh" noises. I noticed Barbara didn't say anything about her own violent family. Maybe she didn't want to interrupt Rose. Rose was on a roll.

"Danny doesn't mean anything," she explained, her voice rising in pitch. "He just yells and makes a fuss." The inside corners of her brows rose too, giving her eyes a pleading expression. Then she looked down at the table again.

Dan Snyder's ramming my car didn't seem to fall into the category of simply yelling or making a fuss, but I kept my mouth shut.

"Danny and Sheila just didn't know what to do with their lives after they left that hippie commune," Rose continued, talking faster now. "They did odd jobs, no real career for either of them. So, after my husband died, I decided to help them out." She looked up. "Did you ever eat at the Good Thyme Cafe?" she asked.

"I have," I admitted. I tried to think up a compliment, but Rose raced on without me.

"The restaurant was Sheila's idea," she told us. "Sheila thought a vegetarian restaurant could make a fortune in Marin. So I gave them the money to buy this building and set up the cafe." Rose smiled softly. Were these memories good ones for her? But the smile faded as she went on. "It was awfully hard work, though. I should have realized that. Sheila worked thirteen hours a day, six days a week. That's one thing I can say about my daughter-in-law, she was a hard worker."

"Was the Good Thyme making money?" asked Barbara.

Rose blinked at her as if she'd forgotten we were there.

"No," she sighed. "Just barely breaking even. And with both Danny and Sheila working full-time. It was hard on both of them. A lot of stress, I guess you'd say. Danny took it out on Sheila. And Sheila took it out on the kids. Oh, she was level-headed enough, especially since she'd stopped drinking. But with Opal and Topaz . . ." She shrugged her shoulders, looking heartsick. "I suppose I shouldn't have gone along with the restaurant idea, but I didn't realize. This cooking class was supposed to make a little extra money. Sheila was taking half the proceeds, but . . ." She faltered.

"It's not your fault," I told her. I knew I shouldn't interrupt, but I couldn't stand to see her so miserable.

"Danny hasn't hurt anyone, has he?" she demanded suddenly, her eyes pleading again.

"Not really," I mumbled. "But you might want to talk to him."

"I'll try, but—"

"Grandma! Grandma!" came a familiar shriek.

We left Rose Snyder to her grandchildren.

On the way out of the restaurant I bumped into Iris Neville. Literally. She was standing, bent over the buzzers by the door, her finger moving toward *B*. Barbara and I were busy whispering as we walked. I felt the impact of Iris's body before I saw her. Luckily, I didn't hit her hard enough to knock her over. I reached out to steady her.

"Oh my, excuse me," she gasped and unbent until she stood ramrod straight. Her deep blue eyes stared into mine for an instant. I stared back, noticing the strength of her bones beneath her expertly done makeup. Then she smiled.

"Well, hello," she chimed. "Such a surprise to see you here." She reached up and pushed loose hairpins back into her French twist, still in place in spite of the impact.

I dropped my hand and was about to apologize for knocking into her, but Barbara was faster.

"What're *you* doing here?" she demanded, then softened her tone. "I mean ... I didn't realize you were a friend of the Snyders."

"Oh, I've known Rose for years," Iris told us, her tone hushed yet animated at the same time. Apparently she took no offense at Barbara's bluntness. "Rose was a Richardson before she married, you know. Her father owned a good deal of Marin County in his time. And her mother was a charming woman, such a wonderful soul. Did you ever meet her?"

"No, I never had the pleasure," Barbara said quietly, her tone almost matching Iris's. "Did you know Dan and Sheila?"

"No, not really," Iris admitted. "I'm ashamed to say I didn't connect either of them to Rose until I saw her the night of the murder." She shook her head sadly. I wondered how well she really knew Rose Snyder.

"You must have met a lot of interesting people in this county," Barbara flattered shamelessly. "I'll bet you know some of the people in the cooking class, too."

"Only Leo Hermann, I'm afraid," Iris told us, a frown on her handsome face.

"Leo Hermann?" echoed Barbara.

"Leo Hermann is lechy Leo," I whispered in her ear.

"Actually, I can only claim a nodding acquaintance with Leo," Iris continued, oblivious to my whisper. "Louise Hermann is more of a friend. Such a good human being. Her parents were quite wealthy. Meat packing, you know. But what she has to put up with from her husband! The artistic temperament can be very trying." She sighed. "It's all very sad."

I nodded knowingly, wondering what exactly was so sad.

"You must know Ken too, then," Barbara prodded.

Iris's blue gaze sharpened. "Do you mean Louise's boy?"

"Yeah, Ken," Barbara answered. "He came with Leo to the cooking class."

Iris's frown gave way to a large smile. "You mean that was Kenny?" she exclaimed in apparent delight. "He's so big now! Why, he was no more than eight years old the last time I saw him."

Barbara and I smiled back, waiting for her to go on.

"Such artistic hands the boy had," she obliged. "Did he become an artist?"

"No," I told her. "An accountant."

The large smile disappeared. I'd have bet that Ken Hermann's hands would never make it to her photo collection now. Unless he was our murderer, of course.

"Well," she said, pulling her shoulders even straighter. "I must let you two go. Such fun meeting you like this."

We made polite noises and left quietly. Then we watched from the Toyota as Iris rang the *B* buzzer and was admitted to the Good Thyme Cafe.

I started the engine.

"How well do you think Iris really knows these people?" I asked Barbara as I pulled away from the curb.

"Not very," she said, shrugging.

That was a pretty short answer for Barbara. She was staring at the dashboard, her forehead crinkled into a frown, her eyes somewhere else. I almost asked her what was wrong, but then decided she'd tell me if she needed to.

I drove in silence for a while, brooding over my own worries. We were almost home when Barbara spoke again.

"Is there a back door to the Good Thyme?" she asked in a whisper.

I turned to stare at her, then brought my eyes back to the road, and my Toyota back into my lane. It had been drifting over the yellow line. I hoped Barbara's driving style wasn't catching.

"Why do you want to know?" I asked her back.

"Suppose the murderer is Dan Snyder, or Rose Sndyer. Or

someone we don't even know about yet," she replied, her voice at full volume now but still grave. "How did they get into the building to murder Sheila Snyder?"

"Through the front door ..." I stopped to think. Would the killer have risked being seen by the members of the cooking class?

"A back door would make more sense," Barbara said after a moment or two.

"Maybe," I agreed halfheartedly. I turned into my street. "But the murderer still had to leave the pantry without being seen."

"That's not as hard," she answered quickly. "A fast look up and down the hallway and you're out."

In my mind's eye I would see a picture of Barbara doing just that. Goose bumps prickled the skin on my arms as I pulled into my driveway.

"It wasn't me," Barbara said. Her voice deepened as she added thoughtfully, "But it could have been someone from the cooking class, someone who was supposed to be outside."

I turned off the engine and took a good look at her. I had rarely seen her beautiful face look so stern.

"We gotta go up to the Good Thyme tonight and check out the doors," she told me.

"Oh no, we don't," I disagreed firmly, getting out of the Toyota. "No midnight visits to murder scenes." I slammed the door.

"Wait, wait!" she called, scrambling out of her side of the car. "Not midnight, Kate. Twilight. The same time that Sheila was killed."

I marched up the stairs, shaking my head violently. "No," I repeated. Suddenly, I was tired of this amateur investigation.

Barbara trotted up behind me. "Come on, kiddo," she cajoled, her voice lighter now. "We don't need to break in or anything. We've just gotta find the door and see what it looks like at twilight."

"Why?" I asked, keeping my voice even with an effort. I didn't want to see the Good Thyme again. Not now. Not ever. I could feel anger rising, cramping my chest.

"Jeez-Louise, Kate! Because I may feel something there!" Barbara shouted. "Don't you see?"

"No, I don't see!" I shouted back. I glared at Barbara. She glared back, her narrowed eyes ugly to me for an instant.

"Why are we arguing?" I asked after a minute had gone by.

"Because you don't wanna drive up with me tonight to look at the back door of the Good Thyme Cafe," she answered loudly, as if I were deaf. Then the glare receded. A foolish grin took its place.

"Oh," I said, feeling a little foolish myself.

"But you will," she told me, the grin widening. She turned and trotted back down the stairs. "See you at seven-thirty," she shouted over her shoulder.

No wonder I was mad at her, I thought, and yanked the front door open.

I almost hoped I'd run into Vesta. I was in the mood to clarify our relationship . . . the hard way. But she was nowhere in sight. I heard her footsteps moving out of range down the hallway and then the slam of her door. Maybe she knew what kind of mood I was in. She'd probably been listening as Barbara and I argued. I wouldn't have put it past her. I let out a long sigh and headed for my desk.

Wayne got home some hours later. I had finished my work for the day on the ophthalmologist necktie and was processing mail orders.

He walked into my office, carrying a grocery bag under each arm.

"Stuffed tomatoes and mushrooms Dijon over spinach noodles, tonight," he announced quietly. There was a shy smile on his face.

I jumped out of my chair to hug him. "How'd you know I needed cheering—?" I began.

"Why doesn't *she* ever cook *you* dinner?" Vesta interrupted, appearing out of nowhere like a bad genie.

I stopped in place, a yard away from him.

"Because that's our agreement, Mom," he explained gently. He carried the groceries into the kitchen. "We each cook our own meals. Kate's a vegetarian. I'm not. Can't expect her to cook for me. This is just a little treat—"

"Are you celebrating throwing me out?" Vesta demanded as she followed him in.

"Now, Mom," Wayne objected. "You know I'll take good care of you."

I went back to my desk, gritting my teeth to keep from speaking. This was their private battle, I reminded myself and sat down.

"Well, don't count your chickens, Waynie," Vesta hissed all too audibly. "I'm not gone yet."

Now my stomach muscles tightened. This was the disadvantage of using my dining room for a home office. I could hear everything they said from the kitchen.

Wayne sighed. I even heard that.

I turned on my adding machine and began humming.

"Got you a nice piece of steak, Mom," he offered. "From my restaurant downtown. Marbled just the way you like it."

"Do you think I can eat when I know you and that woman are plotting to get rid of me?" she asked, her voice suddenly tearful and wavering.

Damn. It was time for the violins. I hurried down the hall to the bedroom, grabbed my boom box and brought it back to my office. I tuned in a classical music station. Orchestral harmony poured forth from small speakers. I let my jaw relax. And yes, there in the background, I could hear violins.

"I'm just scared, Waynie," Vesta's voice intruded from the kitchen. "And I don't feel good. I get these heart palpitations . . ."

I ground my teeth and turned the sound up.

An hour later Wayne tapped me on the shoulder. I jumped in my chair. I hadn't heard his approach over the blare of Schubert's Unfinished Symphony.

My plate was waiting for me at the kitchen table. Unfortunately, Vesta was too. She squinted malevolently across the table at me as I took my seat. I forced a smile onto my face. Wayne sat down on the chair between us.

"Looks great!" I said enthusiastically as I gazed down at my plate. My enthusiasm wasn't entirely feigned. The food was attractive, despite the company.

Two prim, stuffed tomatoes topped with bread crumbs sat next to a mound of green pasta covered in sautéed mushrooms. I sniffed and caught a whiff of wine and mustard.

Wayne was a good cook, much better than I was. I popped a

bite of mushrooms and pasta into my mouth. Yum. Heaven clothed in a tart-and-sweet sauce with onions and red bell peppers. I savored the flavors, then reached over to pat Wayne's thigh in recognition of his culinary skills. He looked pleased and cut a piece from his steak. I have often suspected that Wayne's agreement to cook separate meals was based less on democratic principles than on the needs of his palate. I took another bite of pasta. And another.

I had gobbled all but the last mouthful of tomatoes, stuffed with minced vegetables, herbs and soy cheese, when the doorbell rang. I looked up from my plate. Vesta was still glaring. Her meal remained untouched in front of her.

The doorbell rang again. Wayne rose from the table to answer it. I shoved the last bite into my mouth and sat back in my chair, stuffed.

"Hey, Wayne," came Barbara's voice from the entryway. "How's it going?"

As Wayne mumbled a reply, all the delicious food he had cooked for me congealed into one hard lump in my stomach. Barbara. I had forgotten Barbara.

"Hey, kiddo," she said as she came into the kitchen. "Ready to go?"

"I guess so," I mumbled, looking up at Wayne behind her. His eyebrows were down, his feelings closed off from view. "We'll just be gone a little while," I promised him as I stood up.

"Ask them where they're going," Vesta ordered Wayne quickly.

"Now, Mom," he protested softly, but his face turned in my direction.

"They're going to break into that restaurant, the place where the woman was killed," Vesta informed him.

"We're not—" I began.

"Kate?" said Wayne, his deep voice a question.

"We are not going to break in," I told him evenly. "We're just going to look for entrances—"

"Huh!" snorted Vesta.

"Why don't you come with us?" I suggested to Wayne, pointedly ignoring Vesta.

"I'll get my coat," he agreed, and turned to leave the kitchen. I let out the breath I had been holding.

"Waynie!" Vesta called out.

He stopped in his tracks and turned back. I caught a glimpse of his eyes. They looked desperate.

"You're not going to leave me here alone, are you?" she asked, her voice quavering like that of a woman at least twenty years her senior. She brought her hand up to her heart. "These palpitations . . ." She faltered.

Wayne stayed. Vesta smiled smugly at me from behind his back as I gave him a goodbye kiss. Then she cut into her steak.

"Jeez-Louise," Barbara muttered when we were in the car. "What broomstick did your mother-in-law fly in on?"

"Mother-in-common-law," I corrected automatically.

That about did it for conversation on the way up to the Good Thyme. Barbara's psychic powers must have told her I wasn't in the mood to talk.

Once we got there, things became a little more complicated. We had missed twilight by at least twenty minutes. It was dark now. Very dark.

But at least parking was no problem. I found a space right in front. The CLOSED UNTIL FURTHER NOTICE sign was still up in the restaurant window.

"Do you think Dan Snyder's here?" I whispered as I got out of the Toyota.

"Doesn't matter," Barbara assured me, pulling two flashlights out of her purse. "He'll never see us."

My body didn't believe her. My hand was shaking as I reached for my flashlight.

"You go around the left, I'll go around the right," Barbara ordered. Her voice was vibrating with excitement. It was then that I remembered that one of her favorite TV shows had been *Mission Impossible*. "We'll meet in the back," she added in a whisper. The hair went up on the back of my neck.

Barbara's flashlight didn't stop me from tripping over the bags of garbage around the side of the building. I landed on my knees with a rubbery squish. The smell of rotting vegetables drifted up. I stifled a curse and made my way around to the back of the building, shaking as I went and hoping I didn't have anything too disgusting on my pants now.

Sure enough, there was a door in the back. But Barbara was nowhere in sight. I shined the beam of my flashlight on the frosted glass set in the top of the door. A light was switched on somewhere inside, illuminating the glass. Then I heard the sound of footsteps. I looked behind me, hoping they belonged to Barbara. They didn't. They were coming from inside the building.

I clicked off the flashlight and watched as the shadow of what looked like a man grew in the frosted glass. My shaking hands began to sweat. The shadow turned in profile. It was definitely a man. His hand reached up with something in it.

I gasped without thinking. The something in his hand looked very much like a gun.

- Sixteen -

THE SHADOW IN the frosted glass flickered at the sound of my gasp. Then it slowly moved, the profile changing into something that could have been either the front or the back of a man. Dan Snyder? Dread took hold of my chest and squeezed.

The doorknob squeaked as it turned.

"Barbara!" I screamed.

The door burst open, and still I couldn't see anything but a shadowy figure standing in the doorway. I was blinded by the light behind him.

I screamed again and heard the sound of running footsteps somewhere near me.

"Freeze!" came a shout from the figure in front of me. "Police!"

Police? The word began to make sense to me when my eyesight returned. The man confronting me was in uniform. In uniform and holding a gun out in front of him with both hands. The dread vacated my chest and entered my stomach with a flare of nausea.

"Kate?" came a whispered voice from my side. Then, "Jeez-Louise!"

The officer turned the gun in Barbara's direction.

"Don't shoot—"

"We were just—"

Barbara and I babbled out pleas and explanations until we ran out of words. The uniformed man finally lowered his gun. I recognized him as the same Hispanic officer who had responded to Paula's phone call the evening Sheila Snyder had been killed. Unfortunately, he recognized us too.

"You were there the night of the murder," he accused, his voice deep and vibrating with suspicion.

That was the last thing he said, besides telling us to get in his squad car and accompany him to the San Ricardo police station. And telling us to be quiet.

The police station wasn't any fun. Nor was my phone call to Wayne, explaining why I would be late getting home.

Barbara and I sat on the molded fiberglass chairs in the waiting room, dutifully silent. But my mind was racing. Were we under arrest? No one had read us our rights. Didn't they have to do that if they were arresting us? And what would we be charged with, anyway? We hadn't broken into the Good Thyme. But we probably had been trespassing on private property, my mind chipped in. My mouth went dry.

I turned and looked at Barbara. Her eyes were closed. Her lovely face looked peaceful. How the hell did she manage that? My own body felt weak and nauseated from the recent barrage of adrenaline, and I was sure my face didn't look lovely or peaceful. I stared at her, wondering why she had taken so long to get to the back of the restaurant. What had she been doing?

The front door opened before I could come up with an answer. Wayne strode in, his face as cold and still as granite. I smiled up at him weakly. He didn't return my smile. He was too busy marching up to the officer behind the bulletproof glass.

"What are the charges against Kate Jasper and Barbara Chu?" he demanded.

The officer looked startled.

"I don't know—" he began.

New footsteps sounded from the doorway.

"We just want to have a little talk with them," came Sergeant Oakley's musical voice. She was wearing jeans and a pumpkin-colored sweatshirt that almost matched her red hair.

Wayne turned and glared. Oakley didn't flinch.

"And you are?" she inquired, a warm smile on her freckled face.

"Wayne Caruso," he answered. Then more softly he added, "Friend of Kate Jasper's."

"Well, why don't you have a seat while I talk to Ms. Jasper?" she suggested.

Wayne sat down obediently. I wondered if he would have been so obedient if Sergeant Oakley had been a man. Then Sergeant Oakley nodded at me. I followed her into the interrogation room, adrenaline surging through my body once more.

I told her everything. She was still a good listener. A wave of annoyance passed over her good-natured face when I related what Barbara and I had been looking for at the back of the Good Thyme. I had a feeling the police had already checked for rear entrances. I also had a feeling that Sergeant Oakley had come in on her time off just to talk to us. I was glad to see her expression change to amusement when I described tripping over the garbage and seeing the gun in the frosted glass window.

"You're not going to arrest us, are you?" I asked when I was finished with my story.

"Probably not," she said and stood up. She walked around the table to stand next to me.

" 'Probably'?" I prodded anxiously, twisting my neck to look up into her face. Damn, she was tall. "What does 'probably' mean?"

Her smiled disappeared. She bent down and thrust her face into mine.

"*Probably*, you're not a murderer," she rapped out. Her hazel eyes narrowed. Her voice deepened. "But if you are, we'll get you. That's a promise."

I bent my head back as far as it could go. My neck screamed with pain. Oakley bent her own head closer, all the time keeping her eyes on mine. I swallowed the lump of fear that came up in my throat.

"*Probably*, you won't be a murder victim either," she continued, her formerly musical voice now harsh and atonal. "But you're sure trying hard enough. Do you really want to be strangled like Sheila Snyder?" She paused. A picture of Sheila's dead body rose in my mind. Bile rose in my throat. I swallowed again. "Do you really think your little games are smart, Ms. Jasper?"

I shook my head. The gesture wasn't enough for her.

"Answer me," she ordered.

"They're not smart," I recited.

"Did you kill Sheila Snyder?" Oakley demanded abruptly.

"Huh?" I responded, startled. I looked into those hazel eyes and saw intelligence and curiosity there.

"No, I didn't kill her," I answered belatedly, my voice much too high and squeaky. "I wouldn't. I couldn't. I . . ."

"You can go now," she said quietly as I faltered. She straightened up to her full height, took two long steps and opened the door.

I left in a daze. Then it was Barbara's turn.

Sergeant Oakley finished with Barbara in less than ten minutes. Wayne dropped me at my Toyota, still parked in front of the Good Thyme, and drove Barbara to her apartment. I felt sick with leftover fear as I guided the Toyota home. The officer with the gun had been all too real. And Sergeant Oakley. Did she really suspect me?

I was in the kitchen feeding C.C. when Wayne came in. His face was still stony as he looked at me.

"Please, don't be mad," I requested in a small voice. I didn't want to beg. But I had no energy left to argue.

His face softened. He put his arm around me and led me into the bedroom. We took off our clothes and climbed under the covers of the bed silently. I felt his breath on my neck, then his lips. I moved my mouth to meet his.

Vesta banged on the wall. We sighed in unison and kissed each other goodnight.

Wayne and I slept late the next morning. It was Saturday, after all. When I finally opened my eyes, Wayne was smiling at me, his face pink and drowsy. I smiled back and pulled him closer.

"Hey in there!" Vesta shouted through the door. "You got a phone call!"

I put my robe on and stomped to the phone. Barbara was on the line. She wanted to know if I was coming to Sheila Snyder's memorial service at one o'clock. Sergeant Oakley's questions replayed themselves in my mind, but only faintly. A memorial service would be safe, I told myself. Especially if I took Wayne. I got directions to the Chapel of the Valley in San Ricardo and told Barbara I'd be there.

Wayne and I were late to the memorial service. We had been all dressed and ready to go at twelve-thirty, but as we headed toward the door, Vesta asked Wayne to stay. When he refused, she got heart palpitations. After those had run their course, she said she wanted to go with us. But she had to get dressed. We waited for over half an hour before finally leaving without her. Wayne's expression was grim on the way to the chapel. I wondered what his stomach felt like. Mine was churning.

"I didn't know Sheila Snyder personally," the minister at the pulpit was saying as we slunk into the chapel. The minister was small in stature, but very well-groomed. The chapel was small too, with wood-paneled walls and long, thin, vertical windows. About half the seats were taken. "But I know there were many who loved her ..."

"Excuse me," I whispered and took a place in the back pew next to a young woman I didn't recognize, whose eyes looked swollen with tears. Wayne squeezed in next to me. My heart thudded a little faster. There was no body here, but the presence of death and grief was palpable, betrayed by a sniffle here and a sigh there from the mourners, even an occasional hand raised to brush a tear from an eye.

"... Sheila Snyder was the beloved wife of Daniel Snyder," the minister went on. "The loving mother of ..." He paused to look at the index card he was holding. "Loving mother of little Topaz and Opal. And the dear sister of Stanley Smith ..."

My eyes searched the crowd, wondering if I would spot Sheila's brother. I didn't, but I did recognize Edna and Arletta two rows in front of us. Felix and Barbara were close by too, sitting next to a woman with silver hair in a French twist that just had to be Iris. And there was someone tall with red hair in front of them. I just hoped it wasn't Sergeant Oakley.

"... indeed a tragedy. When such a young person, a wife and mother of two children, is taken from us ..." the minister rambled on. His voice was very soothing. My heart rate slowed.

My gaze traveled to the back of the heads in the first row. Dan Snyder's dark curly one was easily recognizable. And on his right, Topaz, Grandma Rose and Opal. The surprise was the head to his left, Alice Frazier's. There was no mistaking her glossy, well-cut black hair.

"If you will pray with me now," the minister intoned. "Our Father which art in heaven, hallowed be thy name ..."

I bowed my head, suddenly sad. Sheila was dead. There was no getting around it. I felt Wayne's arm come around my shoulder. I squeezed his knee compulsively, glimpsing for a moment the grief I would endure if he were to die.

Once the prayer was over, the minister asked Sheila Snyder's friends and loved ones to speak.

The first one to go up to the lectern was a plump, pretty woman with large, solemn brown eyes. Her name was Julie, and she looked about thirty. She didn't carry any index cards. And her opening line was an attention-getter.

"Sheila Snyder was an alcoholic," she declared. She paused as a buzz of mutters rippled through the room.

"I wouldn't be saying this today if Sheila wouldn't have told you herself," Julie assured us, her voice clear and earnest. "But she would have. Because she was in recovery. She hadn't had a drink in three years. She was proud of that. And she was my sponsor. Without her . . ." Julie's voice caught for a second. Her brown eyes glistened with sudden moisture. She rushed through the rest of her speech. "She was my friend. And she was an inspiration. I'll miss her."

Then she hurried back to her seat, pulling a handkerchief from her pocket on the way. I heard someone else blow their nose in the silence. Rose Snyder put an arm around each of her grandchildren. Dan Snyder's head swayed from side to side. I wondered if he was crying. And I wondered if Julie had been in Alcoholics Anonymous with Sheila. And if so, what had happened to the anonymity?

"Thank you, Julie," the minister said smoothly. He was back at the pulpit again. "That was very moving." He looked down at another index card. "Natalie Westbrook was also a friend of Sheila Snyder's. Natalie," he prompted.

Natalie was a thin, tan woman with a gray frizz of hair pulled back into a barrette. She put on a pair of glasses as she approached the lectern and studied a sheet of yellow ruled paper once she got there. Then she smiled.

"Sheila was one far-out lady," she announced in a high, fluting voice. "I remember the day when I first did her chart. It was a real piss . . . er, a real doozy! She was a Pisces. And not only that—" Her voice deepened. "Mars was in her first house." She gazed out at us significantly. I resisted the urge to raise my hand and ask her what she was talking about.

"I met Sheila at her restaurant," Natalie went on. "She was some cook. Great tostadas!" She made a smacking sound with her lips.

"Of course, with Mars in her first house, she had a temper on her." Natalie frowned here. "But she did her very personal best to control it. And she was *very* in touch with the higher vibrations." She smiled again. "I'm sure she's dancing in the ether with some very far-out folks right now. Not to worry about Sheila." Natalie kissed her fingertips and flung them upward, presumably toward the ether, then left the pulpit.

As the minister introduced Sheila's brother, Stanley, I thought about the words of the last two speakers. Julie had characterized Sheila as a friend and inspiration. Natalie had called her someone in touch with the higher vibrations. I remembered the Sheila I had met, the Sheila of the spike heels, blow-dried hair and short-shorts. The Sheila who had managed to offend at least five people in as many minutes. The Sheila who had struck her own daughter. Which was the real Sheila? All of them?

"My sister had spirit," Stanley announced softly. He was tall and dark with a mischievous look around the corners of his eyes, which his current serious expression couldn't completely erase.

"She was older than me. And with our mother dead, it was up to her to keep me in line when we were kids." A smile crept onto his face. "She was better than me in baseball, better than me at Monopoly. She always ended up with Park Place *and* the Board-walk! But I forgave her. At least she didn't try out for football."

A few people laughed. Then his face grew serious again.

"Anyway, she was my big sister and I'm sorry she's gone," he finished and sat back down.

I felt Wayne shift his weight next to me. I didn't blame him. The pews were hard and uncomfortable. I found his hand and squeezed it, hoping there weren't too many more speakers.

The minister seemed to be tiring of the ceremony too.

"And Dan Snyder," he introduced briefly. "Loving husband to Sheila."

Dan stood up and made his way to the pulpit. When he turned to face us, his eyes were glassy. He swayed a little.

"He's drunk," someone whispered from the row in front of us.

"Looks like he's stoned to me," a deeper voice corrected.

"Shhh," someone else admonished.

"Sheila," Dan began, his voice thick and slow. He swayed again, then grabbed the lectern with both hands to steady himself. "She was . . ." He faltered and began once more. "I loved her. I really did. And now, it's too late to—"

He broke off abruptly, sobbing. Drunk or stoned, he was certainly grieving.

The minister moved to Dan's side and put a steadying hand on his shoulder. Dan's head jerked around like a snake striking.

"What!" he shouted, his hands forming into fists.

The minister stepped back as the shout reverberated through the chapel. I would have done the same. The expression on Dan's face looked fierce enough from the back pew; it had to be worse up close.

"I loved her," Dan began one more time. "Nobody can take that away." Then he just stood, swaying, his eyes on the lectern.

After a few moments, the silent room filled with whispers. Was he finished?

Then a new figure walked up to the pulpit. It was Alice, her substantial body, elegant as usual, in a black silk dress. She put her head close to Dan's, apparently whispering in his ear. Finally, he nodded slowly and allowed her to lead him back to his seat. I heard a number of relieved sighs around me.

Relief was evident on the minister's face, too, as he took the pulpit again.

"Please join me in the Twenty-third psalm," he said, his voice not quite as smooth as before. "The Lord is my shepherd, I shall not want . . ."

I bowed my head, but not so far that I couldn't see the first row. When we got to the part about "paths of righteousness," Alice put her arm around Dan's shoulders. He shook it off. He turned to her and said something I couldn't hear over the sound of the prayer. She said something back and he faced forward again. Then Rose turned his way.

". . . and I will dwell in the house of the Lord forever," the minister finished.

There were scattered "amens," the minister said a few more soothing words, and everyone stood up. It felt good to stretch after sitting for so long on the hard benches. I reached my arms up and bent back, then remembered where I was.

At least the minister hadn't been looking my way. He was busy herding the four Snyders and Sheila's brother, Stanley, to the front of the chapel. Alice Frazier was left behind. I wondered whose decision that had been. A line began to form for those who wanted to pay their respects to Sheila's family. I turned to Wayne.

"Shall we get in line?" I asked softly, hoping he would say no.

He smiled and patted my shoulder, as if he knew why I was asking.

"Hey, kiddo," Barbara greeted me, her voice unusually subdued. She nodded toward the line. "Let's do it," she said.

"Where's Felix?" I asked.

Barbara pointed to the far aisle. Felix was talking to the twins, gesturing frantically with both hands. Arletta was smiling, Edna wasn't. I wondered who was grilling whom. As I turned back, I saw Iris walking toward us, her back as straight as ever under charcoal-gray linen.

"Such a nice service, don't you think?" she asked in a stage whisper.

I nodded insincerely and introduced Wayne.

"Oh my," she trilled, looking up at him.

I bristled. If she said anything about Wayne's face I'd—

"Such beautiful hands," she said instead.

I relaxed. Iris wasn't so bad, I decided.

"May I?" she asked, reaching for his hand.

Wayne blushed, but stoically allowed her to examine it.

"Let me guess," she cooed, holding the back of his hand with one of her own hands and stroking his fingers lightly with the other. "A writer, perhaps?"

"How did you—" I began.

"Hello, again, Ms. Jasper," came a voice from behind me.

- Seventeen -

I TURNED, A social smile ready on my lips. I felt it drain away
when I saw who was standing behind me. Sergeant Tina Oakley,
tall and imposing in a forest-green suit. So she *had* been the redhead sitting in front of Barbara and Felix. No wonder Barbara
seemed so subdued. Oakley turned on her smile. I flinched at the
sight of it, like one of Pavlov's dogs salivating at the sound of
the metronome.

What was Oakley doing here? Looking for the murderer? I
stopped breathing. Did she suspect someone specific? Iris and
Alice were here. And the Snyders. So was Barbara, for that matter. And of course, me. Damn.

I felt Wayne's reassuring hand in mine and took a breath,
thinking of all the suspects who weren't here. Leo and Ken.
Meg. Gary and Paula—

"And hello to you, Ms. Chu," Oakley said, shifting the focus
of her smile onto Barbara's glum face. I could hardly believe I
had once thought Sergeant Oakley's smile was friendly. Now it
looked to me like the big bad wolf's, ready to gobble us up.

"Sergeant Oakley, how nice to see you," Iris cooed. At least
she wasn't afraid of the big bad wolf. "So good of you to come
today."

Oakley's smile flickered for an instant. Barbara and I exchanged glances. I wondered if Iris really was pleased to see Sergeant Oakley.

"Police work must be so demanding," Iris continued, her
voice breathy with apparent fascination. "How did you ever get
into such an interesting field?"

My body relaxed as I watched Iris politely grill Sergeant Oakley. Oakley could dish it out, but she wasn't very good at eating it. She turned and left our little group abruptly after Iris examined her hands and declared them "so wonderfully intelligent and just the tiniest bit manipulative."

Then Iris turned back to the three of us.

"Would you girls consider joining Rose Snyder and myself for lunch tomorrow?" she asked brightly. "And, of course, your lovely friend Mr. Caruso," she added with a nod at Wayne.

"Lunch would be great," Barbara answered for all of us. Her voice had life again now that Sergeant Oakley was gone. "Where do you—"

"Sorry," Wayne interjected quickly. "Another engagement."

"I'd love to come," I put in, trying to pump some enthusiasm into my words to make up for Wayne's obvious reluctance.

We agreed on a time and place, then Iris joined what was left of the line of people paying their respects to Sheila's family. Dan Snyder was swaying in place, his eyes at half-mast as an elderly man spoke to him. Topaz was glowering, Opal was squirming and Rose Snyder was wringing her hands. Only Sheila's brother, Stanley, looked calm at this distance.

"Whaddaya say?" Barbara asked with a nod toward the line.

"Goodbye," I answered and grabbed Wayne's arm. We were out of the chapel in seconds.

The rest of Saturday and the following Sunday morning weren't much more fun than the memorial service. I processed Jest Gifts mail orders and popped antacid tablets as Wayne and Vesta discussed her upcoming departure in the background. Even with my boom box turned all the way up, the shrieks, rumbles and shouts kept intruding.

By the time Sunday noon rolled around, I was only too glad to be going to lunch with Iris and Rose. I didn't even care anymore if one of them might be a murderer. I kissed Wayne goodbye and ran for the quiet of my Toyota.

Barbara was waiting for me in the lobby of her apartment building. She waved through the glass and then came racing out to my car.

"Hey!" she greeted me, jumping in. "Ready for some more sleuthing?"

I didn't answer her. I took a deep breath instead and asked her, "How come it took you so long to get to the back of the Good Thyme Friday night?" It had been worrying me all weekend.

"Huh?" she replied with a frown.

"Friday," I repeated. I turned the key in the ignition. "When we went to look for back entrances. The cop. The gun—"

"Oh, that," she said, her frown disappearing. "There was a full dumpster blocking the side the way I went around, so I came back around your side and stepped in some more garbage. Jeez-Louise, those people have a lot of garbage . . ."

She chattered on happily as I got back on the road. I was relieved by her explanation. Apparently her absence was based on nothing more sinister than garbage. I tuned back into her words once I had steered the Toyota safely onto the highway.

". . . gotta be someone in the class. Or one of the Snyders. All we have to do is—"

"Maybe this murder will never be solved," I cut in. I'd had plenty of time for brooding while Vesta and Wayne had been arguing. My conclusions hadn't been happy ones. "It's been almost a week, and I don't think the police are any closer to an answer than we are."

"Kate!" Barbara objected. "Don't give up. It's not like a mugging or something. There're only a few people who could have done it—"

"But which one of them?" I asked, my jaw tight with impatience.

"Well," she said. Her eyes went out of focus. "How about Ken? You saw him after the murder, smiling that weird, nerdy little smile. And he hasn't answered our phone calls—"

"He's out on an audit," I interrupted, my impatience growing.

"Maybe, maybe not," Barbara answered thoughtfully. She looked at the dashboard absently for a moment, then started back up. "What about Meg Quilter? She's another weird one. That woman's so pale, she looks like a vampire. I mean, she's obviously way out there, some kind of genius. Her artwork's fantastic! So why's she so shy? It's like she's hiding something."

"Shy doesn't mean murderous," I argued.

"Which brings me to Alice," Barbara continued, her voice deepening now. "Alice, who's in love with Dan Snyder. You saw her at the funeral yesterday. A week hasn't passed and she's already putting the moves on him. And . . ." Barbara paused significantly. "She set up the class."

"But if Alice did kill Sheila to get Dan, why's she so obvious about him?" I demanded peevishly. I took a deep breath and went on in a more reasonable tone. "She's not stupid. She must realize how it looks."

"Who knows?" Barbara dismissed my question blithely. "Leo's another one. Drunk as a skunk all the time. Maybe he killed her and just doesn't remember."

"Barbara, you've named four people already—" I began.

"And how about Paula?" she continued, oblivious to my interruption. "She'd do anything to protect Gary—"

"Now you've named another!" I shouted in frustration. I gripped the steering wheel so hard, I would have choked it if it had been a neck. "How do we narrow it down to *one* person?"

Barbara turned to me, startled by my outburst. "But Kate, that's why we're investigating," she said slowly, as if explaining the concept of God to a three-year-old.

I sighed, and Barbara continued with her theories until we took the highway turnoff. Then she directed me to April's Garden, the restaurant where we were meeting Iris and Rose.

April's Garden was hung with a collection of ceramic pots filled with all-too-perfect flower-laden plants. I would have bet they were silk, but they were too high to check.

"Yoo-hoo," Iris called to us. She sat with Rose at a sunny table by the window. She waved and smiled.

As we walked toward them, I was struck by the contrast between the two women. They were probably close in age, each with a head full of silvery hair. But Iris's silver head was held erect, while Rose Snyder's drooped. Iris's strong face was all planes and angles, Rose's doughy curves.

"We were just talking about children," Iris told us as we sat down. "Do either of you have any?"

Barbara and I both shook our heads.

"Ah," said Rose, her voice a sigh. I couldn't tell if that sigh denoted disapproval or sadness. Or maybe envy.

"So nice to be born in an age where you have a choice," Iris commented brightly. "When I was married, we didn't question having children."

"We just did it," Rose added glumly.

"What are your children like, Iris?" asked Barbara.

A flush tinted Iris's skin. I hadn't seen her flushed before. I felt a tingle of curiosity.

"Oh, my," she said with a little nervous laugh. "My children are . . . well, different than I am. Really quite their own unique selves. I've always thought it was such a mistake to expect one's children to share one's interests."

"Wasn't your girl a violinist?" Rose asked, perking up. There was genuine interest in her face now. She looked more alive, less doughy.

"Not anymore," Iris answered briefly. "Married an insurance salesman. She has five kids now. That keeps her busy." She sighed. "We had such hopes for her." She shook her head, then made a dismissive motion with her hand. "Of course, it's her own life. She's quite . . . quite contented."

"How about your son?" Rose pressed.

Iris flushed again. "He's really a very well educated boy. He took his M.A. in art, you know," she told us, her voice a little too high. "Such a bright, bright, artistic boy. He's in Great Britain now." She paused and whispered across the table. "He's incarcerated, you know. Some misunderstanding about drugs with the authorities there."

Rose clicked her tongue, and their roles seemed to reverse for a moment, Rose sitting straight, Iris drooping. But then Rose slumped again.

"Our Johnny was killed in an auto accident before he even had a chance to finish college," she murmured. "They said he was driving too fast. We should have trained him better, I guess." She shrugged her shoulders as if attempting to shrug off the pain.

My stomach knotted in pity. Losing a child that way had to be hard. And her son Dan couldn't be much consolation right now.

"So, so tragic," Iris breathed, her own shoulders straight again. "And your Daniel—"

"Have you decided yet?" a young woman in a flowery apron demanded. Our waitress, I assumed.

"Decided on what, dear?" Iris asked, a reproof in her tone.

The waitress paused for a moment to think. "What to eat," she explained finally.

"It might be a little easier if we had menus," Iris told her.

"Uh-oh," the waitress muttered and trotted away.

She brought us the missing menus within a minute. April's Garden offered lots of salads, a few sandwiches, soups and more salads. Iris pointed out the vegetarian choices. The Spring Salad (assorted greens and vegetables with marinated beans) looked good. I closed my menu. Iris was talking again.

By the time the waitress asked us for our orders the second time, Iris had drawn the conversation back to Rose's son Dan. There was a flicker of annoyance on Iris's face as the waitress interrupted her once more.

"I'll have the Sunshine Salad," Iris said with uncharacteristic brevity.

Suddenly, I realized that this wasn't just a social luncheon for Iris. She was sleuthing. Either that or she was helping Barbara and me sleuth. I was sure of it.

I looked across at Barbara, wondering if she'd caught it. She winked back. Of course she had. That's why she had allowed Iris to so fully dominate the conversation.

"Such a shame your poor boy has to go through all of this," Iris said to Rose once the waitress was gone. "He was so . . . so upset at the memorial service."

It was Rose's turn to flush. A tide the color of the rouge circles on her cheeks washed across her entire face.

"Danny was drunk," she said sharply. Finally, she was showing some spirit. I felt like cheering. "I told him there was no excuse. His own wife dead, and he pulls a stunt like that." She sighed, and the spirit was gone again. "I guess he was upset, though," she amended.

"Oh my, yes," Iris cooed. "The shock of coming home and finding his wife dead must have been terrible."

"He was out with his friend Zach," Rose told us, swallowing the bait without a struggle. "Zach is an awful influence on Danny." She lowered her voice. "Zach takes drugs, I think. And he doesn't work. Oh, he says he's a house painter, but when I asked him for a quote to paint my house, he never gave it to me. Now what kind of house painter is that?"

Iris shook her head sympathetically. "Our children's friends can be such powerful influences," she commented encouragingly.

"Danny was always out with Zach. Left Sheila in a lurch at the Good Thyme as often as not. I just don't know what I did wrong with that boy." Rose sighed. "He wasn't a very good husband to Sheila."

"But he loved her, didn't he?" Iris asked softly.

Rose sighed again, a big sigh that heaved her shoulders and bosom like a wave. "I guess he did," she said in a small voice. "I mean, they argued all the time, but look at him now. I guess he didn't realize how much he loved her till she was gone."

Our salads came. I pondered the truth of Rose's last statement as we ate. Not that I thought she was lying. I felt sure she was telling the truth as she understood it. Unless she was a lot trickier than she looked. I took a bite of vinegary beans. I believed Dan Snyder had loved his wife and grieved her loss. But there were so many kinds of love, I thought as I swallowed. I speared an artichoke heart and wondered. Was there a kind of love that could encompass the murder of the loved one?

"So nice that Sheila's friend spoke at the memorial service," Iris threw out after a few moments of quiet chewing.

I was beginning to see the pattern in her questions. Did she have a checklist in her mind? Find out where Dan was the night of the murder. Check. Find out how he felt about Sheila. Check. Find out about Sheila's friends—

"Most of Sheila's friends were from AA," Rose said. "She spent too much time working to have a real social life. Maybe I should have offered to help more. Maybe . . ." She faltered, her eyes on her salad, unseeing.

I wanted to tell her she wasn't to blame, but I was afraid to interrupt Iris's act. I took another bite of salad.

"Sheila certainly seemed well loved," Iris assured Rose. "Did her friends visit much at the Good Thyme?"

Rose's head came up with a jerk. She stared at Iris for a moment, squinting through her wire-rimmed glasses but not answering. Had she just figured out she was being interrogated?

"No, they didn't," she said brusquely and began eating her salad in earnest.

Iris, Barbara and I all made small talk after that. Rose held back for a long time, but finally joined in a discussion about gardening as we were dividing up the check. Then she stood, laid some bills on the table, and said goobye. The rest of us stood too as she disappeared through the doorway.

"Such fun," Iris cooed as we walked out to the parking lot.

"You're all right, Iris," Barbara said and gave her a quick hug.

Iris's eyebrows jumped at the sudden attack. Her mouth dropped open for an instant as Barbara released her. But then she smiled.

"Thanks for lunch," I said.

"My pleasure," she sang. "So good of you girls to come." Then she strode off to her car, her back as straight as ever.

I was surprised to see Barbara frowning as she got into the Toyota.

"What's wrong?" I asked.

"Zach," she answered. "We forgot about Zach."

Barbara had found another suspect. We hadn't narrowed our list. We had widened it. Damn.

When Barbara asked if I wanted to come up to her apartment for a while, I said yes. I wasn't ready to go back to the house and listen to Vesta and Wayne quarreling just yet. Unfortunately, Felix was waiting when Barbara opened the door.

"Howdy-hi," he greeted us as we walked in. He had something in his hand that looked suspiciously like a fried chicken leg.

"Goddammit, Felix!" Barbara shouted. "You're not supposed to eat that stuff anymore."

"But, babe," he shot back. "My gout's disappearing faster than the ozone layer. My toe hardly hurts anymore—"

"Because of your diet, Felix," Barbara snapped and ripped the chicken leg out of his hands. Pieces of greasy batter dropped to the floor. She looked at the leg for a moment, then took a bite herself. "If you eat this stuff," she mumbled through the chicken, "you'll just get sick again."

"But I'm hungry!" he exploded. "I am sick to friggin' death of vegetables. Do you know how many bags of groceries I have to carry for one friggin' low protein, low fat, low acid meal?"

"See you later," I interjected. I could go home if I wanted to listen to an argument.

"Hold your horses," Felix called out as I got to the door. "I have zee informations about zee suspects." He twirled his mustache in a continental manner and grinned as I turned back. "You wanna do a deal? My dope from the police department for a little scuttlebutt on your end?"

I opened my mouth to answer.

"No, Felix!" Barbara hollered. "This isn't a game! Tell us what you found out right now."

"But babe—"

"Right now, Felix," she repeated, her voice dangerously low, her eyes narrowed and angry. "Give."

Felix gave. It wasn't much. Paula Pierce had racked up a few arrests associated with various political protests. That wasn't surprising. Dan Snyder was a little more interesting—an arrest for possession of cocaine a few years ago. It was a small amount, and he was sentenced to community service instead of jail. But, still, it looked like his friend Zach wasn't the only one doing drugs. Leo's record was predictable, a series of drunk driving citations resulting in the loss of his driver's license.

I thanked Felix for the information and left before he and Barbara could start arguing again.

My own house was surprisingly quiet as I stepped in the door. Wayne was waiting for me on the living room couch. And he was smiling. I smiled back and felt all the muscles I hadn't realized I'd tensed relaxing.

"Nurse came out from the registry to visit while you were gone," he told me as I sat down next to him. "Real nice woman. Left us her home number. Retired psychiatric nurse." He whispered in my ear, "I think Mom actually liked her—"

The phone rang. Wayne ran and caught it before the answering machine kicked in. It was for me. Barbara. I grabbed the receiver impatiently.

"Listen, kiddo," she said, her voice vibrating with excitement. "You'll never guess who called after you left."

"I wouldn't even try," I drawled.

"Ken Hermann," she told me anyway. "He said he'll be home the rest of the day. His audit's over. He wants to talk to us."

"Barbara," I groaned, my muscles all tense again. "I'm in the middle of something here."

"Yeah, I know," she said good-humoredly. "The thing with Vesta. That's cool. I'll go by myself."

"Wait!" I yelped, a vision of Ken Hermann's strange smile flashing into my mind. "Don't go alone." I sighed, then yielded. "I'll pick you up in a little while," I promised.

"I thought you would." She giggled and hung up.

I turned back to Wayne. His brows were low over his eyes. He wasn't smiling anymore. I felt a spasm of misery squeeze my chest.

"How'd you like to come with us?" I asked, shaking off the feeling.

"I hate to leave Mom," he said softly. "But maybe—"

"Oh, don't worry about me, Waynie," Vesta shrilled. I jumped, startled. I hadn't even seen her come down the hall. "Not that you ever do," she spat at him. "I'll be fine."

She fastened her steely eyes onto Wayne's. He began shrinking in place, beginning with his shoulders, which rolled inwards. She smiled.

"By the way," she added in a low, almost seductive tone. "I called that nurse of yours. I told her we wouldn't be needing her services—now or ever."

- Eighteen -

"OH, MOM," WAYNE sighed.

My own heart contracted just hearing the pain in his voice. Then I got mad. My face was burning when I turned to Vesta.

"Don't you see what you're doing to him?" I exploded.

Wayne put up a quick hand to stop my words. He was right. This was between the two of them. I swallowed the rest of my tirade, unsaid. My stomach churned angrily, unable to digest it.

"Waynie," Vesta said softly. She put her hand on her heart. "If that condo you were looking at is big enough for two, why can't we both live in it? We won't be any more trouble to Kate. And—"

"No, Mom," Wayne said quietly. He straightened his shoulders.

I gave a silent cheer. He wasn't going to cave in. He was going to fight. He didn't need me here anymore.

"I'll see you in a couple of hours," I told him, standing on tiptoes to kiss him goodbye. He bent down to meet my lips.

"Waynie!" Vesta shouted. "You listen to me when I'm talking to you!"

Wayne's head popped up like a jumping jack. My hands clenched into fists. I took a deep breath and unclenched them, resisting the urge to turn toward Vesta. Then I reached around the back of Wayne's neck, pulling his head back where it had been. He closed his eyes and kissed me gently. I gave him a quick hug, then let him go.

I left the house without looking back. I made it halfway down the stairs before I heard Vesta's shriek and Wayne's answering rumble. I ran the rest of the way to my car.

Wayne was a big boy, I told myself as I drove to Barbara's. He could handle his mother. I sighed. At least I hoped so.

"So how's Vesta?" Barbara asked as she climbed into the car.

"Fine," I grunted unencouragingly.

"That bad, huh?" she said with a wink. "Okay, I'll talk about something else. Like Ken, for instance. I think he's the one, Kate . . ."

I should have let her talk about Vesta.

By the time we reached Ken's condominium I was trying to remember exactly what we were doing there. If Barbara was right and he was the murderer—

"Here's his name," Barbara said eagerly before I could finish my thought. She pushed the lobby intercom button.

"Who is it?" came a distorted voice that could have been Ken Hermann's.

"Barbara Chu and Kate Jasper," Barbara answered.

"How do I know it's you?" the voice said.

I looked at Barbara. She looked back, shrugged, and then spoke into the intercom again.

"We met at the vegetarian cooking class," she told him.

"Okay," he said and buzzed us in.

I got a sinking feeling as we took the elevator up. And it wasn't just the elevator. It was Ken. Did he think he was safer with people he'd met at the scene of a murder than with strangers? Was he crazy?

Ken opened his front door the two inches his chain lock allowed when Barbara rang the doorbell. He peered out for a moment. I caught a quick glimpse of his nose, then saw the glint of his glasses as he turned his head.

Finally, he opened the door. As we stepped over the threshold, I got a perverse urge to sell him encyclopedias—or magazines—or rug cleaner. Anything to compensate for the trouble we had gone to in order to get in.

"Hey, Ken," Barbara greeted him, her voice filled with camaraderie. "How's it going?"

Ken stared at her through his thick tortoiseshell glasses without answering. I took a closer look at him as he chewed a fingernail. Now that I knew he was Leo's son I could see the family resemblance. The pear-shaped body and close-set eyes were a dead giveaway.

"Do you want to sit down?" he asked after a few moments. The words were right, but the shrill tone of his voice robbed them of their graciousness.

Barbara and I seated ourselves on the gray leather couch he indicated. He flopped down onto another identical couch across from us. They were nice couches. They didn't seem to match the rest of the decor, which included a couple of dilapidated bookshelves bursting with science-fiction paperbacks and an unframed poster of a buxom young woman in a space helmet fighting off the advances of what looked like a ten-foot-tall lizard. Ugh.

I lowered my gaze to the coffee table between us and noticed the glass terrarium built into it. I looked closer, expecting to see plants, but saw only one branch, a rock and a scaly, greenish-brown lizard staring back at me. I flinched involuntarily and lifted my gaze to Ken's face. He was smiling now. And his smile looked genuine.

"He's an American chameleon," he told us, his voice less shrill than before. "He's really quite attractive, isn't he?"

I nodded, forcing a smile onto my face. The best thing I could have said about the lizard was that he was small, maybe five inches. I hoped he wouldn't grow up to be the size of the one on the poster.

"Beautiful," Barbara cooed. "The throat sac is a great color."

I kept the smile on my face. Throat sacs, ugh.

"What do you feed him?" Barbara asked.

"Live crickets, every other day," Ken answered. I flinched again, but he continued without appearing to notice. "I pick them up from the pet store on the way home from work."

"How about when you're out on an audit?" Barbara pressed.

"Oh, my mom feeds them then," he said blithely.

God, the poor woman, I thought. Married to Leo and feeding live insects to her son's lizard.

"I've got an ant farm in the bedroom," he told us, his voice vibrating with excitement. "Wanna see it?"

"Maybe later," I said. Was this offer his version of "come up and see my etchings"? I looked at his face. His open smile looked like a ten-year-old's. I nixed the etchings theory.

"I'm gonna get an iguana, too," he went on happily. "And maybe some scorpions. They're really neat. I saw some at the insect zoo."

Even Barbara's bright smile faded when he mentioned the scorpions. And even more amazing, Ken seemed to notice. He stared at her for an instant, then changed the subject.

"So, are you guys investigating?" he asked, his eyes widening under his thick glasses.

We both nodded in sync. I thought about explaining that we weren't official investigators, but Barbara poked me with her elbow as though she had heard the thought. I kept my mouth shut.

"I'm sorry I was unavailable before," he said. He rubbed his hands together, massaging his knuckles. "I was out on an audit."

"That's what your receptionist told us," Barbara commented softly. She was smiling again. "It must be tough at Rutherford, Rutherford and Kent."

He leaned forward. "It's a jungle," he whispered. Even his whisper had a shrill edge. "People think that accounting's an easy profession. That there's no competition." He shook his head violently. His voice grew louder and shriller still. "Uh-uh! You have to be on your toes all the time. And if you want to make partner, boy, do you have to work hard."

"Oh, my," Barbara trilled encouragingly. She was beginning to sound like Iris.

"At Rutherford, Rutherford and Kent, people argue all the time," Ken went on, whispering again. He popped one of the knuckles he had been massaging. "They even throw things. This one guy who got passed over for promotion threw his hamburger really hard. Right in front of a client! It hit the wall with this big *splat* and then sorta slid down to the floor. It was really gross."

"What happened to him?" I asked, my curiosity piqued.

"Gone the next day," Ken said, cracking another knuckle. "He'll never be able to get a job with one of the top firms again."

"Well, at least the receptionist is on your side," I assured him.

"Huh?" he said.

"The receptionist," Barbara explained with an exaggerated wink. "She likes you."

Ken's brows were furrowed in confusion. He began to chew his thumbnail, then suddenly his eyes widened. He dropped his hand.

"She likes me?" he yelped. His skin turned a deep, hot pink.

"Back to the night of the murder," I said hastily, sorry I had mentioned the receptionist. "Did you notice anything important?"

"That woman who owned the restaurant sure made people mad," he answered after another therapeutic bout of nail chewing.

"Like your father?" Barbara prodded.

"Oh, Dad," Ken said dismissively. He lowered his eyes. "He's always, you know . . ."

"Coming on to women," Barbara filled in for him.

"Yeah," he agreed, his eyes still lowered. "And they get mad at him most of the time."

"Who else was mad?" I asked.

"The older lady with the gray hair who was dressed in a linen suit like Dad's," he said. He tapped the glass of the terrarium absently. Was he losing interest?

"That was Iris," I told him.

"And the lady who's married to the black guy," he added. I followed his gaze down to the terrarium. The lizard was frozen in place, its skin a brighter green than I remembered.

"How about you?" Barbara asked softly.

"Huh?" he yelped, his head jerking up.

"She made fun of you when you told her about the poisons in dairy products, didn't she?" Barbara pressed.

"But everybody does!" he objected. He waved a hand in the air. "Nobody ever takes me seriously. I even tried to tell Mr. Rutherford about the stuff in the water—you know there's awful stuff in tap water: industrial waste, tin, cadmium, aluminum— and he told me I'm not allowed to talk about it anymore—"

"Back to Sheila Snyder," Barbara said.

Ken shook his head violently. "The police asked me about arguing with her, too. I tried to explain what I meant—about the growth hormones and antibiotics and stuff—but they wouldn't listen. No one ever does."

I believed him. He probably did tell everyone. And they probably did all laugh at him. So why would he have killed Sheila Snyder?

I asked Barbara that question on the way back to her apartment. We hadn't learned much more from Ken. He claimed he couldn't remember anything else suspicious. Barbara had even asked him why he had smiled after the body had been discovered. After a few minutes of thought, he told her he'd probably been thinking about the iguana he was going to buy, to distract himself from thinking about the dead body. It sounded strange enough to be true.

"Just because we don't know *why* Ken killed Sheila doesn't mean that he didn't," Barbara said, but there wasn't much heart in her voice. I stole a glance at her. She looked tired. Her face was showing its age for once.

I dropped her off at her apartment and drove on home. When I opened my front door, Wayne and Vesta were still standing right where I had left them.

"You just don't love your mother," Vesta was telling him. Her voice was barely above a whisper now, both of her hands crossed over her heart. "Is it too much to ask for a little love, a little kindness?"

Wayne's face showed nothing, but his shoulders were rounded again, his head hanging. "Mom, you know I love you," he muttered.

"Hi, sweetie," I interjected brightly.

He bent down to give me a kiss.

"Goddammit, Waynie!" Vesta shouted. "I'm not going to allow adultery under my roof!"

Wayne's head popped up obediently. I turned to Vesta and thought about telling her this roof was mine, not hers. She squinted back at me malevolently. I thought about disputing the adultery charge one more time. She crossed her arms and smiled smugly. I thought about strangling her with my bare hands.

Wayne sighed. I looked up into his face and saw misery there.

"Let's go," I said softly.

"What?" he asked, his expression of misery giving way to a look of confusion.

"We're going for a ride," I told him. I turned to Vesta. "We'll be back in a few hours."

Vesta's mouth opened but nothing came out. I grabbed Wayne's hand and pulled him toward the door. We were almost out when Vesta regained her powers of speech.

"You can't leave!" she screamed.

"We'll be back," Wayne promised over his shoulder.

I dragged him the rest of the way through the doorway.

"Where are we going?" he asked once we were in the car.

"The Holiday Inn," I told him.

His eyebrows lifted. I saw a glint of light in his eyes. The beginnings of a smile tugged at the corners of his mouth. That was all I needed. I let out the breath I had been holding and turned the key in the ignition.

The Holiday Inn was great. We made love, ate a dinner ordered from room service, made love, talked a while and then made love again. The only pall over the evening was the ever-present image of Vesta alone in my house. What would she do while we were gone? Wayne seemed to sense what was on my mind.

"I don't think she'd actually destroy anything," he murmured unconvincingly as we drove home.

I pushed the gas pedal a little harder, thinking about fire.

"If she does," he added, "I'll repair the damage."

My jaw muscles tightened. What if she got at my Jest Gifts paperwork? She could ruin my business in a matter of minutes. And we had left her alone for hours. What about my cat? My heart stopped.

"It's okay, Kate," Wayne growled. He put his hand on my shoulder. "Really."

I took a deep breath and smiled. But I kept my foot on the gas.

When I pushed the front door open, I couldn't see anything out of place. I peeked into my office. The usual mess of papers was moldering on my desk. And my cat, C.C., was dozing in my chair. I let myself breathe again.

"No, they're splitting up. Really," came Vesta's voice from the kitchen. I stepped over to the doorway and saw her sitting at the kitchen table, holding the telephone receiver to her ear.

"This is your chance to make your move," she continued, her voice low and seductive. "She's ready for the taking."

Wayne walked up behind me. "Mom?" he asked. "Who are you talking to?"

Vesta waved him away with her hand.

"Come over now," she said. She paused to listen. "No, really," she added. "It'll be fine."

"Mom?" Wayne pressed.

"What?" she hissed, jerking her head up to look at him.

"Who is on the phone?" he asked, each word distinct and ominous.

"Her husband, Craig," Vesta answered triumphantly. She pointed at me and grinned. "He wants her back."

"Craig is my ex-husband—" I began.

"Give me that phone, right now," Wayne said, advancing into the kitchen. His voice was cold and steady.

"But—" Vesta protested.

"Now," he hissed. I had never heard such a nasty sound from his mouth before.

Vesta handed him the phone, then stood and crossed her arms.

"There has been a misunderstanding," Wayne enunciated carefully into the receiver.

I could hear the responding squeak of Craig's voice from where I stood. I turned and went back to my office.

A few minutes later Wayne said goodbye and hung up.

"Well, just don't try that again, Waynie!" Vesta spat at him.

There was a silence. I wondered what Wayne was doing. I stood up from my desk.

"That's it, Mom," he said, his voice as hard as marble. And just as cool. "You're going back to Shady Willows."

"But Waynie!" she cried. Then she whispered, "You wouldn't."

Wayne didn't answer.

"I didn't mean any harm," she said, her voice suddenly soft and placating. Then she began to sob. "I'm sorry," she whimpered. "I'm sorry. Please don't send me back—"

"If you don't want to go back, you have to cooperate," Wayne interrupted. "It's your choice."

He strode out of the kitchen into my office. His shoulders were straight. His face was stiff, devoid of feeling. I shivered involuntarily. He was frightening this way. No wonder Vesta had pleaded.

"Let's go to sleep," he suggested quietly.

I followed him into the bedroom.

Hours later, I awoke to a rasping sound I couldn't identify at first. I reached out sleepily and touched Wayne's face. It was wet with tears. I pulled him to me.

"It'll be all right," I chanted and held him close as he cried. "It'll be all right."

I just hoped that I was telling the truth.

Monday morning was not one I would want to repeat. Vesta, Wayne and I ate breakfast in uncongenial silence. Wayne's face was rigid and pale, his mouth the only moving part as he methodically ate each and every bite of his bacon and eggs. I strained to swallow the first few spoonfuls of my own oatmeal, then gave up and got some juice from the refrigerator. Even that was hard to swallow. Vesta kept flicking angry glances my way in between sobs and bites of toast.

"Mom, get dressed," Wayne ordered brusquely once he had cleaned his plate. "We're going to interview more nurses."

Vesta did as she was told. Ten minutes later she meekly followed Wayne out the front doorway. She turned back to glare at me just before the door closed. I looked away, but not before I saw something besides anger in her eyes, something in the way the inside corners of her eyelids curved upwards. Something that looked like fear.

The look replayed itself in my mind's eye as I did Jest Gifts paperwork. I had no sympathy with Vesta when she was malicious. But when she was afraid? She had spent twenty years overmedicated in a mental hospital—a snake pit, filled with writhing lunatics. She had good reason to be afraid of going back. My stomach clenched. I didn't want to feel sorry for her—but I did.

When the phone rang, I was almost grateful for the distraction.

"Hey, kiddo," Barbara said when I picked it up. "Are you ready for class tonight?"

– Nineteen –

I SHIFTED THE phone to my other ear.

"What class?" I asked Barbara, jotting down the last number my adding machine had spit out.

"The reassembled vegetarian cooking class," she told me. "Monday night, remember?"

"Oh," I whispered. I set the pencil down gently.

"Alice and Meg got hold of most of the people," Barbara went on. "Iris, Leo, Gary and Paula. I called Ken." She paused. "They're all coming, Kate," she breathed. "Every single one. Maybe we'll get the killer to confess—"

"We don't even know who the killer is," I interrupted.

"Not yet," she answered cheerfully. "Pick me up at five-thirty—"

I groaned.

"Unless you want me to drive," she offered. I could hear the grin in her voice.

"All right, all right," I said, caving in.

I managed to get through another hour's worth of paperwork before the doorbell rang. I stomped to the door and flung it open. How the hell was I supposed to get anything done if bells kept ringing?

A tall, handsome man with razor-cut hair and brown, puppy-dog eyes stood on my doorstep. Damn. It was my ex-husband, Craig. Apparently Wayne's damage control hadn't worked. From the eager smile on Craig's face I guessed that he still hoped Vesta had been telling the truth when she told him I was ready for the taking.

"How are things, Kate?" he asked me, his voice hushed and expectant.

"Fine," I snapped. "Just fine."

Craig flinched and blinked. The eager smile disappeared. His puppy-dog eyes filled with an expression of hurt that those kind of eyes can evince so well.

I sighed. It wasn't his fault that Vesta had set him up.

"Listen," I began. "Wayne's mother is—"

"Yoo-hoo," came a call from the bottom of the stairway. I looked down and saw Iris's silvery head bobbing up.

"Such an attractive house," she cooed when she reached the landing. "I hope you don't mind a little unexpected visit."

"I have work to—" I began. I stopped myself with an effort, swallowing the rest of my honest words unsaid. I started over. "It's great to see you," I lied. "What are you doing . . ."

I forgot what I was saying as a familiar rental car pulled into the driveway behind the other cars. The twins were here.

"Iris, this is Craig." I introduced them absently, watching Edna and Arletta alight from their car. "Craig, this is Iris. Would you like to come in?"

At least I didn't have to introduce Arletta and Edna. They remembered Craig from a couple of years back. And they had already met Iris. Of course. I should have remembered. The twins had probably met everyone in the cooking class by now.

I led the party into the house with a gracious smile on my lips and very ungracious thoughts on my mind.

Thirty minutes later they were all gone. I couldn't tell you exactly what they had talked about. Vacations, gardening, the weather. As I sat down at my desk again, I realized I had no idea why the twins had come by. Or Iris, for that matter. My back stiffened. Why had Iris visited?

I was still trying to figure it out when I picked Barbara up that evening to go to class. "Why do you suppose Iris came by?" I asked her.

"She's probably just investigating," she replied reasonably as we got on the highway to San Ricardo. "We visited *her* when *we* investigated."

"I guess so," I said slowly, unconvinced.

"Iris wouldn't kill anyone," Barbara added. "She's too much of a lady."

"Strangling is a fairly ladylike form of murder as murders go," I argued, an unfortunate image entering my mind, an image of Iris wearing a clean pair of white gloves as she wrapped a white cord around Sheila Snyder's neck and twisted it. My stomach did a back flip.

"I hope Meg's gonna give us some food tonight," Barbara said, blithely changing the subject.

"I just hope we're going to *live* through tonight," I countered.

"Kate!" Barbara objected and lectured me about positive thinking until we reached the Good Thyme Cafe.

The CLOSED UNTIL FURTHER NOTICE sign was still in the restaurant window. But there was another familiar sign back on the door, reading "Welcome, Vegetarian Cooking Class Tonight."

Barbara pushed the door open energetically. I followed her in, thinking woefully negative thoughts.

Most of the chairs were still upended atop the tables in the dining room. But ten or twelve had been set right-side up and placed around two tables that had been shoved together in the center of the room. Three women and a tall, thin black man stood by the tables. I shivered. They were the same four people who had stood waiting for us the first night of class.

"Hi, you guys!" Alice called out. Her heart-shaped face was as friendly as ever as she jogged toward us, her high heels tapping on the floor. She looked completely relaxed and unafraid. I wondered why. My whole body was stiff and tight with fear.

"Dynamite outfit," Barbara told her.

Alice giggled and did a model's turn to show off her slinky plum-colored jumpsuit. "The lines take off about ten pounds," she whispered.

I smiled in spite of myself. Here I was, worried to death about murder, and Alice was still worried about her weight.

"Yo, Meg!" Alice shouted. "Come and say hello."

Meg Quilter was living proof that there was such a thing as too thin. I considered and rejected the idea of pointing this out to Alice as Meg shuffled our way, looking like an anorexic teenager in a white cotton blouse and baggy gray pants. Her silky blond hair was pulled back and stuffed into a plastic barrette.

"Hello," she mumbled. She looked up for a moment, her sea-green eyes large in her pale, freckled face. I caught a glimpse of the lines radiating from the corners of those eyes, lines marking her as an adult. She lowered her gaze. *At least someone has the sense not to be cheerful*, I told myself.

"Tell Kate and Barbara about the food you made for tonight," Alice prodded Meg.

"Oh, just some more appetizers," she mumbled.

"Meg never does herself justice," a new voice declared from behind us. I turned and saw Paula Pierce, stocky and severe in a navy blue business suit. She frowned. "Meg's a talented woman," she reminded us. "A very good artist."

"And very modest," Gary said softly. He smiled a kind, reassuring smile. Then he put his long arm around Paula's shoulders. "Unlike some of us," he added.

A quick grin appeared on Paula's face, then disappeared again just as quickly. "Aren't you going to collect the money tonight?" she asked Alice abruptly.

"Oh, yeah," Alice said, her face crumpled with thought for a moment. Then she laughed. "I almost forgot. Let me go get my checklist."

Once she was gone, Paula leaned toward us. "Any progress?" she demanded brusquely.

"Not really—" I began.

"We've found out a whole bunch of interesting stuff," Barbara interrupted. "We'll talk later," she added in a whisper.

Paula nodded solemnly. Barbara winked at her. I controlled the urge to scream at Barbara. She might as well have put signs around our necks saying, "We know who the murderer is. Kill us." Meanwhile, Gary and Meg just stared.

"So," I said to Paula, trying to think of a neutral subject. "How are your dogs doing?"

"My dogs?" she repeated, her eyebrows rising. I should have asked about the weather.

"They're probably ripping apart the living room as we speak," Gary answered, his voice soft with amusement. "Paula can never turn down a stray. Canine or human."

I smiled at Gary gratefully. He smiled back for a moment, then turned away. I tried to think of something else to say as my own smile ebbed. Meanwhile, Gary fished around in his pocket with his free hand and pulled out a crystal. At least he was set for the evening. Paula continued frowning, and Meg studied her feet.

"I have a cat, myself," I threw out desperately.

But nobody caught the conversational ball. My armpits dampened with perspiration. I turned to Barbara for help. But she didn't seem to see me. Her unsmiling face was wrinkled in heavy thought now. I opened my mouth to ask her what was wrong.

The tapping of Alice's returning heels saved me from asking. Whatever was wrong with Barbara, it probably wasn't something she wanted to talk about aloud.

"Okay, you guys," Alice said with a smile. She shook her notepad in our direction. "It'll be fifteen dollars each." It was worth every cent to have someone who could talk back on the scene.

I was digging through my purse to find the money when the front door swung open. Iris walked in and paused at the doorway, erect and elegant in jade-green silk. There were even what looked like real jade chopsticks poked into her French twist.

I waved to her, wondering once again why she had been to my house earlier.

"Well, hello everyone," she trilled and stepped up to our little group. "It's so good to be meeting again. So important to go on, don't you think?"

We all nodded silently. Let Iris take the conversational burden for a while, I thought as I handed some crumpled bills to Alice. Iris could handle this crowd. Iris could handle any crowd.

"And such delightful cooking, I must say," Iris went on with enthusiasm. "Are we in for some more treats tonight?"

"You bet," Alice answered as she marked down a check from Paula and cash from a still-frowning Barbara. "Steamed dim sum, stuffed grape leaves, homemade crackers, zucchini relish—"

"Oh my, it all sounds simply delicious," interrupted Iris. She turned her gaze on Meg. "How do you find time to do it all?"

Meg looked up at her for a moment in silence, then blinked and straightened her shoulders. "Organization," she replied briskly. "Many of the ingredients can be prepared in bulk ahead of time . . ."

"Kate," Alice whispered in my ear. I jumped. I hadn't noticed the click of her heels behind me.

"What?" I whispered back.

Alice jerked her head toward the back of the restaurant as

Meg went on about food preparation technique. Iris's eyes flickered. I was sure she had noticed Alice's gesture.

I stood there for a moment holding my breath, wondering if I could ignore Alice. I knew she wanted to talk to me about the murder, but I was much happier listening to a lecture on cooking. She tapped my shoulder and jerked her head again, then walked slowly away, her heels still noisy on the floor. By this time, I was sure that everyone had noticed her.

I let out my breath in a quiet sigh and followed her. I didn't even try for nonchalance. I just stomped along behind her until we reached the far wall.

"So?" she whispered as she turned back to me. Her eyes were wide with something that might have been interest, or excitement. Or even fear.

I shrugged my shoulders. That wasn't enough for her.

"Who is it?" she asked, her whisper a little louder. I watched her as she ran a hand through her glossy black hair, and wondered if she was "it." She had motive and opportunity. She had set up the class—

"You can tell me," she breathed, bending close enough to me that I could smell the minty aroma of her breath. I could even see the gray eyeliner that traced her eyelids and the tiny clumps of mascara on her lashes.

"I don't know who it is," I whispered back.

Her eyes narrowed, wrinkling the gray eyeliner. She tapped her foot, still staring at me. I stared back. After a heartbeat or two, her face softened. She smiled again.

"Really?" she asked, tilting her head.

"Really," I assured her.

She gave my shoulder a little pat and seemed about to say something. Then her gaze focused on something behind me. I swiveled my head around to see what had drawn her attention. Ken and Leo had arrived.

"Hello, ladies," Leo greeted the group still standing near the door. His smiled was lopsided tonight, his eyelids drooping in a drowsy leer.

In greeting the ladies, Leo seemed to have missed a gentleman. Had he mistaken Gary for a woman? Maybe. Even from here, Leo looked drunk enough. His short, pear-shaped body was swaying in place as he stood. He lifted a hand to his face and managed to poke himself in the eye with a stray finger.

"Whoa," he muttered and brought his hand down to his beard. He gave it a slow stroke.

"Dad," Ken burst out shrilly. "Why don't you sit down?"

"Leo," his father corrected him, his voice low and sleepy. "Call me Leo, good buddy." But he didn't resist as Ken led him to a chair and sat him down at the table.

"Such a shame when a man lets himself drink to excess," Iris's clear voice rang out.

No one argued with her. The room was filled with silent disapproval. Meg, Paula and Barbara gazed unsmilingly at Leo. Leo's head slumped forward, his long dark hair spilling into his face for a moment. Gary averted his eyes.

"Whoa," Leo said again and jerked his head up.

"Dad'll be all right," Ken insisted, his voice even shriller now. He glared at Iris through his thick glasses. "He just had some wine, that's all. He has a bad heart, you know."

My own heart squeezed. I wondered how many times he had felt the need to defend his father before. And how many times he would again.

Even Iris softened. "Such a good son," she said warmly. "So kind of you to take care of your father." She clasped her hands together in front of her chest. "You're Ken Hermann, aren't you? I'm Iris Neville. I met you years ago, when you were just a boy."

Ken goggled at her for a moment, then seemed to remember his manners. "Oh," he mumbled and shuffled toward her with his hand held out. "I'm sorry I didn't recognize you before."

"No, no. Don't give it a thought," trilled Iris, shaking his hand. "And how is your dear mother, Louise?"

"Okay," Ken said. He dropped Iris's hand and began massaging his knuckles.

I turned my head back to Alice. I knew he'd be popping those knuckles soon.

"I'm betting on Leo," Alice whispered with a wink. Then she strode back to the tables in the center of the room. I muffled a sigh and followed her.

"Okay, folks," she announced enthusiastically, flashing a big master-of-ceremonies smile. "It looks like we're all here. A few of you still owe us your fifteen dollars. So, pay up. Then we'll get this show on the road."

Ken obediently reached into his jacket pocket and drew out a checkbook. Iris opened her purse.

"Why doesn't everyone just take a seat?" Alice continued. "Then Meg will begin—"

She broke off abruptly and turned to face the hallway that led to the kitchen, pantry and rest rooms. She wasn't smiling anymore. I turned too, wondering what she saw. Then I heard the voices. It wasn't what she saw, I realized. It was what she heard. Men's voices, moving toward us.

"Hey, it'll be cool," said one of them, high with excitement. "Really cool."

"One of those fuckers killed her," said the second deeper voice.

Dan Snyder. I guessed before I could see him.

Then he emerged from the hallway, big and burly as ever in jeans and a T-shirt, his curly black hair wild. He squinted out at the people gathered in the dining room. It was not a friendly look. My stomach tightened.

Another man stepped around to his side, a tall, thin man with protuberant eyeballs. I recognized him from the Monday before. He was Dan's friend Zach. He looked at us and grinned. A big, goofy, stoned grin. That grin scared me even more than Dan's glare. The skin on my arms prickled into goose bumps.

Iris didn't seem to be afraid, though.

"You must be Mr. Snyder," she sang out, smiling graciously. "Such a . . ."

Dan focused his glare on her. Her smile faded along with her words.

Zach giggled into the silence.

"Dan," Alice whispered and trotted toward him, her heels tapping all the way. She extended an arm as she reached him. He raised his own arm high in warning. There was something in his hand.

I took a closer look. It was a gun.

- Twenty -

"DAN, WHY?" ALICE whispered, her voice hoarse with disbelief. I watched from behind as her extended arm floated slowly down. The back of her head didn't move at all. I wondered what her eyes looked like. Was she staring at Dan Snyder? Or maybe at the gun he held?

"What are you trying to do?" she asked finally, her voice a little stronger. "Why are you here?"

"Don't worry," Dan told her, his own voice gentle for a moment. "I know what I'm doing." He even reached out for her, then seemed to remember the gun in his hand. His voice hardened. "Get back, Alice," he ordered brusquely. "Sit down."

But Alice remained standing, the back of her head still unmoving. Dan squinted at her angrily.

Zach emitted another high-pitched giggle. Nausea rose from my stomach into my throat. I turned to look at Zach as he rocked on his heels, grinning. He wiped his nose with the back of his hand, then giggled again. I took a deep breath. He was stoned all right. But on what? His eyes looked like boiled eggs, even more protuberant than I had remembered from the time before. Were his pupils dilated? It was hard to tell from here, but I thought so. And his nose was red. Was cocaine his drug of choice?

"I told you to sit down!" Dan shouted. I jerked my gaze back to him. He was the one with the gun. Who cared what drug Zach was on.

"Alice, do it now!" Dan shouted again. He raised his gun arm and pointed it at her head.

Alice's body went rigid. As she turned, I saw that her face was shiny with tears, mascara and eyeliner bleeding from her eyelids. She walked back to the table carefully on stiff legs, almost stumbling once on her high heels. She sat down next to Leo, then sank her wet face into her hands.

"Okay," barked Dan. He surveyed the lot of us with angry eyes. I looked closer. His pupils might have been dilated too. "Everyone else, stay where you are." He lifted the gun again to make his point. "Don't move."

Move? I couldn't even breathe.

"One of you fuckers killed my old lady," he continued. "And I'm going to find out who."

He surveyed us once more, very slowly this time. My eyes followed his gaze, and I noticed the rest of the class members for the first time since Dan had pointed his gun at us. Leo looked astonishingly sober, sitting up straight in his chair, his close-set eyes round with fear. Meg's shoulders were straight too, but her eyes were cool as she stared back at Dan. Ken was goggling as usual and popping his knuckles one by one. Paula Pierce looked angry. Her shoulders were hunched forward, and her mouth was tight with disapproval. I shivered for a moment, hoping she wouldn't tangle with Dan, wouldn't set him off.

Paula's husband, Gary, stood with his eyes half closed as if he were sleepy. But a look at his hand convulsively squeezing his crystal told me he was wide-awake. Barbara looked more puzzled than frightened. I craned my neck to study her face, trying to decipher the message behind her expression. I realized abruptly that Dan Snyder might just flush out his wife's murderer this way. Everything might be all right after all. This is, if he didn't shoot one of us in the process. Dan's gaze landed on Iris. She seemed to grow taller as he looked at her

"Do you think your mother would approve of what you're doing?" she asked Dan evenly.

Dan took a step backward as if she had pushed him. His mouth opened, but nothing came out.

"You're an intelligent man," Iris went on, her tone friendlier now. "Such a shame to waste—"

"Who made you God?" Zach demanded. He laughed at his own words, then rattled off some more. "Dan's got a right, you know. He's got a right to find out what happened to his old lady. Right? So keep your mouth shut, you old bitch—"

"Young man," Iris interrupted him. "I was speaking to Mr. Snyder." She turned to Dan again. "I-m sure you're not thinking clearly now," she said quietly. Dan seemed to be listening to her. His eyes were on her face in any case, his mouth still open. "Grief is such a terrible thing—"

"Ask her if she killed your old lady," Zach cut in. He put his hand on Dan's shoulder. "Come on," he prodded. "That's what we're here for. Right?"

Dan closed his mouth and narrowed his eyes. Zach removed his hand.

"Did you kill my wife?" Dan asked Iris. He wasn't shouting anymore. His words were muted, but they shook with tension.

Iris's shoulders slumped. "Of course I didn't kill her," she murmured.

Dan stared at her a while longer in the silence. Iris stared back. Finally he nodded, as if he believed her.

"Dan," Alice said softly. "Iris is right. This is really stupid—"

"Be quiet!" Dan shouted, lifting his gun again.

Alice obeyed. Everyone obeyed.

"Okay," said Dan, dropping his gun hand. "I'm gonna question all of you. So just wait your turn."

"Let's start with the men," Zach suggested eagerly. Suddenly, I wondered if *he* was our killer. He was certainly close enough to psychotic to count. But hadn't he been with Dan at the time of the murder?

"Bunch of assholes," Zach went on. He tapped his fingers on his thigh. "You got 'em under control now. Right? Right?" He didn't wait for Dan to answer. "Then we'll get to the ladies. This is gonna be really cool," He swiveled his hips lewdly. The hair went up on the back of my neck.

"How about him?" Zach suggested, pointing at Leo. "Look at the asshole. He's pissing in his pants. D'you think he's the one?"

Dan took two long strides toward the table where Leo was sitting, then stopped, still a few yards away.

"Stand up," he ordered.

Leo stood up, his arms stiff at his sides. He wasn't swaying anymore. He was shaking.

'You're a drunk and a dirty old man," Dan rumbled. "What else are you?"

Leo shook his head violently, his long dark hair dancing with the motion. Was he denying Dan's charges or just unable to speak?

"Well?" Dan prodded.

Leo's eyes widened, but he still didn't answer. It was fear that kept him from speaking. I was sure now.

"Hey, I'll take care of the asshole," Zach offered. He grinned. "I'll get him to talk. Right, Dan? Right?"

Dan continued to glare, not seeming to hear his friend's offer. Zach scurried up to Leo and grabbed the front of his shirt. A button popped off and rolled onto the floor as Zach yanked Leo closer to him.

"What are you hiding, asshole?" Zach demanded. He pulled Leo upward by his shirt until Leo was on tiptoe looking into Zach's eyes. "Tell, me or I'll—"

"My heart!" Leo cried.

Zach let go of his shirt and Leo flopped onto the floor. He grabbed his chest, gasping, his face grimacing in pain.

"Dad?" Ken whispered. Then more shrilly, "He's had a heart attack!" He started across the room toward his father. "Call an ambulance, he's—"

"Stop right there," Dan ordered.

Ken stopped and goggled through his thick glasses at Dan for a moment, then took another step toward his father. He was either very brave or very distracted. Or maybe a combination of both.

"Stop!" Dan shouted. He raised the gun to point at Ken. Ken stopped walking. But he didn't stop talking.

"You've gotta do something!" he wailed. "He's got a heart condition. He could die—"

Zach stepped forward and grabbed Ken by the shoulder. Ken's head jerked back.

"It's a trick," Zach hissed. "It's a trick, but we're not buying it, you little weirdo."

Ken's face went slack with disbelief.

"What'd you do?" Zach demanded. "Make a pass at her?"

"At who?" Ken asked, his forehead wrinkling with confusion.

"Dan's old lady!" Zach shouted. He gripped Ken's shoulder and shook it. "You made a pass at her and she turned you down—"

"I wouldn't make a pass at anyone," Ken objected through clattering teeth. "I don't even like women that much."

Zach stared at Ken for a moment. It was his turn for disbelief. Then he jerked his hand away from Ken's shoulder.

"Are you telling me you're a faggot?" he demanded.

Ken shook his head. "I'm not gay," he answered, twisting his hands together. "Women just make me uncomfortable—"

"Is that why you killed her?" asked Dan.

"I didn't kill anyone," Ken insisted, his voice almost steady. He turned toward Dan. "Listen, we've got to do something about my father. He's not faking it. He has a heart condition." I would never think of Ken as a wimp again.

I stole a look at Leo. He was still lying on the floor. The red had drained from his face, leaving it the color of old ivory. His lips were purplish. And he was still breathing in short gasps.

"Let me take his pulse," Iris requested. She took a step in Leo's direction.

Dan swiveled his head toward her, his eyes uncertain.

"It's a trick," Zach piped up. "Don't let the old bitch near him."

Dan turned back to Zach.

"He looks like he really has had a heart attack," Iris insisted, drawing herself up even taller than before. Her blue eyes were sparkling. "If he has, he should try to breathe deeply. An ambulance should be called—"

"The asshole's faking it," argued Zach. He pounded a fist against his own thigh. "Don't let them fool you, Dan. You've got more questions to ask. Right?"

Dan nodded slowly, then reached up a hand to rub his eyes. He wasn't looking a lot better than Leo. His skin wasn't as pale as Leo's, but it was pale enough. And his shoulders sagged. Even his head sagged.

"You should listen to Ms. Neville," Paula put in, projecting her words as if in court. "If Mr. Hermann dies because of your actions, you will be legally responsible for his death. Do you understand—"

Dan whirled toward her, pointing the gun. "Just shut up," he yelped. His eyes were as wild as his hair. I almost felt sorry for him. Almost.

Paula's head jerked up. Her mouth opened. Gary put his arm

around her shoulders and squeezed. She clamped her mouth closed with an obvious effort. Her hands formed into fists.

"Okay, you," Dan growled, pointing his gun at Gary. "What do you know about my wife's death?"

"Very little—" Gary began.

"Oh, yeah. Sure," Zach cut in. "Big black professor man like you doesn't know anything. Right? Big fuckin' professor—"

"Let the man talk," Dan barked.

Zach's eyebrows rose for a moment; then he shrugged. I felt a surge of hope that warmed my cold and shaking limbs. If Dan was going to control Zach, we might just get out of this thing without any real damage. If only Leo was all right. I glanced at him again. His eyes were closed, but he was breathing deeply now. Maybe he had heard Iris's words of advice. His color looked slightly better too.

"What do you know?" Dan prodded Gary again.

"I know very little about your wife's death," Gary answered carefully. "Probably much less than you. I know she was killed last Monday night. I know that the killer might or might not have been one of the members of our class. I certainly didn't kill her myself."

Dan nodded, apparently satisfied. But Zach wasn't.

"Oh, yeah?" he snarled. "You were talking with her that night, weren't you? Coming on to her. So she put you down. And you got mad. Right? Right?" I listened to the venom in his voice and wondered if we were actually hearing Zach's motive for murder. Maybe *he* had made the pass at Sheila and been put down. But would he have done that in front of Dan? Then I wondered if he had really been with Dan that night.

"My husband did no such thing," Paula declared, bringing me back to the present. Her head jutted forward as she spoke. "Ms. Snyder and my husband exchanged a few words, nothing more. Whether or not you believe in his good character, there was simply no opportunity for him to do anything more than that—"

"You like to argue, don't you," Zach interrupted.

Paula pulled her head back and tilted it. Was she confused by Zach's comment? I certainly was.

"Bitches like you think you can take the place of men," he continued, glaring. I was no longer confused. Zach was just launching into a new tirade. "Take away our jobs. Bust our balls ..."

I threw a pleading look at Dan, hoping he would stop Zach again. But Dan just looked tired. His eyes were on the floor as he rubbed his temple with the gun in his hand. *There ought to be a way to get that gun from him*, I thought. There were nine of us and only two of them. But when I tried to think of a specific strategy, my mind just balked.

". . . And little Miss Priss Bitch, here," Zach continued, turning to Meg. "She'd cut off your balls, without batting an eyelash. Right? Right?"

Meg looked Zach in the eye without flinching, her slender shoulders pulled back military style. She was another one I would never underestimate again.

"Were you jealous of my wife?" Dan demanded abruptly. I jerked my head in his direction, wondering if he was speaking to me. But his eyes were on Meg. I let my startled breath out slowly.

"Certainly not," Meg replied coolly. "I had no interest in her, one way or the other. She just owned the space we were renting for our class."

Dan stared at her for a few more heartbeats. Had he taken offense at her cool answer?

"How about this one?" Zach said, his attention focusing on Barbara. He grinned and waggled his pelvis. He probably thought he looked like Elvis. He didn't. "Nice looker for a gook. Real pretty. Right?"

This had gone far enough, I decided. Whatever Dan's original plan had been, sexual terrorism couldn't have been part of it. At least I hoped not. I opened my mouth to object. But Barbara beat me to it.

"Mr. Snyder," she murmured. "Could you please ask your friend to stop?" Her tone was gentle, almost crooning, despite its underlying tremor. "None of this is going to help you find out what happened to your wife."

"Hey, bitch," Zach objected. He wasn't grinning anymore. "It's not up to you. Right, Dan? It's not up to her."

"Zach," Dan said wearily. "Why don't you just sit down for a while?"

Zach whirled around to face him. "Waddaya mean, sit down?"

he demanded shrilly. He drew his skinny body up to its full height. "We're in this thing together, buddy. Right? That's what you said—"

"Okay, okay," Dan muttered. His eyes traveled down to the gun in his hand. His shoulders sagged even more. Was he just beginning to realize the mess he was in?

A flicker of movement from the darkness of the hallway drew my attention away from Dan. I held my breath. Maybe it was the police. Or even someone else, someone who could size up the situation and call for help. But as the flicker moved forward, it became a little girl. It was Topaz Snyder. I let out the breath I had been holding. It was hopeless. Topaz wasn't going to help us out of this situation. She crept up silently behind Dan, a frown distorting her small face.

"Yeah, well just don't tell me to sit down," Zach told Dan.

"Fine," Dan snapped, raising his gun.

Would he actually shoot Zach? Somehow the notion didn't bother me as much as it should have.

"Come on, buddy," Zach chided him. "One of these assholes is a killer. Right?"

"Right," Dan agreed, straightening a little.

He turned his gaze on me. My mouth went dry.

Zach looked my way too, then trotted toward me. I could see his eyes clearly now. His pupils were dilated, all right. He waggled his pelvis again and I noticed the bulge in his pants. Damn. I averted my eyes quickly, but not before my hands began shaking. And sweating. I turned to Dan.

"I didn't kill your wife," I volunteered. My mouth was so dry it kept sticking as I formed the words. Could Dan hear it sticking? Would he take this as a sign of guilt? "I don't know who did," I added for good measure.

"I'll bet you don't know," Zach mocked me. "You're lying, bitch. But I know how to take care of you." I felt rather than saw his face come closer to mine. I kept my eyes averted. But he was so close I could hear his breathing, even smell the garlic on his breath.

"No," growled Dan. I let out a sigh of relief. He was going to keep Zach away from me. "I'll take care of her myself," he finished. The sigh stuck in my throat.

"Why have you been asking so many questions?" Dan demanded. He peered at me intently.

"I just—" I began.

"What's going on, Daddy?" came Topaz's question from behind him.

Dan jumped in place, clearly startled. Zach let out another giggle. Dan glared at him for an instant, then turned toward Topaz and swung with his gun hand in one motion.

"Don't!" I called out too late.

Dan's gun hand came slashing down to connect with the side of his daughter's head.

Topaz shrieked and grabbed her temple.

I watched the back of Dan's head as he looked down at the gun in his hand. Had he forgotten it was there? He reached out for his daughter with his other hand. Her eyes were round and staring. And there was a thin red line of blood at her temple.

"I'm sorry, honey—" he began. His words weren't enough.

Topaz turned and ran. She disappeared down the hallway.

"Daddy hurt me!" came her wail floating back to us a minute later. Then we heard the sound of rushing footsteps.

Rose Snyder burst from the hallway, dressed in a lavender chenille robe, with quilted slippers on her feet. She pulled her wire-rimmed glasses from her pocket and put them on. She took a hard look at her son. Her eyebrows rose when she saw the gun in his hand. Then her head reared back.

"Stop it, Danny!" she shouted. "Stop it right now!"

Dan Snyder lifted the gun slowly and pointed it at his mother.

– Twenty-one –

"DANNY!" ROSE CRIED out. She stepped backwards, her eyes widening behind her glasses.

Dan didn't move. He kept his arm steady, his gun still pointing at his mother. I wished I would see his face, his eyes, but all I could see was the back of his head.

"Danny," Rose repeated, this time in a near whisper. Her eyes filled with tears. "What are you doing? I don't understand this."

Dan lowered his arm slowly.

"I was trying to find out who killed Sheila," he mumbled. It was hard to make out his words. His voice was thick, his words slurred. "I didn't mean . . . I didn't mean . . ."

He never finished his sentence. He slumped to the floor as if someone had dropped him there. His shoulders moved up and down spasmodically. Was he crying? Then I heard the clatter of his gun hitting the floor, and I didn't care if he was crying.

I sprinted around Zach, toward Dan, toward the gun. But Zach caught on. He reached out a long arm and grabbed me by my shoulder. I spun around, throwing off his hand, and faced him. He moved closer, clenching a fist. I raised my hand and knee simultaneously and felt the satisfying impact of my knee in his groin. My upthrust fingers didn't jab him in the throat the way they were supposed to. They just grazed his chin. But I didn't care. He was down and squirming on the floor. I blessed my tai chi teacher as I turned back toward Dan.

I wasn't the only one who had seen the gun hit the floor. Alice was trotting toward it, amazingly fast on her high heels. Iris was hurrying Dan's way too. And Barbara had just broken into a run.

I took a couple more steps, then gave up the competition, satisfying myself with watching as Alice took the lead. She landed on her knees next to Dan and reached down, scooping up the gun triumphantly.

Then everyone got in the act.

"I'm calling the police," announced Paula Pierce, hunching her shoulders forward as she took a step toward the phone.

I let myself breathe. Everything was going to be all right.

"How about my dad?" demanded Ken shrilly, kneeling down next to Leo. Leo was sitting up, scowling, his skin color back to normal.

"Perhaps an ambulance too, Paula," Iris sang out.

In the midst of the confusion, I heard the front door open behind me. I turned just in time to see Zach's backside disappearing. No one ran after him. Good riddance, I thought.

"Paula, wait a minute," Alice called out. She stood up, the gun in her hand pointing Paula's way. My shoulders tightened. Maybe everything wasn't going to be all right. "There's no need to call the police. Zach's split and Dan didn't mean anything—"

Paula stopped in her tracks and turned toward Alice. Her mouth was tight, her eyes stony. "Are you threatening me, Ms. Frazier?" she asked calmly.

Gary darted across the room to stand in front of his wife. Alice didn't seem to notice.

"No, of course not," she answered Paula, but she didn't lower the gun. "It's just that I don't want Dan to get in any trouble. The police are gonna give him a hard time—"

"Don't worry about it, dear," Iris interjected quietly. "The San Ricardo police are not monsters. So kind as human beings, many of them. They'll handle your Dan fairly. They know he's a grieving husband."

Alice frowned. Then she looked down at Dan. He was still turned away. And his shoulders were still heaving. It didn't look as if he was going to give Alice any guidance in the matter.

"A very dear friend of mine used to head the San Ricardo Police Department," Iris went on, her words forming a soothing melody, far more soothing, I would have guessed, than the police would be once they got their hands on Dan Snyder. "Such a compassionate man he was. I'm sure the new chief is just as kind. They'll give Dan the help he needs."

Alice lowered the gun, then turned her head to look at Rose Snyder. Rose was sobbing, great gulping sobs that sounded as hopeless as the situation itself.

"Mrs. Snyder," Alice prodded her gently. "Whaddaya think? Should we call the police?"

Rose stared at Alice with an expression of cartoon surprise on her face. Her eyebrows arched. Her mouth was shaped in a perfect O. But no sound came out of it.

"Mrs. Snyder," Alice began again. "What should—"

Rose closed her mouth and shook her head. "I don't know," she whispered. She pulled her chenille robe tighter around her body. "I don't know about anything anymore." Then she turned and headed back down the hallway, her slippers softly scuffing the floor.

"Wouldn't you like to give me the gun, dear?" Iris asked brightly. Alice's heart-shaped face was slack and undecipherable as she stared at Iris. Would she take Iris's suggestion?

Do it, Alice, I ordered silently, tensing as I tried to send the mental message. Maybe Barbara wasn't the only psychic around here. *You don't want the gun, Alice*, I thought as hard as I could. *Hand it to Iris. Do it. Do it now.*

Alice looked down at the gun for an instant longer, then held it out to Iris, butt first. Had it been something I thought? I held my breath and waited for the moment of transfer.

It wasn't a long wait. Iris glided forward and reached out her hand slowly, palm up. There was nothing abrupt in her motions, nothing that could startle Alice. Alice placed the gun in Iris's hand. I sucked in a long, deep breath. It was done. Iris had the gun. Paula continued on her way to the phone. Alice collapsed onto the floor next to Dan.

"All right!" I heard. It took me a moment to realize that I was the one doing the shouting. "All right, Iris!" I shouted again. The relief buzzing through my body was exquisite.

"Right on!" Barbara chimed in. "Way to go!"

A pink flush rose in Iris's cheeks. She lowered her eyes demurely for a moment, looking truly shy. I could have kissed her. But I didn't want the gun to go off. Iris lowered it into her purse gingerly. I wondered if it had a safety catch, but before I could ask she had turned back to Alice.

"You did the right thing, dear," she cooed reassuringly. "Absolutely the right thing. It would have been such a shame if—"

"I hope they lock the two of them up and throw away the key!" Leo bellowed, his face red and ugly now. I supposed it was better than deathly pale. Maybe. "I could have died—"

"Dad, calm down," Ken said, patting Leo's shoulder. "You don't want to have another attack."

"Are you feeling a bit better?" Iris asked Leo. I couldn't be sure, but I thought I detected a note of mockery in her question.

"I suppose I'm okay," he muttered ungraciously. He tossed his long black hair out of his face. "No thanks to those punks. I hope they rot."

"But Dan didn't mean anything," Alice protested, on her feet again. Her eyes were wide with sincerity. "It wasn't Dan's fault. I'll bet it was all Zach's idea. Dan wouldn't really hurt anyone—"

"He hurt his daughter," Paula said coolly, back from the phone now.

"But . . . but that was an accident—"

"Don't hassle it, Alice," came Dan's mutter from the floor. "Okay?" The words sounded thick, waterlogged.

Alice blinked, then knelt down again next to him, whispering urgently. I couldn't hear her words, but I could guess their general content. Dan Snyder was in a heap of trouble. And he'd better figure out how he was going to handle it. Grief was only going to go so far as an excuse for his behavior.

"Perhaps we could all sit down while we wait?" suggested Iris, breaking into my imminent depression. She smiled winningly. "All this standing can be such a strain."

She was right. I was tired. Damn tired.

We all sat down at the tables that had been set up for the cooking class. All but Alice, that is. And Dan, of course.

We weren't a real perky bunch. Ken helped Leo to the table, then sat down next to him. Leo was glowering and muttering under his breath. Something about what he planned to tell the police. Ken sighed and looked down at his hands. He popped one knuckle, then started on the next one. Ugh. I turned my eyes to Paula and Gary. They sat next to each other in silence. Paula's mouth was tight, her eyes disapproving as she stared at Leo. Gary's eyes were almost closed. I couldn't see his hands, but I would have bet one of them was fondling a crystal under the table. It was better than popping his knuckles, anyway. Meg was staring wide-eyed into the space above our heads. She made no effort to organize what was left of her class.

Only Barbara and Iris were smiling. I certainly wasn't. I felt too shaky and nauseated to manage a smile. True, with the exception of Topaz and possibly Leo, we were all alive and unharmed. But after all the fuss, none of us had learned who Sheila Snyder's murderer was. Of course the murderer knew his or her own name. And I had a feeling that murderer was somewhere in the room, if not at this very table.

"Well, Meg," Iris said cheerfully. "Would you like to tell us about the food you've planned for tonight?"

"What?" said Meg, lowering her eyes slowly to focus on Iris. Maybe Meg needed Alice to kick-start her. She wasn't doing too well by herself.

"The food, dear," Iris prodded, her voice a little too tight to carry off the chatty tone. "Some lovely appetizers as I remember—"

She stopped abruptly. I heard the sound of sirens.

We waited in silence until the police burst into the dining room. They were the same pair as before, the muscular young policewoman, and the tall Hispanic officer who had caught Barbara and me snooping at the back of the restaurant three nights before. Damn. They were both in uniform and they both held guns out in front of them. The hair went up on the back of my neck.

"Who placed the call?" the Hispanic officer demanded.

Paula rose. "I did," she answered with quiet authority. "Please lower your weapons, Officers. We have had enough of guns for the evening—"

"The punk that attacked us is over there!" bellowed Leo, apparently unable to contain himself. He pointed at Dan, still sitting on the floor with Alice, his back to us. "Arrest him! And find his friend. They tried to kill me—"

"Dan didn't try to kill anyone!" Alice protested, jumping to her feet. Her face was alive again, lit up with righteousness. Both police officers swung around to face her, guns still raised.

"Perhaps we should start from the beginning, Officers," Iris suggested mildly. She pulled Dan's gun from her purse.

"Hold it!" shouted the female officer, turning to point her gun at Iris. Iris froze, Dan's gun still in her hand, her mouth open with surprise.

"Place the gun on the table, ma'am," the officer recited slowly.

Iris placed the gun on the table, then smiled. "So silly of me," she trilled. "I should have warned you."

"Forget about her!" Leo bawled. "Arrest Snyder! He's the one. Right over there."

Dan Snyder stood up and faced the police officers. His eyes were red and swollen. "It's my gun," he growled.

The Hispanic policeman sprinted over to Dan. The muscular policewoman holstered her own gun and gingerly picked up the one that Iris had been holding.

"Please do not talk among yourselves," she warned us. "We will interview each one of you separately—"

The door behind her opened before she could finish. Sergeant Oakley marched in, her rangy body clothed in an emerald-green sweatsuit tonight. Her red hair was tousled. Had she been called in from home? She bared her teeth in a wolf's smile. I flinched involuntarily.

"Everyone's here and accounted for, I see," she commented, her musical voice mild. Her eyes flickered from face to face and then settled on mine. "So whose idea was this little party?" she asked.

I squirmed in my seat, afraid to look over at Barbara. I opened my mouth to answer.

"Arrest that man!" Leo hollered, saving me the trouble. He pointed at Dan Snyder.

"For what?" Oakley inquired softly.

Leo's jaw dropped for a moment. "For attacking me, for attacking all of us," he answered finally. His voice grew stronger. "He held a gun on us. A gun! And his punk friend—"

The paramedics bustled through the door before he could finish his speech.

"Heart attack victim?" asked one of them.

Five different fingers pointed to Leo. Leo himself slumped in his chair, looking suddenly ill. So ill that I wondered if he had faked the earlier heart attack.

After a whispered consultation with the paramedics, Oakley allowed them to take Leo away.

Then she turned back to Dan Snyder.

"Take him in the kitchen," she told the Hispanic officer, the music gone from her voice abruptly. She turned to the rest of us. "Okay, what happened here?"

Paula took the lead. "Mr. Snyder and his cohort—I believe his name is Zach—held all of us here at gunpoint," she recited calmly. Too calmly. "Apparently Mr. Snyder wished to question us about his wife's murder—

"His friend roughed up my dad," Ken put in.

"Mr. Snyder also hit his daughter with his gun," Paula continued. "I believe she is upstairs with her grandmother now—"

"Dan hit Topaz by accident!" Alice protested from where she stood, alone now. "And Zach did all the rest of the mean stuff. And Dan let me have the gun. And—"

"That's enough," Sergeant Oakley interrupted. "We'll talk to you each one by one." She switched on her wolf smile. "You know the routine."

I did by the end of the evening. The routine was a rerun of the night of Sheila's death. Except that there was no corpse. And Dan Snyder came out in handcuffs after his interview. Much to Alice's loud distress. Her pleas did no good. She was led into the kitchen by one officer as Dan was led out the restaurant door by another set of officers who had apparently been called for that purpose. After Alice, the rest of us were interviewed individually by Sergeant Oakley. Paula, Gary, Iris and Barbara had already taken their turns by the time the female officer called my name. I took a deep breath, squared my shoulders and walked into the wolf's den.

Sergeant Oakley was mercifully brusque. Maybe she was tired. She didn't smile. She didn't stare at me with warm, concerned eyes. She didn't even try to draw me out. She just leaned back in her chair and demanded my version of the night's events, then listened with no visible reaction to my words except for the briefest flicker of a smile when I described kneeing Zach in the groin.

"And tonight's class was your idea," she stated when I was finished. It wasn't a question.

"Well," I temporized, squirming in my chair. She narrowed her hazel eyes. "Mine and Barbara's, I guess," I told her.

"You guess?" she barked.

"I think Barbara suggested the idea to Meg and Alice," I explained hastily. "And they actually set it up."

Sergeant Oakley stood up the better to glare down at me. "Keep out of it," she warned, her voice a quiet snarl. "I mean it."

I nodded as hard as I could without nodding my head right off my neck.

"You can go now," she told me.

I didn't need to be told twice.

Barbara was waiting for me in the dining room. We left the restaurant quietly, then broke into a run once we were out the door. Barbara beat me to the Toyota by a nose. I let her in, then climbed in myself. Safe in the Toyota's womb, I took a series of deep breaths before sticking the key in the ignition.

As I turned the key, I heard a high, keening note from beside me. I swiveled my head toward Barbara. Her hands were over her eyes. Her mouth was wide and wailing. Damn. The night wasn't over yet. I put my arm around her. Her wailing turned to sobs. I squeezed her shoulder helplessly.

"Jeez-Louise," I muttered, unconsciously purloining Barbara's own phrase.

Barbara's hands dropped from her wet eyes. She frowned at me.

"What did you say?" she asked.

It took me a minute to remember. "Jeez-Louise?" I answered finally, still not sure.

She smiled moistly. "I knew I'd rub off on you sooner or later," she told me.

I turned off the Toyota and handed her a Kleenex. She blew her nose loudly.

"You *have* rubbed off on me," I assured her. "I even psychically willed Alice to drop her gun tonight." I felt foolish saying it, but I wanted to cheer her up.

It didn't work. Barbara's smile disappeared. New tears squeezed out of her eyes.

"What did I say?" I asked her desperately.

"Kate," she whispered. "I've lost them again."

"Your psychic powers?" I asked, understanding dawning.

She nodded. "I tried to tune in to people's minds," she said, her voice taking on speed. "But all I got was a garble of disjointed thoughts. Like a dozen TV sets playing at once. It was awful!" She began to cry again.

"Did you lose it when Dan and Zach came in?" I asked, trying to distract her. She looked up, frowning. "Maybe the fear scrambled your signals," I went on. I liked this theory. "Once you get over the shock—"

"It won't wash, Kate," she interrupted. At least she wasn't crying anymore. "I started getting the weird signals before Zach and Dan ever showed up."

I tried again. "Maybe you're getting the murderer. Maybe a killer's mind is so messed up it gives off weird signals."

"That's interesting," she murmured slowly. She sat for a minute staring at the dashboard, lost in thought. "You know what?" she said finally.

"No, what?" I replied. "Have you figured out who did it?"

She laughed. "No," she said, shaking her head. "I was just going to tell you I was hungry."

It took a moment for her answer to sink in. I was waiting for wisdom and she was giving me hunger.

My stomach let out a loud growl. That made it two against one. I looked at my watch. It was nearly eight o'clock. I turned the key in the ignition and pulled out from the curb.

By the time we were seated at the nearest Chinese restaurant, Barbara was cheerfully playing Guess-the-Murderer again. The Chinese restaurant had been my choice, not hers. Barbara had grown up on pot roast, potatoes and hamburgers. Chinese food held no nostalgic appeal for her.

"It's Leo," she whispered once the waiter had taken our order, pork chow mein for Barbara and moo shu vegetables for me. "I don't think he actually had a heart attack. He was just afraid to answer Dan's questions."

"But why would he murder Sheila?" I demanded irritably. "What's his motive?"

"Maybe it's something Freudian. Maybe Sheila reminded him of his mother," Barbara suggested.

"But Freud would have him kill his father, not his mother—"

"Maybe Sheila was blackmailing him," Barbara went on, ignoring my brief interruption. "Maybe she saw him do something

illegal. Maybe Leo didn't like the way she hit her kid. Maybe
Leo and Sheila were distant cousins, the only heirs to a mutual
uncle's fortune . . ."

The moo shu vegetables almost made up for listening to another hour of Barbara's theories. Shredded black mushrooms,
zucchini, green onions, bean sprouts, and cabbage sautéed and
wrapped in thin pancakes with plum sauce. I savored my last bite
and tuned back in to Barbara. She had covered Leo, Ken, Meg
and Paula. I was glad she was enjoying herself. But I was really
tired of murder. She was working on Alice now.

"Maybe Alice murdered Sheila because the commune did
something wildly illegal twenty years ago and now Sheila was
going to spill the beans," she proposed. "Maybe Sheila did
something to her twenty years ago that she's never forgiven.
Maybe Topaz is really Alice's illegitimate kid and . . ."

I flagged the waiter for the check.

It wasn't until I had dropped Barbara off at her apartment that
I began to wonder if she might have hit upon the murderer's motive in her long bout of supposition, much like a few zillion
monkeys at typewriters will, given enough time, theoretically
bang out the collected works of Shakespeare. Maybe I should
have listened more carefully.

Wayne was waiting for me when I got home. His face looked
worn and tired. His shoulders slumped. Then I remembered that
he had spent the day with Vesta. I wondered if it had been worse
than my evening with Dan and Zach.

"How'd it go?" I asked him cautiously.

"Talked to a lot of nurses," he sighed. "Looked at a lot of condos."

I put my arms around him and squeezed.

"And Vesta?" I asked softly as I released him.

He swiveled his head around to look behind him. Vesta was
nowhere in sight.

"Fought me every step of the way. Didn't like any of the
nurses. Didn't like any of the condos," he whispered. "I don't
know, Kate." He sighed again as he rubbed his temples. "I really
may have to put her back in an institution. I can't just kick her
out. She can't take care of herself. She'd end up on the street."

I put my arms around him again and held him tight, trying to
squeeze away his troubles. Trying to squeeze away my own. I

didn't know what the answer was for Vesta. I didn't know what the answer was for Dan Snyder, either. How did Rose Snyder end up with Dan for a son, anyway? How did Wayne end up with Vesta for a mother?

I stepped back, shaking off the thoughts.

"Let's go to bed," I whispered.

Vesta didn't bang on the wall that night. Maybe the universe wasn't completely unjust after all.

In fact, Vesta didn't make a peep the next day either. She ate her breakfast without a word. Her facial expressions were eloquent, though. Hurt, anger and hatred were the major themes. After she had swallowed her last bite of toast, she stomped back to her room.

By eleven, I was beginning to worry. I had only heard her leave her room once and that was for a quick trip to the bathroom. Should I check on her?

The phone rang before I could decide. It was Barbara.

"Felix called," she said without further introduction. Her voice was tingling with excitement. "Dan Snyder's been charged with a whole boatload of crimes, beginning with assault with a deadly weapon." She paused. "Guess who got him out on bail?" she asked.

"Alice," I answered. That one was too easy. "What about Zach?" I asked back.

"He's disappeared, Kate," Barbara told me. Her voice held a new note. Was it concern? "The cops can't find him."

"Do you think Zach is still in the county?" I wondered aloud, remembering my knee in his groin. My hands went cold. "Do you think he's mad at me?" I whispered.

"Is the Pope Catholic?" Barbara replied.

- Twenty-two -

"You kicked the doofus in the balls," Barbara reminded me. As if I needed reminding. "He's not gonna be very happy about it."

"But he was the one . . ." I faltered.

I wanted to tell her that Zach had deserved the knee to the groin, but somehow I had a feeling Zach wouldn't agree with me on that point.

"So how would he find me?" I demanded instead.

"He could try the phone book," Barbara suggested.

My mouth went dry. In my mind, the sound of my pulse pounding in my ears became the sound of Zach's fist pounding on my door. And I hadn't even told Wayne about Zach. Damn.

"Don't panic," Barbara advised. "He probably doesn't know your last name."

The pounding diminished. Maybe Barbara was right. If I didn't know Zach's last name, he probably didn't know mine.

"Unless he got it from Dan," Barbara added helpfully.

"Barbara!" I yelped. "Stop it. My head feels like a tennis ball—"

"Never mind, kiddo," she interrupted. "You'll be safe. You're going to spend the afternoon with me."

"I am?"

"Yeah," she said. Her voice took on a husky tone. "First thing, we're going over to the city to take Alice out to lunch—"

"No way!" I objected. "You heard Sergeant Oakley. It's dangerous to talk to these guys! One of them's a murderer—"

"Not Alice," Barbara said quietly.

I paused for a moment. Not Alice?

"But last night you said Topaz might be Alice's illegitimate daughter," I reminded her, keeping my voice even with an effort. "And then there was the theory about the commune—"

"That was last night," she cut in again. "I don't think it's Alice anymore. And Kate, Alice knew Sheila. Think about it." The phone was silent for a moment. It wasn't enough time for me to figure out what I was supposed to be thinking about. "Alice knew Sheila longer than anyone else did," Barbara added. "She'll have some answers for us."

"Answers to what?" I demanded. "What the hell are you talking about!"

"I'll tell you when we get there," she promised and hung up.

Twenty minutes later I heard a car in my driveway. I peeked through the curtains, afraid for a moment that Zach might be driving up. But all I saw was Barbara's Volkswagen. That wasn't a whole lot better. I had work to do, I told myself. This whole thing was too dangerous, I added. There were boundaries even in the best of friendships, and Barbara was pushing the limits of those boundaries. I stood up straighter. I wouldn't go with her to San Francisco. That was all there was to it.

Ten minutes of arguing later, I was driving over the Golden Gate Bridge with Barbara next to me in the passenger's seat. Vesta hadn't replied when I shouted goodbye.

"Vesta'll be fine," Barbara assured me. "She's manipulating you, kiddo. You let people push you around too much."

"Is that a fact?" I drawled with a pointed glance in her direction.

Barbara had the grace to quietly avert her eyes for a moment, pretending to find great interest in the license plate of the car next to us. Or maybe she wasn't pretending. The silence didn't last long, though.

"Don't worry," she said, turning back to me. "Alice isn't going to do anything to us in the middle of downtown San Francisco."

Barbara had a point. But it turned out to be a moot one. We made our way through the downtown traffic, parked in the underground parking lot, walked four blocks and took the elevator up to Alice's office. But Alice wasn't there. And the woman at the desk claimed to have no idea where she'd gone. In fact, the woman at the desk was mighty annoyed. Alice was supposed to be covering the phones. And Meg was gone too. The woman was still muttering angrily as we left.

"Any other bright ideas?" I asked Barbara as we exited the lobby to the sidewalk. I'll admit it wasn't a friendly question. Or an original one. But I wasn't feeling very friendly or original.

"How about lunch?" Barbara suggested with a grin.

I glared at her.

"My treat," she added. She put a hand on my shoulder. "Come on, kiddo. I didn't know Alice wouldn't be here."

"No, I suppose you didn't." I sighed and gave in.

Barbara bought me a tofu dog with mustard and onions from a cart in the plaza a few blocks from Alice's building. Then she got two of the meat versions with chili for herself. We stood on the sidewalk and devoured the dogs, oozing chili and mustard respectively all over our hands. I closed my eyes as I licked my fingers. They were almost as good as the tofu dog itself.

"Jeez-Louise," Barbara commented, handing me a paper napkin. "You sure you don't want another one?"

I shook my head.

"Good," she said. "It's time to visit Rose Snyder again."

I said no, emphatically. Barbara said yes, more emphatically. I said it was too dangerous. Barbara asked me if I really thought Grandma Snyder was a killer. I said no, but what if Dan showed up? She said she'd go alone. I told her not to. She said Dan wasn't really dangerous, anyway. I said he was, too . . .

I was thinking about assertiveness training as I parked in front of the Good Thyme Cafe an hour later. How come Barbara always won our arguments? Maybe she was a hypnotist as well as a psychic. Maybe she was just good at being stubborn.

She jumped from her side of the car energetically, striding up to the Good Thyme before I had even opened the door on my side. I got out reluctantly and walked up behind her as she pushed the *B* buzzer.

"Hello?" came Rose Snyder's low, lifeless voice through the intercom.

"Hi!" Barbara greeted her with all the enthusiasm of a charity fund-raiser. "This is Barbara Chu again. I'm here with Kate Jasper." I flinched when I heard my own name. The poor woman's son was in trouble. Her daughter-in-law was dead—

"We wanted to talk to you about Dan," Barbara went on. I

wished she hadn't said "we." Then she said it again. "May we come up?" she asked.

"I guess so," Rose answered slowly, uncertainty evident in her tone.

It was gall, I realized as we waited for Rose to come down and open the door. Pure and simple gall. That was why Barbara won all our arguments. If she could learn to lie, she might have a career in politics, I thought. I looked at her beautiful profile and shivered. What if she had already learned to lie? And to kill? I shook off the thought as Rose Snyder arrived at the door.

Rose looked tired, very tired. Her soft, round body sagged incongruously under her bright, gaily flowered dress. She wore no rouge today. Her skin looked pasty without it. Even her permed silver hair drooped. Her eyes were bleak as she stared at us through her gold wire-rimmed glasses.

"Come in if you like," she offered tonelessly.

She led us down the hall and up the stairs to the apartment above the restaurant. Then she opened the apartment door, and we were transported back to the sixties. The Grateful Dead, Ravi Shankar and Jefferson Airplane posters decorated the bright yellow walls. The moldings were painted purple. A frayed velvet couch whose maroon had mostly faded to brown sat against one wall. Large, mismatched pillows were scattered nearby. And there were a couple of easy chairs draped in purple velour. The strings of multicolored beads that hung in the two inner doorways completed the picture. I could almost smell the patchouli oil.

"I'm sorry the living room looks so funny," Rose apologized softly. "Danny likes it this way." She shrugged her shoulders gently and sighed. I had a feeling she would have rolled her eyes if she'd had the energy.

"Don't worry. I love it," Barbara assured Rose. From the rapt look on Barbara's face, I assumed she wasn't just being polite. "It's far out. I haven't seen anything like this for years—"

The curtain of beads in one of the doorways rippled as Opal Snyder came rushing through. Her brown eyes were round, her hair held in place by yellow butterfly barrettes today. Topaz stalked behind her little sister, her thin arms crossed over her chest.

"Grandma," Opal said breathlessly. "Topaz says I can't have another cookie. I can, can't I?"

Rose closed her eyes for a moment and sighed.

"Can't I?" Opal repeated shrilly.

"One cookie apiece," Rose ruled finally. "Topaz, you get them out of the cupboard. You can both eat them in the kitchen."

Rose asked us to sit down as the little girls disappeared through the dangling beads of the other doorway. We lowered ourselves onto the old velvet couch. A musty smell of damp and decay rose into my nostrils as we sank into its flaccid cushions. Rose took a seat on one of the easy chairs.

"I don't know how I can apologize to you about Danny," Rose whispered once we were seated. She folded her hands neatly in her lap and stared down at them. "I've been awake all night, trying to figure out where I went wrong with him."

Pity tightened my chest as I listened to her. "Maybe it isn't anything you did," I suggested.

Her head jerked up as if startled. She looked at me for a moment, then shook her head. "There's no excuse for his behavior," she murmured. Her cheeks flushed. "None. How could I have raised a boy who would hit his own daughter with a gun?"

I looked over at Barbara. When was she going to ask her questions? I didn't want to watch Dan's mother suffer anymore. But Barbara just stared at Rose Snyder without speaking. It was an effective technique.

"And Topaz," Rose continued, her voice a little stronger. "She's getting as bad as Danny. She hits her little sister. And the foul language she uses." Rose clicked her tongue. "I don't know what to do with her." She sighed again.

"Mrs. Snyder," Barbara began. It was about time. "Have you been told the names of the people in the vegetarian cooking class?"

Rose nodded, her eyes widening a little.

"Did you recognize any of the names?"

Rose shook her head gently. "No, though I suppose I should have. I've certainly met Iris Neville before," she told us. "And Danny tells me I was introduced to Alice Frazier some years ago." She sighed once more. "My memory's not as good as it used to be. The police asked me the same questions."

"How about last night?" Barbara persisted. "You saw all the

people in the dining room. Did you recognize anyone else besides Alice and Iris?"

"Well, there was Danny, of course. And his friend Zach,"
Rose answered hesitantly. "And I think I recognized the rest of
you from the night Sheila was . . . was killed. And, let's see, I
saw you two at the memorial service." She closed her eyes for
a moment. Maybe she was trying to summon up another memory. Apparently it didn't work. "I'm sorry I'm not more help,"
she said finally, opening her eyes again.

"You're doing great," Barbara assured her. "Now about
Zach—"

The phone rang, interrupting whatever question Barbara had
been going to ask.

"Oh dear," Rose murmured as she stood up. "Excuse me,
please." She shuffled her way over to the phone that sat on a
small table below the Jefferson Airplane poster. Her back was to
us as she picked up the receiver. I averted my eyes anyway, not
wanting to intrude on her conversation.

"Hello?" Rose answered. I could still hear her, averted eyes or
not. "This is she."

Then there was a long silence. I glanced at Barbara. She was
sitting upright on the edge of the couch, her face stricken. What
the hell was wrong with her?

"Oh, my God!" Rose cried out.

Barbara was on her feet in an instant. She ran across the room,
but stopped two feet away from Rose as if she were waiting for
something. Rose hung up the phone slowly, then turned, not
seeming to notice Barbara standing nearby. Her face was paper-
white and drawn, her eyes focused ahead of her on something
that wasn't in the room. A chill raised the hairs on the back of
my neck.

Topaz came marching through the strings of beads in the
kitchen doorway, her face sullen.

"What's wrong?" she demanded, staring at her grandmother.

Rose Snyder looked down at Topaz slowly. It took her a moment to focus on the girl.

"Grandma?" Topaz prodded, her voice softer now. Her face
seemed to open, looking like a little girl's to me for the first
time. Was she afraid? I was. "Grandma, are you okay?" she
asked.

"I'm fine," Rose replied in a zombie's voice.

"But—" Topaz began.

"Can you take your sister downstairs for a moment?" Rose asked, her voice still lifeless.

"What's—" Topaz tried again.

"Please," Rose said quietly.

Topaz nodded, her face sullen once more. She stomped back into the kitchen and emerged seconds later, dragging Opal by the hand through the living room and out the apartment door. Every time Opal tried to ask a question, Topaz told her to shut up. And Rose didn't correct her once.

Once the children were gone, Rose's body seemed to lose its stuffing. Barbara put an arm around the older woman's waist and half led, half carried her to an easy chair.

"Danny is dead," Rose said. There was no emotion in her voice.

"What?" I asked, thinking I must have misheard her.

"Danny is dead," she repeated and slumped forward in her chair.

I jumped from the couch and ran to her. Barbara's fingers were already on Rose's pulse.

"Did she have a heart attack?" I asked, my voice shrill and shaking.

"I don't think so," Barbara said, her voice no better. "I think she just fainted."

"I'll call an ambulance," I told her and turned to the phone.

"What'd you do to Grandma?" came a voice from behind me. I turned and saw Topaz scowling at me. Instantly, I wondered if it was true that Dan Snyder was dead, that Topaz no longer had a father.

"Honey—" I began.

"Danny!" yelped Rose. She was sitting up again, her white face tight with misery. At least she was conscious, I thought gratefully. I wouldn't call an ambulance. Not yet, anyway.

"What did Daddy do to you?" demanded Topaz, running toward Rose.

"Nothing, honey," Rose sobbed. She held her arms wide for her granddaughter.

Topaz hesitated an instant, then crawled into Rose's lap. Rose wrapped her arms around her granddaughter, resting her chin on the girl's head as she cried. God, I was glad that Rose and Topaz had each other to hold.

I looked over at Barbara. She was motioning for me to join her on the couch.

"You'd think the police would be a little more sensitive," I whispered to her once we were seated.

"Maybe it wasn't the police who called," she whispered back.

I looked at her, puzzled. "But who else would have told her that Dan was dead?"

"Sheila's murderer, maybe," Barbara mused. "Who knows?"

"You mean as a joke?" I breathed. "Do you think Dan's still alive?"

Barbara shrugged. "No, probably not," she answered finally. She frowned as she looked back over at Rose Snyder. My eyes followed her gaze. Rose was crying quietly now, her arms still around Topaz. It would be too cruel a joke to tell Rose that Dan was dead if he wasn't.

"How can we find out?" I asked.

Barbara frowned for a moment more, then answered, "Felix."

But when she got up from the couch, she walked to Rose Snyder's side.

"Mrs. Snyder," she prompted gently.

Rose looked up at her, eyes bleary with tears.

"Who called you, Mrs. Snyder?"

Rose pulled a handkerchief from her pocket and blotted her eyes. "Topaz, honey," she said gently. "Go play with your sister downstairs."

"I wanna stay with you, Grandma," Topaz protested.

"And I want to stay with you, too," Rose said with a catch in her voice. "But you have to go downstairs right now."

Topaz jumped out of her grandmother's lap and scowled at her, then at Barbara. Then at me.

"Please, Topaz," Rose said. "Do as I say."

Topaz walked heavily across the room and slammed the door on the way out.

"Who called you?" Barbara asked Rose again, wasting no more time.

"Alice," Rose replied, her eyes drifting around the living room, unseeing. Was she going to faint again?

"And what did she say?" Barbara pressed, her voice gentle but clear.

"That someone murdered my son," whispered Rose. Her eyes came back into focus. "Danny's dead," she said as if she just now understood. She began to cry again, sobbing more loudly than she had before.

Tears moistened my own eyes. I blinked them back and went to Rose, putting my arm around her shoulders as I crouched by the side of her chair. I didn't know if I could do her any good that way, but I didn't know what else to do. Her son's life wasn't mine to offer. And that was probably all that mattered to her right now.

"It's all right," I whispered, knowing it wasn't.

I patted Rose's hand and murmured words of consolation as Barbara phoned Felix. Barbara kept her voice low, but I got the gist. Felix was going to check on the story with the police department and then get back to us. Barbara was back by my side a moment after she hung up the phone.

"I have an idea," she whispered in my ear.

"What?" I asked, standing to hear it, keeping one hand on Rose's shoulder. I hoped I wouldn't hate Barbara's idea. I hoped I wouldn't get talked into it anyway.

But Barbara's idea turned out to be a surprisingly good one. She suggested calling Edna and Arletta and asking them to come take care of Rose Snyder and her grandchildren. Actually, it was a great idea. The twins would know what to do. I was sure of it. I gave Barbara the name of their hotel and she went back to the phone. I squatted down next to Rose and put my arm around her again. Her sobs were quieter now.

It wasn't until Barbara came back and told me that Edna and Arletta were on their way that my mind turned to the inevitable question *Who killed Dan Snyder?* Assuming he was dead, that was.

I looked up at Barbara. I knew she was asking herself the same thing. The faces of the members of the vegetarian cooking class flashed through my mind. Alice's face stayed the longest. If she had told Rose about Dan's death, was she the murderer? But she was in love with Dan. Why would she kill him?

Then I thought of Zach. Maybe Dan had lied when he told the police he was with Zach the night Sheila died. Had Zach convinced Dan he needed an alibi, then offered to provide one? Had

Dan finally realized that Zach needed that alibi for himself? Had he challenged Zach?

After a while, another face floated into my mind—Topaz Snyder's. Her mother had hit her, then died. Her father had hit her, then died. Had Topaz had a hand in their deaths? That was too spooky to bear thinking about.

I shifted my crouched position next to Rose. My legs were beginning to cramp.

"'Mrs. Snyder," I said softly. "Would you like to lie down?"

"What's wrong with Grandma?" came an angry voice from the doorway. I started. It was Topaz.

"I'm fine," Rose told her. "I'm just going to lie down for a minute."

The buzzer sounded just as I helped her to stand. Barbara found the intercom and shouted instructions, then raced down the stairs. Moments later, she escorted the twins in.

Arletta was holding Opal's hand as she came through the door. Edna strode up to Rose and wrapped an arm around her waist, then took Rose's arm and put it over her own solid shoulder. She supported her to the couch and helped her lie down. Then she took her pulse.

"How are you feeling?" she asked brusquely.

"Just a little dizzy, I guess," Rose answered in a nearly normal voice. She wasn't sobbing anymore.

"Any chest pain?" demanded Edna.

Two down and one to go, I thought and turned to watch Arletta approach Topaz.

"Can you read, young lady?" Arletta asked. The tremor in her voice made her sound almost as frail as she looked.

"Of course I can," Topaz answered impatiently.

"Oh, maybe you can help me, then," Arletta warbled. "I have something downstairs I just can't make out with these old eyes. Could you come and read it for me?"

"Okay," agreed Topaz ungraciously. She followed Arletta and Opal out the door. I could hear their three high voices mingling as they descended the stair.

I looked at Barbara. She winked back. I let myself breathe a long, sweet breath.

Then the buzzer sounded again. Was that Felix? I should have known he'd show up.

"Just up the stairs, dear," I heard Arletta call out.

The footsteps didn't sound like Felix's, though. Unless he was wearing high heels these days.

Alice Frazier came tip-toeing into the apartment. She was dressed as beautifully as ever in a well-cut turquoise suit, but that customary elegant look was missing. Maybe it was her swollen red eyes, her drooping body. Whatever it was, today she looked like the middle-aged, overweight woman she'd always claimed to be.

Her red eyes widened when they lit on Barbara and me.

"What are you . . . ?" she began. But she looked away without finishing her sentence. Then she saw Rose lying on the couch.

"I'm so sorry, Mrs. Snyder!" she cried out. She took a couple of steps toward the couch.

Rose sat up slowly without speaking. She fixed her eyes on Alice. Edna turned to stare at the younger woman too.

"I got Dan out of jail this morning. He used the restaurant building as security for his bail . . ." Alice said hesitantly. She kept on talking when Rose didn't reply, her speech suddenly racing as if it had gotten away from her. "After he got out, I took him to my apartment. He lay down on the couch to sleep. I made some breakfast for him in case he got hungry. Then I left to go to work."

She stopped for a moment. "When I got back, he was dead on the couch, strangled!" she burst out.

Rose narrowed her eyes at Alice, no longer looking like Mrs. Santa Claus, even on a bad day. There was no comfort in her eyes, only pure hatred.

Alice turned her head away from Rose's eyes.

"You weren't at work when we visited your office," Barbara said slowly.

Alice's body jerked. She turned to Barbara.

"I called, and Dan didn't answer the phone," she explained. "So I went back home.'

When Barbara didn't comment, Alice looked at me. I didn't know what to say. Alice turned her eyes back to Rose Snyder.

"Believe me, Mrs. Snyder," she pleaded. "I didn't kill your son."

No one spoke.

"Goddammit!" Alice screamed. "I didn't kill him!"

- Twenty-three -

ALICE SEARCHED OUR faces slowly, one by one in the ensuing silence. My chest tightened when she turned her swollen eyes in my direction. She looked so absolutely and sincerely miserable. I wanted to tell her that I believed her. I wanted to tell her that I knew she hadn't killed Dan Snyder. But I didn't know.

There were just too many points against Alice. As far as I could tell, she was the only one in the vegetarian cooking class who had known both victims previously. And she had arranged that class. Had she arranged it in order to be lost in a sea of suspects when Sheila was found dead? And Dan had been in her apartment when he was strangled. Actually, a little voice protested in my head, that was too obvious a point against her. If she had wanted to kill Dan without getting caught, why would she kill him in her own apartment?

I was about to ask her if someone else could have gotten into her apartment, but I was an instant too late.

"I didn't!" Alice cried once more. "I didn't kill him!" Then she turned on her high heels and ran straight out the door.

I thought I heard her stumble on the stairs, but then I heard her heels clattering again. And finally, I couldn't even hear that anymore. She was gone.

I let out a big whoosh of breath. Rose lay back down on the couch. And Edna pulled an easy chair over to Rose's side. I told myself I could relax now.

"We gotta talk to Meg," Barbara whispered in my ear with all the urgency that a whisper can carry.

I glanced over at Rose. Her eyes were closed. She looked al-

most peaceful. Edna turned and jerked her head toward the doorway. Barbara and I took the hint and crept quietly out. I was glad
to close the apartment door behind me.

Downstairs in the dining room, Topaz was reading aloud from
what looked like an often-used cookbook. Opal's eyes fluttered
drowsily as she leaned against Arletta's frail body, but Arletta
herself seemed engrossed.

"Meanwhile, sauté two medium onions in one-quarter cup of
oil," Topaz vocalized ponderously. Arletta nodded in rhythm
with the girl's voice. Was this the only book she could find?
"Add one-half cup of whole-wheat flour . . ."

No one seemed to notice Barbara and me sneaking by. It must
have been a really great cookbook.

Once we were out the door, Barbara took off down the street,
going as fast as she could on foot without actually running.

"Hey!" I called out. "Where are you going? The Toyota's
right here."

"There'll be a pay phone at the bar," Barbara shouted back.

I jogged to catch up with her. The way we were yelling,
they'd hear us at the Good Thyme.

"Why do we need a pay phone?" I asked breathlessly once I
caught her.

"To call Meg," she answered without breaking stride. "We
don't want to miss her like we did Alice."

"Why do we need to call Meg?" I pressed. Sometimes talking
to Barbara was like talking to someone from another planet.

"Because Alice is innocent," Barbara explained briefly.

I stopped in my tracks, surprised by her assessment. Barbara's
back grew farther away. I started jogging again.

"Then why did you give Alice a hard time about not being at
work this morning?" I demanded once I was even with her.

"I didn't know she was innocent then," Barbara replied.

There was a phone in the bar. Barbara was right about that. I
still wasn't sure if she was right about Alice's innocence, though.
Or why she now thought Alice was innocent, for that matter.

"Meg's at home," Barbara told me when she got off the
phone. "Let's go."

We went. I didn't even bother to argue. Forty minutes later, I
parked in a space across from the Victorian building that housed
Meg's flat, still uncertain of our exact purpose here.

Meg had opened the door at the top of the steep stairs by the time we got there.

"Um, hello," she greeted us. Then she sniffed.

"Allergies?" I asked.

"What?" she replied, her sea-green eyes wide in her pale face. For a moment, I wondered if she did cocaine. She was certainly skinny enough—her slight body couldn't have weighed more than a hundred pounds. And her mental processes seemed none too sharp today. I reminded myself that she was an artist. Artists at work could be notoriously absent-minded. Once I had forgotten three appointments in a row while immersed in a design for a new optometrist mug. And Meg was a real artist. She shifted her wide-eyed gaze to the ground as I stared at her.

"I just wondered if you had allergies," I explained. She looked up at me blankly. "Never mind," I told her hastily. "May we come in?"

"Um, okay," she said.

Meg's living room was filled with the same drawings, paintings, books and electronic gear I remembered from the last time we had visited. I averted my eyes from the writhing figures in the pen-and-ink drawings and gazed instead at the painting of the four-foot carrot still lounging on its canvas, looking as sensual as ever. I stepped forward to examine it more closely.

"Would you like some tea?" Meg asked in a near whisper.

"That would be great!" Barbara replied with far too much enthusiasm. It seemed to bowl Meg over. She blinked uncertainly for a moment, then scurried into the kitchen.

Barbara and I followed her in and took seats at her yellow Formica table as she put the kettle on the stove.

"Did you happen to see Alice at work this morning?" Barbara asked Meg casually.

"Alice?" repeated Meg, turning on the gas flame. She reached for a yellow ceramic teapot.

"Alice Frazier," Barbara enunciated carefully as if for a deaf person. "Where you work. Did you see her this morning?"

"Let's see," Meg whispered hesitantly, staring up at the ceiling. "What day is this?"

"Tuesday," Barbara replied impatiently, stiffening in her chair.

"Oh, Tuesday," Meg said. "I must have been here all day,

then." She reached for a canister of tea. "I think so, anyway," she added.

Barbara watched in silence as Meg stuffed the loose tea leaves into a bamboo tea ball.

"This is useless," I whispered in Barbara's ear. "Let's just go."

Barbara shook her head angrily. "I'll get right down to it, Meg," she said bluntly. "Do you think Alice is capable of murder?"

Meg's mouth opened in a little O of surprise. Her eyes were even wider than before as she stared at Barbara.

"Capable of murder?" Meg repeated. Then she closed her eyes for a moment, apparently thinking. Had Barbara finally gotten her attention?

"You know Alice pretty well—" Barbara began again.

Meg straightened her shoulders as she opened her eyes. "No," she interrupted Barbara crisply. "I don't think Alice is capable of murder." I felt like applauding.

"Why not?" Barbara pressed.

"Alice lacks the necessary passion to commit a murder," Meg replied thoughtfully. "She has small enthusiasms, but none of them go very deep. Or last very long. One month she's ready to save the homeless personally. The next month she's forgotten all about them and wants to become a vegetarian. Next month she'll be campaigning for a woman president." Her eyes narrowed. "You'd do better to forget about finding Sheila Snyder's murderer and concern yourselves with the children."

"The children?" Barbara repeated with a frown.

"Opal and Topaz Snyder," Meg told her. "They've been abused by both their parents. Don't you wonder what that will do to their lives?"

"I *know* what it'll do to their lives," Barbara retorted, obviously stung by the question. "I was abused myself." She paused for a moment, then spoke more calmly. "On the other hand, half the people I know have been mistreated by their parents. Like Kate's boyfriend. He was beaten and tormented by his mother when he was a kid, and now the old witch is living with them."

Meg turned and looked at me.

"Vesta's not that bad," I objected half-heartedly. My cheeks felt uncomfortably warm. These weren't my secrets Barbara was telling. They were Wayne's. Too late, I realized that I should never have shared the ugly details with Barbara if I hadn't wanted them to go any further.

"Not that bad?" Barbara mimicked. "Jeez-Louise, Kate, look what she's done to Wayne! And now she's in your house, trying to break up your relationship."

"Barbara," I hissed. "Forget about Vesta, all right?"

She opened her mouth to argue with me some more. I glared back at her. She closed her mouth just as the teakettle began to sing. I certainly hoped the Snyder murders would be solved soon, if only because I needed a vacation from Barbara. A very long vacation.

"Do you mind if I take a look at your paintings?" I asked Meg abruptly.

"No," she said with a shrug of her shoulders.

I strode back into Meg's living room, seething with anger at Barbara. I squinted at a new abstract in bold strokes of purple and blue that sat on one of the easels. The paint was still wet. Maybe Meg had been working on it when Barbara called. No wonder she'd been so distracted when we arrived. My mind jumped back to Barbara. How in hell had I previously found her outspokenness so endearing? I turned to look at the oversized carrot again. Now that was my kind of painting—

"Hey, kiddo," came Barbara's voice from my side. "Do you want your tea?"

I jumped, startled, then turned to her with a curse on my lips. Meg stood behind Barbara with her arms crossed, her sea-green eyes narrowly focused now. I swallowed my curse and forced my face into a smile.

"I'm sorry," Barbara mouthed in my direction. The expression on her face was vulnerable for a change, without a trace of brazenness. Damn. I should have known I wouldn't be able to stay mad at her.

"It's all right," I told her.

Barbara smiled weakly and handed me a white ceramic mug that smelled of cinnamon.

"How much for the carrot?" I asked Meg, taking a sip of tea.

"Two thousand," she answered. I gulped the hot tea too fast and coughed. I knew it was probably a fair price for all the work that had gone into it, but it was too much for me, and I told her so.

Meg didn't bother to negotiate the carrot's price. She gave us exactly enough time to finish our tea, then herded us out the door, pleading an appointment. She certainly wasn't distracted anymore.

"Well?" I said to Barbara once we were in the car again.

"I just don't know," she answered, her voice low and unhappy. "Sorry, kiddo. I guess visiting Meg was a waste of time."

"Are you all right?" I asked. Barbara without enthusiasm? I couldn't have been more surprised if the health food store had run out of brown rice.

She shrugged her shoulders and stared at the dashboard.

I spent the rest of the drive over the Golden Gate Bridge convincing her the trip hadn't been a waste of time. Every little bit of information counted, I told her. You'll figure it out, I insisted. By the time we got to my house, she was talking again.

"I'll come in with you," she said, life in her voice once more. "We can talk strategy."

I wondered if I had done a little too good of a job cheering her up as we climbed the stairs.

We had made it to the porch when Wayne came trotting out the doorway, pulling on his jacket as he ran.

"Kate," he murmured and came to a dead stop. He looked down at me. For a moment, I thought I saw adoration flashing from beneath his eyebrows. Then he put his hands on my shoulders and bent down to give me a long kiss. Maybe it wasn't adoration. Maybe it was lust. Either one was all right by me, I thought as I eagerly leaned into his embrace.

Barbara giggled behind me. Wayne and I pulled away from each other simultaneously.

"How's Vesta?" I whispered, still dizzy from the kiss.

He sighed. That was answer enough for me.

"So how's everything else?" I amended. "Anything else."

"Glad I caught you," he told me. "Gotta run. Crisis at the downtown restaurant. I'll be there most of the evening." He looked into my eyes again. "Okay?" he asked softly.

"Okay," I agreed reluctantly. I didn't really want to spend another evening alone with Vesta. But business was business.

"Been people calling for you all day," he continued. "Judy at the Jest Gifts warehouse says you didn't leave her enough signed checks. Something about a C.O.D. package that the guy will come back to deliver at the end of his route."

I groaned long and loud. Wayne's brows went up.

"Never mind," I said. "I'll phone her."

He shifted his gaze to Barbara.

"Felix wants you to call him," he summarized. I knew it was a summary. Felix couldn't even say his name that concisely.

Wayne reached for me one more time, limiting himself to a chaste kiss on my forehead; then he ran down the stairs.

I called the warehouse as soon as we got inside. Everything was all screwed up. Even worse than usual. Judy couldn't find the checks. Jean couldn't find the ambulance-chaser mugs for the Trial Lawyers of America convention. (The mug itself looked like a foreshortened ambulance; the handle, an attorney leaping onto the ambulance's rear end, hands and feet outstretched.) And the computers were acting funny. Judy hoped she hadn't erased anything important, but . . .

"I'll be there in an hour," I promised and hung up.

"See you later," I told Barbara and took a step toward the door.

"Wait a sec," she called to me. "Don't you want to know what Felix found out?"

I looked at my watch. It was after three-thirty. I needed to go soon. But I did want to know. And Barbara knew damn well that I did.

"Make it quick," I ordered.

Barbara saluted and dialed the phone. I sat there tapping my foot as she pried information out of Felix.

"Just tell me, Felix," she kept repeating, her voice a little tighter each time. I could just hear Felix stringing out his tale to bargain for an exchange of information.

But he must have let her have the story, because suddenly she made a series of smooching noises into the receiver and told him goodbye.

"The San Ricardo Police Department is interviewing Zach," she whispered after she hung up.

"They caught him?" I breathed.

"Yeah, you'll love it." She grinned. "He was picked up for speeding in Santa Rosa. And he had his whole stash of drugs with him." The grin left her face. "The police think he may be the one who murdered the Snyders. He's got a history of arrests for drugs and violent crimes. And he doesn't have an alibi anymore—"

"But did he really do it?" I interrupted, asking myself the question as much as Barbara.

Barbara sighed in instant understanding. "No," she said. "I don't think so." She looked up at me. "It's up to us," she announced.

"Oh, no," I told her, moving toward the door. "We're out of it."

"But Kate," she objected, following me. "Think about poor Mrs. Snyder. Her first son dead in a car accident . . ."

I didn't hear her next few sentences. I had forgotten about Rose Snyder's firstborn son. My stomach spasmed as if someone had punched me. Poor Rose. Both of her children dead. All of her children dead.

". . . if you're going to the East Bay anyway," Barbara was saying when I tuned back in, "why don't you catch Paula and Gary in Berkeley? And maybe Leo at his gallery on your way back. Find out where they all were this morning. I'll do Iris. I wanna look at her hand collection again. And Ken. Maybe I'll get to see his ant farm this time."

"Fine," I said, too rushed to even think about it. I took another look at my watch. "I really have to go," I told her.

She gave me a quick hug. "Thanks," she whispered and let me go.

I was almost out the door when she called out to me. I turned back reluctantly.

"Find out if Leo really had a heart attack," she ordered with a grin.

"All right," I agreed. "Will you do something in return?"

She nodded.

"Say goodbye to Vesta for me."

I could hear her chuckling as I ran out the door.

It wasn't until I was stuck in rush hour traffic on the Richmond Bridge that I realized I had agreed to see suspects alone. And so had Barbara. In my hurry, I had forgotten the buddy rule. Maybe I had forgotten on purpose. It felt so good to be in my car *alone*, even in the middle of traffic. I reviewed suspects in my mind the rest of the way down the highway to the Jest Gifts warehouse. And I couldn't make any of them into a murderer. Maybe Zach did do it, I thought as I pulled into the warehouse parking lot. It was nearly five o'clock.

Judy had found the signed checks after all, in a locked drawer where she had moved them for safety's sake a week ago. And she had received the C.O.D. package. Only the package wasn't ours. It was full of auto-body parts. Tomorrow, I told her. It will all be straightened out tomorrow. There was probably an auto-body shop in the area wondering why they received a package of gag gifts. All we had to do was find them and make the exchange. It took me ten more minutes to locate the ambulance-chaser mugs, and another five to restore the files that Judy had erased. Then I was on the road again, heading for Paula and Gary's house.

I pulled my car into their driveway hesitantly. I was hot and sweaty from driving. And my mind was shouting out warnings. If either Paula Pierce or Gary Powell was a murderer, one of them would be sure to protect the other. And that would make it two against one in confrontation. I took a long, deep breath and forced myself to climb out of the womb of my Toyota. A light breeze came by to cool my damp skin as I marched up to the stucco house and rang the bell.

I heard the thunder of paws behind the door along with a full chorus of threatening barks and frantic yips. Now it was six against one if you included the poodle, the Labrador retriever and the beagles. I waited five long minutes for the sound of a human voice, but never heard one. Even the dogs seemed to have lost interest by the time I gave up and left, only occasionally yipping half-heartedly.

I was more relieved than disappointed as I returned to my car, my pursuit unrewarded.

But it was a different story when I got to Leo's gallery. I slunk in the Conn-Tempo door, made my way around the seven steel breasts on the metal monstrosity in the middle of the room and came face to face with Leo himself.

"Hello there, beautiful," he purred. His breath almost knocked me over. Either he had spent the day drinking or he was marinating himself in red wine in preparation for broiling. He cocked an eyebrow at me as he stroked his beard. "Haven't I met you someplace—?"

His jaw fell open before he could finish his own sentence. He must have recognized me. He backpedaled frantically, stumbling over the outstretched leg of a bronze nude. His close-set eyes widened.

"I just—" I began, afraid for a moment he was going to have another heart attack.

"Stay away from me!" he shrieked. "Just stay away from me!" Then he turned and ran.

I watched as his pear-shaped body disappeared through the door behind another naked lady, this one carved in stone.

A few minutes later, Ophelia emerged from the same doorway, her long legs showy in sparkling metallic tights under a green miniskirt.

"How may I help you?" she asked, projecting her voice as if from the stage. Then she whispered, "Up there," and pointed toward the front of the gallery.

"He can't hear us now," she explained once we had hustled on up to the front. "So what's the old guy done now?" she asked, her freckled face alive with curiosity.

"I'm not sure," I told her honestly. "Was he in this morning?"

"Nah," she said. "He never comes in before twelve. He rolled in here today around four, drunk as a skunk." She stuck her tongue out, put her finger down her throat and made gagging noises. I assumed she was just commenting on Leo's excessive drinking and not really going to throw up.

"Did he tell you he had a heart attack?" I asked hastily.

She took her finger out of her throat and looked at me with raised eyebrows. "Uh-uh," she said, shaking her head. "Did he?"

I thought for a moment. "I don't actually think so," I answered slowly.

Ophelia straighted her back suddenly.

"He's watching us," she whispered out of the side of her mouth. "Pretend you're looking at something."

So I looked at some expensive abstract paintings, a few even more expensive carvings of naked ladies and one large welded God-knows-what that was priced at twelve thousand dollars. I could have bought a new car if I'd had that kind of money to spare. As I left the gallery, I wondered if Meg's carrot was a bargain at two thousand.

The sky had taken on the luminous quality of twilight by the time I dragged myself back up my front stairs. I was tired, hungry and unhappy. I had three days' worth of Jest Gifts work to do in one evening. I was no nearer to knowing who had killed Sheila Snyder than I had been a week ago. And I was dreading another confrontation with Vesta. I looked up at the sky as I reached the top of the stairs, taking one last moment to enjoy the shimmering twilight.

As I turned the doorknob, I thought I heard a man's voice. I checked the driveway again. Wayne's Jaguar wasn't there. I pushed the door open cautiously.

The house was in darkness. Someone had pulled the curtains closed and turned out all the lights. Vesta? I wondered.

Then I heard the sound of the deep voice again. Or did I? It was gone before I could be sure. For one instant of pure panic, I thought it was Dan Snyder's voice. Then I remembered that Dan Snyder was dead. I stepped toward the light switch quickly. I wanted to see what I thought I had heard.

I didn't think of Zach until my hand flipped the switch.

- Twenty-four -

THE LIGHTS FLASHED on, dazzling my vision. In that instant I assured myself that Zach was in police custody *and* simultaneously realized that the police might have released him by now. My stomach lurched.

But it wasn't Zach who was waiting for me in the living room. Even with the light still dancing in my eyes another instant later, I could tell my visitor wasn't tall enough to be Zach. I let my breath whoosh out of me in relief. My visitor was Meg Quilter. At least I thought so. I walked into the living room, looking closer as I blinked away the light. Was it Meg?

The figure before me had the cooking teacher's height, her coloring and her slender build. But the stance wasn't right. Meg, if it was Meg, stood in a martial arts posture, feet spread wide, knees bent and arms slightly raised as if in readiness to fight. And Meg's face was wrong too. It was more angular than I remembered, the green eyes too narrow and pinched. I could have been seeing a double exposure. It looked like Meg Quilter, but at the same time it looked like a young man, a very angry young man. Maybe my relief had been premature.

"Meg?" I said.

"She ain't here, man," Meg replied in the deep, vibrating male voice I had heard at the door. The hair went up on the back of my neck. That wasn't Meg's voice. It was someone else's, someone who was made of pure rage.

I told myself to breathe evenly, and dropped my center of gravity, bending my knees slightly and trying to find the stillness inside that would be my best weapon. If I needed a weapon.

"Why are you here?" I asked, taking care to keep my voice low and calm.

"We're here to waste the bitch, man," Meg growled. *We?* I scanned the room. Then I saw Vesta, crouching in the corner with her arms crossed over her bowed head. Was Vesta the other half of "we"? Or was she "the bitch"?

"She's gotta die, man," Meg's deep voice ground on. I kept my breathing even, but I couldn't control the shiver that jerked my body. "You know what she is, man. You know what she does."

"Who has to die?" I asked slowly.

Meg raised her hand high and pointed at Vesta. For the first time I noticed the glove on that hand, the kind of disposable latex glove that my dentist had taken to wearing as a protection against AIDS. But I didn't think Meg was worried about AIDS. I thought she was worried about fingerprints. I fought to control the nausea that rose in me.

"She's crazy!" Vesta screamed suddenly, her voice ringing shrilly in the silence. She had taken her arms away from her head and looked up, exposing a face that was twisted in fear.

"Shut up, bitch," Meg snarled, then turned back to me.

"Why does she have to die?" I asked quietly.

"We waste all of them, man," Meg replied matter-of-factly in her deep voice. "Anyone who hurts a little one." Then she bent forward, her voice even deeper, her eyes dark with rage. "Everyone's gotta pay the freight, man. The woman's dead. She's history."

"But—" I stopped speaking as Meg abruptly closed her eyes. In seconds she unbent her knees, shifted her feet closer together and drew her back up straight. When she opened her eyes again, they were cool and competent, the rage erased from their shape. I blinked, unbelieving.

"Stilleto has been responsible for many incidents," Meg said crisply, her voice unarguably female once more. "However, we must not be caught. The children would never survive in prison."

"Stiletto?" I asked, if only to say something while I tried to absorb what I was seeing. What I was hearing.

"Stilleto," she said impatiently. "You have just met him." I searched my mind for something else to say, but could only stare blankly.

"There are many of us here besides the woman who calls herself Meg," she told me, assuming a lecturing tone now. I recognized that tone. It was the one Meg had used when she was teaching her class. She had seemed to change into a different person then, too, I remembered suddenly. Multiple Personality Disorder. My shoulders jerked as the diagnosis came to me.

"The original Meg left to go to sleep the day her mother stuck her hand in boiling water," the lecturer continued. "She was two years old."

My body stiffened. Two years old.

"Another child left when Meg's mother locked her in a box for two days in her own excrement," she went on, unheeding of my horror. "Another when the mother broke her wrist because she had drawn a flower, another when she was held under water . . ."

My mind refused to take any more in as the lecturer spoke of blows and burns and forced sex with her mother's boyfriends. And worse. And as my mind shut off, I glimpsed for a moment how it would be if these things had happened to *my* body, how I might have let the part of me who had the experience leave and create a new person, a new personality, to replace her.

"We had to find some way, someone to bear the pain," the lecturer was saying. "And then later, someone to prevent it from ever happening again. Someone to avenge the children. Stiletto." She looked me in the eye. "Do you understand now?" she asked.

I nodded. I was beginning to. "But what about the Meg I met before, the . . . the shy one—?"

"The airhead?" the lecturer responded drily.

"Yes, how does she feel about—"

"The woman who calls herself Meg is a sniffling ninny," she told me. Then she paused and cocked her head as if listening to someone else. "That's right. She's useless. She couldn't fight her way out of a paper bag."

"But what does she think about you?" I asked, still confused by her attitude.

"She doesn't know us," the lecturer said brusquely. "We know her. Sometimes—" She stopped again to cock her heard. "Stiletto wants to come out again. He wants to complete his mission."

"Wait!" I yelped. *Keep her talking*, I thought. *Keep Stiletto at bay.* "Wait," I said more evenly. "I still don't understand. Can you explain how this all works?"

The lecturer nodded tersely. It was her role to explain. At least I had guessed that much correctly.

"Children should not be hit," she told me. "It is The Rule. Stiletto enforces The Rule. He had to kill Sheila Snyder. And Dan Snyder." She paused and looked into my eyes. I shivered again. The coolness in her gaze was almost as frightening as Stiletto's rage. "Do you understand?" she asked.

I nodded. There's a difference between understanding behavior and condoning it.

"Stiletto met Sheila Snyder when the woman who calls herself Meg went with Alice to arrange the class. Sheila hit the child that day. And we knew that if she hit the child in public, worse would be happening in private. Beatings, burnings, torment. But we waited. There had been too many incidents. We did not want to have to leave California as we had Oregon." She paused, her eyes still cool and competent. I wondered if this part of Meg was completely devoid of feeling. "Then Sheila hit the child again on Monday night. We agreed that Stiletto must act.

"Stiletto called up the stairs after everyone else had left. He told Sheila there was something she must see in the pantry. Then he strangled her there with the cord from the food machine.

"Dan Snyder's death was just as easy to arrange. Alice told the woman who calls herself Meg that she was going to pick Dan up from jail. We followed Alice until she had taken Dan to her apartment and left him there. I rang Alice's doorbell and talked to Dan. Once Dan let us in, Stiletto took over."

She started to close her cool eyes again.

"But Vesta?" I interjected hastily. "Do you have to kill Vesta? She doesn't have any kids to hurt now."

"We know she hit her son in the past," the lecturer argued. "She broke The Rule. And she told us that she still believes 'hitting kids is good for them.' Though perhaps you are right. She will probably do no future harm." She frowned in concentration. "Stiletto wants to come out," she told me. "He says we must kill the old woman. And you. There is some disagreement here. But we will not go to prison." She gazed directly into my eyes. "Will you tell the authorities what you now know?" she asked.

I should have just said no. But I couldn't lie under her cool gaze. "Maybe not," I said finally.

"You must consider the children," she reminded me.

"What children?" I asked.

She closed her eyes and I braced myself to meet Stiletto again. But when she opened her eyes she was smiling a soft little smile.

"Who are you?" I asked.

"Sweetie," she answered in a high voice of childhood. "I'm five years old. Do you have any cookies?"

Before I could answer, she had closed her eyes again.

Her body bent forward into a stoop and the face that looked up at me when she reopened her eyes seemed far more wrinkled than a moment before.

"I'm Granny, dear," she told me in a voice that trembled lightly. It was a kind voice. "I take care of the children. There are many children here. Many. Sweetie and Baby and Joey and Toby, just to begin with. They're afraid they'll be hurt." Her voice cracked as she spoke. "Many of us are tired of the killing, dear. But prison is no place for the children. Stiletto would be the only one left if we go to prison. We don't know what to do."

Then her eyes closed and the lecturer was back. I could tell by the sudden coolness of her gaze.

"Do you understand?" was all she said.

"No," I answered quickly. If I could keep asking questions maybe I could figure out what to do. "What about Meg . . . the woman who calls herself Meg?"

"I have told you," the lecturer said impatiently. "Meg does not know us. She hears us sometimes, but she thinks she's going crazy. Hearing voices. She can't figure out where the paintings come from. She doesn't understand why she can't remember what has happened when we've been out—"

Her eyelids sank to half mast, then popped up again. I could see the struggle there in her face. She clenched her teeth. The muscles around her eyes bulged. And then her eyes were closed. And her body was changing, crouching. When her eyes opened they were no longer cool. They were filled with rage.

I centered myself.

"We gotta waste you too, man," Stiletto growled as she raised her gloved hands. "You're too dangerous, man. You won't keep quiet." She took a step toward me.

I took a backstep without thinking. "Killing me won't protect the children," I said quietly. "They need help, a therapist. Someone who understands."

There was no change in Stiletto's angry face. But in a moment, she lunged at me. I stepped to the side, avoiding her. Stiletto made a noise deep in her throat as she almost fell, then righted herself. I stepped quickly around the couch, nearer to Vesta. Stiletto followed.

"Ain't gonna help you, man," she snarled. "You're dead."

"But I'm a child too, sometimes," I squeaked. My voice was high and frightened enough to pass for a child's, I thought, then hoped.

Stiletto stopped short, her face contorted. Her eyes closed, then opened again. The face staring at me was wrinkled, the body stooped.

"There has been enough killing, dear," the voice trembled. "But you must hurry. Run while you can. I can't—"

Her face contorted again. She kept her eyelids open, but her eyeballs rolled upwards.

"Vesta, come on!" I shouted, not waiting to see what happened next.

"No, Stiletto," Granny groaned.

But Vesta didn't come. I turned and saw the hesitation in her face. Why was she hesitating? Was her hatred for me stronger than her fear of death?

"Come on, dammit!" I bellowed as I ran toward her. I grabbed her hand and pulled her onto her feet. Finally, I felt her body give.

"Run!" I shouted.

And we ran.

- Twenty-five -

"SEE YA LATER, kiddo," Barbara was saying to me the next afternoon. It was the fifth time she had said goodbye. She took one step out the door, then turned back to hug me again. When she let me go, her model-beautiful face stretched into a big grin no model would ever exhibit in public.

"We did it, Kate!" she whooped. She shook her fist in the air triumphantly. "Forget the rest of it. Just remember . . ." She took me by the arms and stared into my eyes, as if she could mesmerize me into jubilation. "We flushed out a murderer. You're a hero."

"Yes, Master," I replied in a B-movie zombie's voice. "I am a hero."

She shook her head and laughed, then gave me yet another hug. "You'll be okay, kiddo," she whispered. "You'll see."

I pasted a smile on my face for her.

Barbara turned back to Felix, who was waving his arms as he yakked at Wayne. She caught his wrist on the downswing. "Come on, sweetie pie," she said, tugging. "Let's go."

"But you just wouldn't friggin' believe it," Felix rattled on, unheeding. Wayne grunted noncommittally. "Holy Moly! Down at the cop shop, she just switched in and out of personalities like something out of *Sybil*," He paused. "Or maybe *The Exorcist*," he said thoughtfully, then resumed his spiel. "They're all totally freaked out down there. Gonzola! Word is it took three beat-pounders just to stuff her in the friggin' paddy wagon—"

"Come on, Felix," Barbara insisted, pulling him down the stairs by his hand.

"Really friggin' bonkers," he mumbled as he went. "Boingy boingy, looney tunes . . ."

Wayne and I stood and watched Barbara's Volkswagen shoot out of the driveway and onto the street, spitting gravel. I heard the screech of brakes and a honk. A genuine smile tugged at my lips for an instant as I shut the door.

But when I sat down on the couch next to Wayne, the last of my energy drained away. My muscles felt like overstretched elastic. I couldn't imagine them ever holding me up again. Even my vision was blurry as I squinted at the litter of glasses and food on the coffee table. Too much excitement, too little sleep, I diagnosed.

Everyone had been waiting for me when I returned home from the police station. Wayne, Barbara, Felix, the twins, Ann Rivera, C.C. Even Iris Neville. And they had all celebrated, raising glass after glass of sparkling apple juice as C.C. yowled for her share. Now everyone but Wayne had gone. Even C.C. I leaned back and closed my eyes.

The images of the night before came pouring into the void. Running across the street with Vesta to my neighbor's. Locking the doors, hoping Stiletto wouldn't break a window. Hearing the sirens. Watching from my neighbor's front window as the police escorted a dazed-looking Meg from my house. Then watching her change into Stiletto again, dropping into a crouch and leaping.

I popped my eyes back open. The litter on the coffee table had its aesthetic merits, I decided.

Wayne put his arm around my shoulder and squeezed gently. "What'll happen to Opal and Topaz Snyder now?" he asked.

"They have their Grandma Rose," I assured him, putting my cold hand on top of his warm one. "Iris says Rose has almost recovered from the initial shock of Dan's death. She's devoting herself to her grandchildren now."

"Good," Wayne said quietly. I waited for him to say something else. Was he angry with me? I had never had the time to tell him the more recent details of my snooping into Sheila Snyder's death. Unfortunately, he had learned most of those details today, from my friends. The silence lengthened.

"I saw Paula Pierce down at the police station," I told him. Anything to fill the silence.

"Paula Pierce?"

"Meg's friend, the attorney," I said. "They called her when Meg started going through her thirty-seven faces of Eve act."

"Think it is an act?" Wayne inquired, eyebrows raised.

"No way," I told him. Gooseflesh formed on my arms as if to prove my point. "Those personalities were real." I didn't want to think about that too long. "Anyway," I hurried on, "Paula told me she's already got a top criminal attorney for Meg *and* a psychiatric evaluation ordered."

"Meg'll probably need both," Wayne commented.

"Did Felix tell you about the notebook?" I asked.

Wayne shook his head.

"Felix talked to someone at the San Ricardo Police Department this morning," I explained. "He wouldn't say who. You know how closemouthed he is about his sources. But whoever it was leaked the information that the police found a notebook in Meg's desk drawer when they searched her apartment."

I took a big breath before going on. "The notebook had a list of over twenty names, with dates beside each of them that spanned twelve years. They ran the information through their computer. They were all names of victims of unsolved murders, each with the corresponding date of the murder. Most of the victims had been raising children at the time of their deaths. And Meg had lived conveniently near each and every murder site. From Portland, Oregon, to San Francisco."

"How about the victims without children?" asked Wayne.

"The first name on the list," I began. I took another breath. "Helen Quilter, Meg's mother."

Wayne reached over and patted my cold hand. After a few moments, he asked, "Think Paula knew Meg was a murderer?"

"Maybe," I answered slowly. "I remember the look on Paula's face when she was talking about the string of Oregon murders—as if something had just dawned on her. I think she may have realized then that it was Meg. Or at least wondered." A sudden tremor shook my body.

"You okay?" Wayne murmured.

I shrugged my shoulders. Was it okay to feel so cold and nauseated?

"I remember telling Barbara," I went on, unable to stop talking about it, "that if someone was killing everyone they saw hitting a child, there would be an awful lot of dead bodies around. Well, there were." I shivered again, then tried to lighten up. "It was lucky I read that book on 'the child within' last year," I joked.

Wayne didn't laugh.

I went back to serious. "If I hadn't confused Meg by telling her I was a child myself sometimes, she might have killed me. She might have killed Vesta." I shook my head and corrected myself. "Not Meg. Stiletto. Stiletto might have killed us."

Wayne put his hands over his face, but not before I saw the look of pain there. I waited for angry words. But none came.

"Just glad you're alive," was all he said when he took his hands away.

"Thank you," I whispered. I leaned over and placed a kiss on his scarred cheek, then saw the moisture in his eyes. I hurried on with my story. "I can't believe I missed it," I told him. "I saw two distinct personalities, space cadet and lecturer. The space cadet never knew what time it was. More often than not, she didn't even seem to remember what she'd been doing. And I saw the different styles of artwork in her house. And those pen-and-ink drawings! God, Wayne. You should have seen them. All those writhing figures stuffed into a woman's head ... Meg's head. Why didn't I understand them for what they were? And all the electronic gear. Another personality must have collected that. And the totally different handwriting—"

"Kate, everyone missed it," Wayne interrupted gently. "Even Barbara."

"Only because her psychic powers were shorted out by Meg," I reminded him. "Or so Barbara claims now. I don't know why she didn't figure it out sooner. She should've noticed that she got the weird readings whenever Meg was around. She thinks it was interference from all the personalities disagreeing." I shrugged my shoulders. "At least Barbara's happy now that she has her powers back."

But I wasn't happy. As I sat back and closed my eyes again, the images from the previous night flashed like strobe lights on my inner eyelids. And the words "a two-year-old child" reverberated. I pulled my eyes open.

"Kate?" Wayne probed softly. I turned toward him. His face looked stern, but I knew him well enough to read the concern there. "I know you didn't sleep last night," he told me. "What will it take for you to feel better?"

"It'll take believing there aren't people out there like Meg's mother," I answered instantly, then stopped to realize what I had just said.

"How about knowing there are at least as many compassionate people out there as sadistic ones?" Wayne offered.

I didn't answer. I wasn't sure. Was compassion enough to compensate?

He knelt down in front of me, putting his hands on my knees. Then he looked up into my eyes.

"When I was a kid, I had Mom," he said gruffly. I nodded my understanding of the pain that statement encompassed. "But I had my uncle too, Uncle Ace." Wayne smiled suddenly, his homely face beatified.

"And Meg has Granny," I said aloud, surprising myself once more.

Wayne nodded slowly.

"Go on about Uncle Ace," I ordered as I absorbed the thought.

"He was great," Wayne obliged. "Big old guy, as ugly as me. Always joking. Always clowning. Could even make Mom laugh." Wayne laughed for a moment himself. I smiled down at him. Damn, I loved him. If only Vesta—

"Where is Vesta?" I demanded, suddenly realizing that I hadn't heard her voice since I'd come back from the police station.

"In a condo on Vine Street with the nurse she fired," Wayne mumbled. His eyebrows descended, obscuring his eyes. "I'm renting it for her now. I'll buy it as soon as I can."

My mouth dropped open. My dazed mind couldn't take it in.

"She's got a new home, Kate," he said.

I felt the warm relief bubbling up from my center all the way to my head. We were free. Compassion was enough. I jumped up from the couch, feeling new snap in my elastic muscles. I had only one more question.

"How the hell did you get her to do it?"

Wayne looked down at the floor. Red color flooded his neck, then rose into his cheeks. "The twins took care of it," he growled.

I leaned my head back and laughed. Wayne looked up, his eyebrows high. Then he laughed too.

"Come on!" I ordered, grabbing his hand and pulling him to his feet. "Let's celebrate."